DE is better

That lovable connoisseur of horror, Alfred Hitchcock, may not be a spring chicken anymore, but he isn't one of those doddering old vultures who keep mourning the bad old days.

On the contrary, Alfie finds that fiendish fun is at an all-time high, helped along by the latest strides forward of sinister science.

The economy of evil is booming. Never has the gross national product of corpses been greater, or killers more free of all the old hang ups. Swing and slay is the motto of the day, and Alfie's delighted to report that for the best in brainy brutality, the time is "now!"

Alfred Hitchcock's
ROLLING GRAVESTONES

ROLLING GRAVESTONES

ALFRED HITCHCOCK,

EDITOR

A DELL BOOK

Published by
Dell Publishing Co., Inc.
750 Third Avenue
New York, New York 10017

Dell ® TM 681510, Dell Publishing Co., Inc.
Printed in the United States of America
First printing—August 1971

Acknowledgments

Copyright © 1969 by H. S. D. Publications, Inc.

A PLACE TO VISIT by *Stephen Marlowe*. Copyright © 1968, by H. S. D. Publications, Inc. Reprinted by permission of the author and the author's agents, Scott Meredith Literary Agency, Inc.

CALL ME NICK by *Jonathan Craig*. Copyright © 1968, by H. S. D. Publications, Inc. Reprinted by permission of the author and the author's agents, Scott Meredith Literary Agency, Inc.

DEAD STOP ON THE ROAD SOUTH by *Robert Colby*. Copyright © 1969, by H. S. D. Publications, Inc. Reprinted by permission of the author and the author's agents, Scott Meredith Literary Agency, Inc.

RUSTY ROSE by *Edward Hoch*. Copyright © 1966, by H. S. D. Publications, Inc. Reprinted by permission of the author.

HENRY LOWDEN ALIAS HENRY TAYLOR by *Helen Nielsen*. Copyright © 1960, by H. S. D. Publications, Inc. Reprinted by permission of the author and the author's agents, Scott Meredith Literary Agency, Inc.

THE ENORMOUS $10 by *Jack Ritchie*. Copyright © 1960, by H. S. D. Publications, Inc. Reprinted by permission of the author, Larry Sternig Agency, and Scott Meredith Literary Agency, Inc.

FIRST COME, FIRST SERVED by *Rog Phillips*. Copyright © 1962, by H. S. D. Publications, Inc. Reprinted by permission of the author's agents, Scott Meredith Literary Agency, Inc.

THE EXPLOSIVES EXPERT by *John Lutz*. Copyright © 1967, by H. S. D. Publications, Inc. Reprinted by permission of the author and the author's agents, Scott Meredith Literary Agency, Inc.

I HATED THE HIRED MAN *by H. A. DeRosso.* Copyright © 1960, by H. S. D. Publications, Inc. Reprinted by permission of the author's agents, Scott Meredith Literary Agency, Inc.

A SINGULAR QUARRY *by Ed Lacy.* Copyright © 1969, by H. S. D. Publications, Inc. Reprinted by permission of the author's agent, Howard Moorepark.

SLEEP IS FOR THE INNOCENT *by Henry Slesar.* Copyright © 1960, by H. S. D. Publications, Inc. Reprinted by permission of the author and the author's agent, Theron Raines.

SORRY, RIGHT NUMBER *by Charles Einstein.* Copyright © 1958, by H. S. D. Publications, Inc. Reprinted by permission of the author and the author's agent, Lurton Blassingame.

FREE ADVICE, INC. *by Michael Brett.* Copyright © 1968, by H. S. D. Publications, Inc. Reprinted by permission of the author and the author's agent, Scott Meredith Literary Agency, Inc.

A SWEET YOUNG THING *by Mary Linn Roby.* Copyright © 1967, by H. S. D. Publications, Inc. Reprinted by permission of the author and the author's agents, Scott Meredith Literary Agency, Inc.

THE PRICE OF FAME *by Richard Deming.* Copyright © 1964, by H. S. D. Publications, Inc. Reprinted by permission of the author and the author's agents, Scott Meredith Literary Agency, Inc.

CONTENTS

INTRODUCTION

Although five years have passed since I last visited Philadelphia, I find myself frequently thinking about the city of brotherly love. Constitution Hall, the Liberty Bell and Betsy Ross's little house all hold proud meaning in our lives.

A recent news item about a deranged ornithologist who'd been arrested while attempting to strike the Liberty Bell with a rubber mallet brings Philadelphia to mind at this time. Needless to say, security guards pounced upon him before he could deliver the blow and the culprit was immediately led off to jail.

This unimportant event instantly recalled the time I'd spent there. The memory is vivid. It was a fine autumnal morning. I had just breakfasted at my hotel and I was walking toward a nearby university where I had been invited by the university's president to deliver and address upon the various types of criminals that I have known and studied.

At any rate I hadn't walked more than two blocks when I detected that I was being followed by a beautiful young brunette. My first impression was that she was merely going in the same direction where I was heading. This soon proved erroneous for when I deliberately stopped to gaze at a store window she kept her distance and only resumed walking after I had started again.

It amused me at first, then after I had walked about half a mile my curiosity came to the fore and without further ado I made an about face and confronted her.

Her frightened face told me that something was definitely wrong and in an attempt to put her at ease I said, "Miss, is there something amiss?" At the time I was certain that this sparkling witticism would do the trick. Imagine my astonishment, if you will, when her face contorted and she burst into tears. Momentarily, I was taken aback at this emotional display, but my recovery was quick. "Why are you crying?" I said. "What's the matter?"

Her reply was a series of incomprehensible blubbering sounds, which drew an immediate crowd, including an uncouth type in a plaid shirt who said to her, "Girlie, is this character bothering you? If he is, just give me the word and I'll flatten him."

Luckily for him, she replied, "I'm quite all right," just as I was about to strike him with a punishing karate shop for his unwelcome intrusion.

After he and the crowd had disbursed I led the distraught young woman into a coffee shop. We sat in a booth and I said, "Now, what's this all about?"

She hesitated. "I'm in terrible trouble. I've been following you trying to get up my nerve."

I waited without comment so she could tell me in her own time.

She spoke in a small voice and it took her ten minutes to tell me what was at the root of her problem. She had been married three weeks ago. While honeymooning in Mexico she and her husband Richard had been kidnapped by bandits. They had held them both, then she had been released for the purpose of returning to the United States to obtain the ransom money in exchange for her husband's release.

What it all boiled down to was that the bandits had insisted that I act as an intermediary to deliver twenty thousand dollars to them in exchange for her husband's life. Jo-Ann added that any attempt to bring in the police would result in her husband's immediate demise.

It was an opinion with which I concurred. Unfortunately, there were a few unanswered questions about the whole business that stirred uneasy feelings for me.

To begin with I believed that Mexican bandits were something out of the past, and if they did exist, why had they selected me to bring the ransom money instead of merely having Jo-Ann bring it to them? I considered the possibility that I might be held captive. I even considered the possibility that her story might be part of a ruse designed to place me in a position where I myself might be kidnapped.

Jo-Ann explained it all. The kidnappers had chosen me to bring the ransom money because of my reputation as an expert in the field of crime who would definitely realize that going to the police would jeopardize her husband's life. Jo-Ann on the other hand would also realize the situation for what it was, but they were apprehensive that she might unwittingly create problems, whereas if I handled the matter things would proceed smoothly. She dug in her purse and produced an envelope stuffed with bills which she handed to me. I accepted with some doubt and misgivings.

I canceled my lecture at the university and we departed via the next flight to Brownsville, Texas, where it was prearranged that we would cross over into Mexico.

The custom guards who recognized me on both sides of the border waved me right through without even bothering to inspect our luggage.

We followed the kidnappers' instructions. We rented a car and drove southward on a major highway, leaving it for a lonely road after about ten miles. On a desolate stretch of road, I stopped and deposited the envelope containing the money under a large rock marked with a red X. I found a note instructing us to proceed to an abandoned shack about four miles down the road. A second note pinned to the door of the shack advised us to return from whence we had just come. Trickery upon trickery. I drove back at breakneck speed. Approaching the marked rock I found her husband.

Jo-Ann and Richard embraced amidst tears and laughter. Then I shook his hand. He explained that he and the kidnappers had actually seen us drop the ransom off. They had sent us off on a wild goose chase to the shack to gain time to make their getaway in a small helicopter. We left.

The only holdup we had occurred at the border. I told Jo-Ann and Richard that I had to call the university to inform them that I was returning for my speaking engagement.

And once again the border guards recognized me and waved us through. At the airport for my flight Jo-Ann and Richard thanked me profusely and said good-bye.

Unfortunately for them they were arrested before they got to their car. I had called the police and alerted them rather than the university as Jo-Ann and Richard believed. The police found a large quantity of diamonds in Richard's money belt.

One of the arresting officers wanted to know how I had known that the kidnapping story was false. I explained that I hadn't fully believed the girl's story and that I had sprinkled nondectable Cavendish powder on the envelope containing the ransom money and a smear of Bilgar's salve on the palm of my right hand. When I shook Richard's hand there was a slight electrical reaction set up by the powder and the salve. I felt a tiny tingle and I knew at once that he had retrieved the ransom envelope himself. I realized that the kidnapping story was an elaporate hoax neatly designed to conceal another form of skullduggery, which in this case turned out to be diamond smuggling.

The lengths criminals will go to in their efforts to turn a shady buck is amazing, but I can assure you that even greater effort has gone into the discriminating selection of the stories that follow.

Alfred Hitchcock

ROLLING
GRAVESTONES

A PLACE TO VISIT

Stephen Marlowe

The sign outside, in big white letters, said *Pepe's*. That much, in keeping with the geography, was Spanish, but the rest of the place was Greenwich Village with maybe a little Soho thrown in.

The canned music, as I opened the door and entered the dim interior, was a beatnik caterwaul. The waiters all wore tight white duck trousers, scarlet shirts tied at the waist, and peroxided hair. A drunk in the corner, wearing a Hemingway beard, a baseball cap, and a pair of steel-rimmed glasses low on the bridge of his nose, was shouting something about a bullfighter. Three limp-wristed types at the bar were discussing the war in Vietnam in disparaging terms. A girl, not quite drunk, sat on the end stool fiddling with a pair of castanets and saying "olé" over and over again without spirit.

She wasn't the girl I was looking for. Nobody paid any attention to her, or to me, Chester Drum, until I hoisted myself up on a stool and said, "Pepe."

"Not here," one of the peroxide boys told me. "You're drinking?"

"Beer."

"One cerveza coming up."

He plunked the bottle and a glass down in front of me, and a chit that said I owed Pepe sixty pesetas, muchas gracias. Sixty pesetas is a dollar. Pepe is the diminutive of José, which is Joseph in Spanish. The girl I was looking for was living here in Torremolinos, in the south of Spain, with an American expatriate named Joe Cummings.

I said, "Señor Cummings charges a lot of dough for a bottle of beer."

The peroxide boy shrugged. "You can always do your drinking elsewhere, amigo. We got class. You pay for class."

". . . simply so *aw*ful I hardly knew what to *say,*" one of the limp-wristed set whined.

". . . madman with a cape," pontificated the man with the Hemingway beard, "but did anyone ever see him do a single decent *natural* to the left?" He was talking to himself.

The girl at the end of the bar went on clicking her castanets.

A bad Spanish imitation of the Beatles took over on the canned music.

I finished my beer. "When do you expect him?"

"Pepe?"

"Pepe," I said.

"He comes and he goes."

"I'll wait," I said.

Waiting earned me another beer and another one of Pepe's IOU's. It was swell beer.

An old man wearing one of those electric blue work jackets you see all over Spain, a pair of dirty white ducks and a beret came by sweeping the floor with a twig-broom. He was dark enough to be a gypsy, and he was the only Spaniard in the joint.

The door opened and a guy wearing the red and white team colors strolled in. He was big and his blond hair was no peroxide job. He had wide-spaced, mean-looking eyes and a complexion as pink and soft as a baby's bottom. Still he managed to look tough.

He slapped the old man's back. "Glad to see you're minding the store, partner," he said in English, and laughed, and went around to the business side of the bar.

"No comprendo," the old man said contemptuously.

The big blond guy moved down the bar to where the girl sat alone with her castanets. "You're drunk, Fran," he said. "I told you not to hang around here when you're drunk."

"I had a few," she protested.

"I say you're drunk. The Guardia could lift my license on me."

"I am not drunk."

"Beat it," he told her.

She stared at him with inebriated defiance.

"Drinks are on me," he said with a small smile, picking up her chits and tearing them in half. "Now blow."

"Well, in that case," she said, and lurched toward the door and through it. The three limp-wristed types snickered.

The peroxide boy whispered something to the big blond guy, and he came over to me. "You wanted something special?"

"Pepe? Joe Cummings?"

"So?"

"Joyce Addams," I said quietly.

"Never heard of her." The wide-spaced eyes narrowed.

"You got together in San Sebastián a couple of months ago," I said slowly. "You stayed at the Hotel Plaza in Madrid for the Festival of San Isidro. You drove down here by way of Granada, and she's been here ever since."

"Sorry, wrong number," Joe Cummings said.

"Her father hired me to bring her back to Geneva, no questions asked," I said. "She goes to the university there."

He laughed. "Been cutting a lot of classes, hasn't she?"

"No questions asked," I repeated.

"Better check with the operator," he said. "Or hey, have you thought of the Yellow Pages? They're full of dames who want a free ride in the south of Spain or the south of anywhere."

The three limp-wristed types, who had been listening, snickered again.

"This is the part that hurts," I said, "because ordinarily I wouldn't do it this way. I've got a blank check of her old man's in my pocket. It's yours, filled in with a reasonable figure, if she drives back with me tonight, and that's the end of it."

"What's a reasonable figure?" he asked, now showing some interest.

"I thought you never heard of her."

"I'm just curious."

"It could go as high as a grand," I said. My client, who was loaded, worked for an American government agency in Geneva, had his eye on a big political appointment and couldn't afford adverse publicity, had told me I could go as high as five thousand.

"Okay. I heard your pitch. I don't know your pigeon. Now get lost."

"You're making a mistake," I said.

"I'll take it up with my tax accountant."

He didn't offer to pay for my drinks. I paid and went out the door into the plaza that was lighted as bright as day. If he wanted to do it the hard way I'd go along with him. Torremolinos had grown from a fishing village to a jet-set watering place, but that still didn't make it any big city. I decided I could find Joyce Addams without any help from the guy she was keeping house for, but I didn't like it. Her old man had insisted on no fuss and no publicity. Well, she was his daughter.

"Señor."

I turned around. The Old Spaniard who had been sweeping the floor of Pepe's was behind me.

"You will continue to walk," he said. "Turn at the first street to the right. It is dark. Then we can talk."

I followed his instructions. The street was dark all right. It smelled of charcoal, garlic, and the sea. I heard the old man's shuffling footsteps. "The señorita," he said in Spanish, "every day she cries. She wishes to go home."

"Then why doesn't she?"

"He will not allow it."

"Where is she?"

The old man said nothing.

I sighed. "All right, how much?"

The old man spat on the pavement. "*Nada.* For *nada,* señor. I only wish to know that you are the man who can do it."

I saw no way I could establish that fact. "Her father thought so," I said. "He sent me over a thousand kilometers to find her."

"A thousand kilometers," the old man said musingly, and I realized I had said exactly the right thing. "It is like the other end of the world. He must have much faith in you."

"Where can I find his daughter?"

The old man's thoughts were elsewhere. "His partner," he said. "I am his partner. It must be so as no foreigner can commence a business in Spain otherwise. But he treats me like dirt. You have seen? And of course the money all goes to him. Yet should the Guardia Civil learn of his various enterprises, señor, I too would be punished."

"Where is she?"

"That also is her problem. She knows, so he cannot let her go. Sooner would he kill her. That is clear, señor. Every day she cries. Every night."

I said nothing.

He walked away from me and then came back. A match flared and he was smoking. "A thousand kilometers," he said. "The father must have great faith in you. You are *norteamericano* also?"

I said I was an American.

He let out a long breath. "In the old days, before this of the *bodega* called Pepe's, I worked as a gardener in my village of Churriana, in the mountains. The Americans who stayed there were always good to me. Sí, sí, they were. It meant much to me. But the one who calls himself Pepe, he is an abomination."

"Then help me," I said.

He was going to, of course, or he wouldn't have followed me, but he had to wait for anger to trigger courage. I waited with him. Finally he said, "With the gypsies. On the beach. You walk down the Calle San Miguel to the mill tower, and follow the steps down to the water. There you will see caves where the gypsies live. Ask for the *gitano* named Rafael. And you understand as well that we never spoke?"

I said I understood.

"Then vaya con dios, hombre."

His footsteps shuffled away. He was gone.

Caves pockmarked the sandstone face of the cliff. Outside each one a cook-fire was smouldering to ash. Along with the sea breeze I smelled frying fish and saffron and olive oil. A high tenor voice shouted a flamenco lament at the dark sky. There was no moon but the stars were bright.

Half-seen gypsies directed me to the cave of Rafael. They were just shadows in the night, and they wanted to stay that way, but as I passed I left excited whispers in my wake. It wasn't every day, and sure as hell not every night, that the gypsies had visitors.

A pregnant woman was frying fish in a pan outside Rafael's cave. The olive oil spattered, and she drew a hand back from it. She looked up at me with dark, steady eyes. Large gold earrings swung from the lobes of her ears. In the firelight her face was dark and seamed, but still drawn tight like old parchment over the fine bone structure. I decided she once had been pretty. Gypsies, particularly gypsy women, age fast.

"I'm looking for Rafael," I said in Spanish.

"There is no one here who calls himself that, señor."

"How do you call yourself?"

"I have no name."

"Whose cave is this then?"

"The cave of my man," she admitted grudgingly.

"Does he have a name?"

"Yes."

"Rafael?"

"Go away, señor."

The gypsies are secretive, and their lives are weighted down with superstitions ten centuries old. To know the name of a gypsy, if you are a stranger, is to have power over him.

"Tell Rafael I came from Pepe. Pepe, the norteamericano."

She took the large pan of fish off the fire, set it on a rock and disappeared barefoot into the cave. I lit a cigarette and waited.

In a few minutes she was back. She replaced the pan on the fire. Right away the olive oil began to sizzle. She sat hunkered down near it like an Indian squaw.

"She said, very softly, "Is it the girl?"

"What about the girl?" I said.

"You will take her away? Señor Pepe wants her back?"

"Maybe," I said.

"It would be well, señor," she said. "The girl does not belong here."

"Why doesn't she leave?"

The woman looked up at me. "Have care, señor," she said slowly. "You do not come from Pepe if you ask that."

I realized I had made a mistake, and then I wasn't so sure. The gypsy woman said, "Take the girl and go then, with my blessings. But have care." She got up suddenly and grasped the lapels of my jacket. "Every day it is more. The way my man looks at her, the way he must touch her every chance he gets—I know what he is thinking. I know what it is he wants." Her hands dropped to her belly, that was big with child. "I have this. Always I have this. Tell my man that you are from Pepe, as you told me. You are an *estranjero,* otherwise what would you be doing here? Then take the girl and go."

I started toward the entrance to the cave.

"I do not want to be responsible for killing her," the woman said to my back.

The walls were rough-hewn, but there were old, almost threadbare carpets on the floor. The light of candles revealed a few battered old chairs, a table, even an armoire. I heard a baby crying somewhere. Low doorways with curtains hanging across them led to other rooms. I was in an apartment carved from the soft sandstone of the cliff.

"Anybody home?" I said brightly in English.

A curtain parted and a man came out. He was wearing rags, and he was filthy. He hadn't shaved in a week. His skin was gypsy-dark and his eyes, sunk deep in a narrow skull, were shrewd and calculating. As he approached me I began to smell him.

"The girl," I said curtly. "Where is she?"

He shrugged one shoulder. It was more like a twitch.

"Come on, come on," I said then in Spanish. "Where is she?"

"You are from Señor Pepe?"

"Of course not," I snapped at him. "The Guardia Civil sent me."

He opened his mouth and revealed three yellow fangs. A sound emerged. I realized he was laughing. He jerked a large and dirty thumb toward the curtain behind him. He made the sound that he thought was laughter again. "That is good," he said. "The Guardia."

I passed through the curtain and saw Joyce Addams.

She was sitting on the edge of a bare mattress and wearing a skirt and blouse that had seen better days. A candle burned on a table near the bed. She pouted at me, the same sulky and spoiled pout that I knew from the picture I carried in my wallet. She was a lithe little brunette, twenty years old, very pretty, and at the moment trying to affect a go-to-hell look in her eyes but she was scared blue.

"I don't know you, do I?" she said quickly. "I guess I don't recognize you without the peroxide job. I'm not much good at recognizing Pepe's boys without their peroxide jobs. It's good for business, he says. It gets the swish trade of which there is gobs in Torremolinos, he says. You can't tell one of Pepe's boys without . . ." She began to cry.

"Who has your passport?" I asked. "Pepe or the gypsy?"

"What? My passport?"

"Your father sent me. I'm getting you out of here."

She was still crying. I patted her shoulder and made comforting sounds. I felt awkward.

She blew her nose, hard. She looked up at me and put on the brittle act again, or tried to. Her voice broke a couple of times as she spoke. "Pepe has it. Trust Pepe to know how to turn a buck. After he kills me he'll sell it. Doctored, of course. You can get a thousand dollars for a valid American passport."

"I'll remember that for when I go broke," I said. "Why should he want to kill you?"

She gave me an impatient look, as if my not knowing her life was in danger was somehow denigrating. Then her eyes opened wide and fixed on something over my shoulder. I started to turn, but the room was small and the gypsy Rafael was both quiet on his feet and very fast, and what I did was turn toward something that smashed against the side of my head.

The candle guttered, or maybe it was just me. Whatever happened, I was in no condition to question.

A voice said, "His name is Chester Drum. He's a private detective licensed to operate in——"

Another voice cut that one off. "I can read. Hand it over." The second voice belonged to Joe Cummings.

I opened an eye and saw a ceiling the way a ceiling looks when you are very young and have been on a carousel too long. I shut the eye.

"There's water if you want," Joyce Addams said.

I touched my head and brought away a sticky hand. I swung my legs to the side of the bare mattress, where someone had thoughtfully deposited me, got them over the side and leaned toward the floor with my head between my knees. After a while I lurched to my feet and made it to the curtain hanging in the doorway. I pulled the curtain aside. Joe Cummings and one of the peroxide boys and the gypsy were out there. Cummings had my wallet. He gave it to the peroxide boy. He was preparing to leave.

"See you later," he said to no one in particular. "About midnight?"

The gypsy, in English that would have won no elocution prizes but still English, said, "Midnight, sure. What about the girl?"

"Both of them," Cummings said.

"Got you, boss," the gypsy Rafael said, not liking it, and I knew how I had been made so fast. Who would have thought the gypsy understood English?

Cummings looked at me, grinning. "I saw my tax accountant," he said, and went out. The peroxide boy pointed a gun at me. It was a Luger. "You get to go back inside with sweetie-pie," he said.

I let the curtain drop.

"It's crazy," Joyce Addams said in what for her was a subdued voice.

She cleaned my blood-matted hair with a damp cloth. I sat back on the mattress feeling sick but not moribund, smoking a cigarette and staring up through the smoke at the rough-hewn stone ceiling.

"I mean," she said, "everything was so predictable. I'd finish school, and there was this boy back home, my father liked him, he's going to be a lawyer, but he's so damned stuffy. I just couldn't stand it, really. Everything was all mapped out for me. I didn't like school anyway. I'm not very good at school. I took off."

"You took off," I said.

"Hitchhiking south, complete with rucksack. After

a few days I wound up in Spain. San Sebastián? I was
never in Spain before."

"San Sebastián," I said. "Where you met Pepe."

"I was in a bar, alone. I shouldn't have been, not a
girl, not in Spain. They began to make a fuss. Joe
came along and after that it was all right. I was feeling wild and free, you know? I mean, in New York or
Geneva I never would have let myself get picked up
at a bar. It's why I ran away, I guess."

She looked away from me. "I went back to Joe's
hotel with him. I never——"

"Look," I said, "save it. You don't have to tell me
the story of your life."

She didn't hear me, or didn't want to hear me. "I
was smashed, really smashed. I didn't even know what
I was doing. Joe saw to that. Spanish brandy all night.
Boy, that Fundador. Anyway——"

"You stayed with him. You came down here. Okay.
How did it begin to go sour?"

"I was drunk off and on, mostly on, till we got here.
It was my revolt with a capital R. You know? Just the
opposite of the life I'd led."

"What you needed was a low type. Joe is a low type.
I get you."

"You don't have to be cynical. You don't understand me at all."

"Your father didn't pay me to understand you."

"Sometimes you sound just like him. My father."

"Look, Joyce," I said patiently, "the sooner you tell
me what kind of trouble you're in, the sooner——"

"That's what I'm trying to tell you. You're not even
listening."

"I mean right here. Right now. Joe's going to kill
you, you said. I want to know why."

"I'm getting to it."

I looked at my watch. It was eleven-thirty. "Get to
it now."

"I guess I came to my senses. I mean, if I didn't
want to lead the kind of life my father had in mind,

that didn't mean I had to—well, you know. I had an argument with Joe. I said I was leaving and he said he couldn't care less. That didn't bother me—much. A clean break and all, you know. But then Joe said I was going just the way I came—one skirt, two blouses, a pair of jeans and the rucksack on my back. I started getting mad.

"I followed him that night, after Pepe's closed. I don't know why. I was curious. He was always spending half the night somewhere. He went to the beach. There was a boat. A bunch of gypsies began unloading things, wooden crates. They took them up the beach to a truck. One of the cases dropped on the rocks and broke open. It was full of cameras."

"Sure," I said, "and maybe the others had automotive parts and Swiss watches and like that."

Her eyes widened. "How did *you* know?"

"Spain's a smuggler's paradise," I said. "They get the contraband in Gibraltar and sell it on the black market here."

"I went right up to Joe and said if he didn't at least give me air fare back to Geneva, I was going to snitch on him. He got real mad. 'You shouldn't have seen this,' he said. 'You shouldn't have said that.'

"One of the gypsies wanted to kill me on the spot. He had this big knife and he kept looking at it and looking at me. But Joe shook his head, no. He said there was no hurry. He took me here and talked to me. He said, 'Look at the position you put me in. You can blow the whistle on me any old time, can't you?' I was scared, but I was still mad. I've got this temper, you know? I said it was for me to know and him to find out if I ever told on him. It's crazy, but it was almost like a game, arguing with Joe like that here in the cave. Finally he said, 'Okay, baby, you asked for it,' and went away. That was last week. They haven't let me out of here since. The old man keeps looking at me and trying to paw me, and the old lady doesn't like it, and they have four children and the old man has a gun and the only thing Joe can do is kill me. He's got to, you know?"

She sat there, watching me. She'd told it all like a small child who'd run away from home, maybe took a streetcar to the end of the line or something, and then got hungry and used her pocket money on an ice cream and then walked home and got sent to her room without any supper, tired, hungry, but proud of her exploit.

Then, when I'd said nothing, she gulped a couple of times, and the second gulp became a sob, and she said, "I'm scared. I'm so scared. I just wish it never happened, not any of it. I'm twenty, I ought to feel all grown up after what I've been through, but it was all a mistake and I feel like a little girl. Take me home. Please, you've got to take me home."

Pepe, I thought, might have his own ideas on the subject.

Midnight came and went, and then it was one o'clock, one-thirty, and pushing two.

I got up and pulled the curtain aside. The gypsy Rafael was seated at a table with a plate in front of him and fish tails on it and a gun alongside his fork. Near his right elbow stood a bottle of wine, almost empty. Rafael took a swig. He was a little drunk, but not so drunk that he didn't look up at me and raise the gun and shake his head. I let the curtain drop.

One of the peroxide boys showed up at two-thirty. He looked tired. His white ducks were wet almost to the hips.

"All right, let's get moving," he said in a bleak voice. There aren't a whole lot of people who like to commit murder.

The boat was riding at anchor about fifty yards out in the surf. In silhouette against the starlit night it was a fair-sized cabin cruiser. Its inboard engine was throbbing powerfully. It would be a big engine, of course; big enough to outrun the Guardia patrol boats

if it had to; big enough to take us a few miles out in
jig time, drop us, and still make it back before dawn.
Not that when it got back would be of any importance
to us.

Half a dozen gypsies were hanging around, their
trousers wet. They had been unloading contraband. At
first their presence surprised me, and then I realized
that taking Joyce Addams for a ride had probably
been their idea more than Pepe's. Life is cheap in
Spain and cheaper still among the gypsies, and they
were hanging around to see that Pepe did what they
thought had to be done. After all, it was his *mujer*
who could put the finger on them for spite.

We reached the edge of the surf. It lapped up at the
sand and hissed back out to sea.

One of the gypsies approached me. He said politely,
"Your shoes, señor."

I just looked at him, not getting it. He smiled. It was
not an unfriendly smile at all. He pointed down at his
bare feet.

"Where you are going," he said, still in that polite
voice, "you will need no shoes."

"What?" I said.

"But I, I need shoes. For a favor, señor?"

It hardly makes sense that you can laugh at a time
like that, but I managed it as I bent down and removed
my shoes. He took them from me gravely with a little
bow. He tried them on and laced them. He took a few
tentative steps forward and back. He began to smile.
"They are a good fit. I thank you, señor."

The Guardia, I thought. *Maybe a Guardia foot patrol would come along the beach.* But I knew they
wouldn't. Contraband runners from Gibraltar have to
worry only about the patrol boats, unless they miss a
payment at the local Casa Cuartel.

A voice called across the water: "What's holding
you up?" It was Pepe.

Joyce came close and looked at me. She was trying
hard not to cry. I was trying hard to smile. Once we

were on that boat, and once it began to move, I knew we were dead.

The peroxide boy motioned with his Luger. He and the gypsy Rafael moved out into the surf with us.

When we were still about twenty feet from the boat, a figure leaned over the side and heaved up at the anchor line. It didn't have far to come. There was a slight splash and the anchor clanged on board. By then we were thigh-deep in water. The surf was gentle but the footing uncertain. Shells and sharp rocks cut into my bare feeet.

Joyce stumbled. I moved toward her, but the peroxide boy waved me off. "Rafael can handle it. He likes to."

"Keep your filthy hands off me," Joyce said. The gypsy snickered.

The boat was bobbing as we neared it. Waves lapped its hull. Two figures were leaning toward us from the cockpit—Pepe and a young gypsy. I was standing up to my hips in water that reached Joyce's waist. Rafael was still holding her.

"Easy does it," Pepe said. "He comes first."

I looked at the peroxide boy. He stood just far enough away so I couldn't go for him. He jerked the muzzle of the Luger toward the boat.

"All I came here for was the girl," I said slowly, looking up at Pepe. "Your business is your business. We could fly out of Malaga tonight."

Pepe glanced at the young gypsy, who shook his head slowly. "It's too late for that," Pepe said. "They'd cut my throat. Better come aboard."

"You're making a mistake."

"Move!"

I grabbed hold and pulled myself up over the side and into the cockpit. It was awkward work, starting in hip-deep water. Pepe got a grip on my jacket and yanked. The young gypsy on board stood nearby with another Luger, his legs planted unnecessarily wide against the slight rocking motion of the boat.

I got to my feet in the cockpit. It wasn't a huge

boat, maybe a thirty-footer, and the three of us made a crowd in the small open area behind the cabin. I looked forward and saw a figure standing at the wheel with his back toward us, ready to take her out—another of the peroxide boys. I faced starboard again and saw Joyce's head, her hair drenched from her ducking, appear over the side.

Suddenly it dropped back out of sight, and she cried out. She had lost her footing. The young gypsy with the gun started to laugh.

Rafael was grinning, half-helping, half-fondling Joyce as he levered her up to where Pepe could get hold of her.

The young gypsy was staring down at them. "Now there," he said in Spanish, "is a man who enjoys his work."

Rafael pawed at Joyce and lifted her.

"Damn it, cut the comedy," Pepe said.

The young gypsy began to laugh. Rafael, with a final prodigious effort, heaved Joyce aboard.

There was a moment's confusion as, soaking wet, she got slowly to her feet.

The young gypsy was still laughing when I hit him.

He slammed back against the padded bench in the rear of the cockpit. I was on him before he could get up. I got the Luger and shouted to Joyce. "Get down flat!"

She dropped obediently to the floor of the cockpit and I waved Pepe back to where the young gypsy was. "Hands all the way up," I said, "and keep them there." He obeyed. I moved to the port side of the cockpit.

A shot rang out. It was the peroxide boy in the water. He hadn't hit anybody, but now I heard yells from the beach. I aimed for his shoulder and let one go with the Luger in my hand. He screamed and flopped into the water, gun and all. Rafael was floundering back through the surf toward the beach. I saw a line of foam and dark shapes approaching us fast: the gypsies from the beach.

"Take her out," I shouted to the peroxide boy at the wheel. He just stood there.

I fired past his head. The windshield shattered, spraying him with glass. I was leaning against the gunwale on the port side of the cockpit, trying to look port and aft at once.

"Take her out now," I said. "Fast."

The engine roared. The boat began to move.

I watched the beach and the gypsies fade behind.

We stood a couple of hundred yards offshore and the big manmade mole that gave Malaga its harbor, ten miles up the coast from Torremolinos. I could see the lights of ocean-going ships in the harbor, and the city lights of Malaga beyond, strung along the hillside above the bay.

"This is where you get off," I told Pepe.

He looked at me. He licked his lips. "You're crazy," he said. "You can't."

"Why can't I? You can swim, can't you?"

"The gypsies. I told you. They'll slit my throat."

Joyce looked at him steadily. There was something in her eyes that I hadn't seen there before. "I wonder what they'll find when they do," she said quietly.

They went over the side one at a time, the gypsy with a sneer, the peroxide boy stiffly, his face frozen with fear, Pepe with a last pleading look at Joyce.

I put the spotlight on them while they were swimming. In a few minutes they clambered up on the mole, then they were gone and I cut the light and made my way forward to the wheel.

The lights of Malaga grew ahead of us, and spread out, and became a city.

CALL ME NICK

Jonathan Craig

"He'll see you in just a few moments, Mr. Wilson," the incredibly beautiful secretary said as she put the intercom phone back in its cradle and smiled at him across the width of the anteroom.

"Thank you," Harry said, trying not to stare at her, and failing completely. She wore no clothing. No one here did, of course; but then, not everyone here was a curvaceous movie star who had been dead only a few years. He rubbed his eyes.

"It might help if you were to say something nice about his horns," the secretary said.

"What?" Harry asked.

"His horns," the secretary said. "He's an old dear, but he *is* a little vain about his horns. It would please him if you were to compliment him on them."

"I'll do that," Harry said, still trying unsuccessfully not to stare at her. "Thanks for the tip."

The secretary smiled at him again and went back to her typing.

"Miss?"

"Yes?"

"Does he interview *all* the newcomers like this?"

"Oh, goodness no," she answered in the soft, enticing voice he remembered from the sound tracks of a dozen motion pictures. "He couldn't possibly. There are thousands of arrivals every day, you know. Tens of thousands, some days."

"Then I guess, whatever it is, it must be pretty serious."

"I wouldn't worry about it," the secretary said. "I'm sure everything will work out all right."

"I sure hope so," Harry said. "I've been here only four hours, but . . . Well, they've been the happiest, the most wonderful hours of my life."

The secretary laughed. "Well, not of your *life,* exactly," she said. "But I know what you mean, Mr. Wilson. All the newcomers feel the same way."

The intercom buzzed softly. The secretary lifted the phone, listened for a moment, then nodded to Harry. "You may go in now, Mr. Wilson."

Harry rose, walked to the black door with the initial *S* inlaid at eye level in fuming brimstone, and reached for the doorknob.

"Don't forget, now," the secretary whispered. "Say something nice about his horns."

"Right," Harry said, and stepped into the inner office.

The being seated at the massive executive desk smiled, got to his feet quickly, and extended his hand.

"Nice of you to drop by, Harry, and *very* nice to meet you." He had a deep, melodious voice, powerful but controlled, like the controlled strength of the hand that clasped Harry's own.

"Thank you, sir," Harry said.

"Call me Nick," the being said, motioning Harry to a chair beside his desk. "We don't stand much on formality here, Harry. Sit down and let's chat a bit."

When they were seated, Nick leaned back in his chair, folded his hands behind his head, and regarded Harry warmly.

Harry was certain the friendliness was genuine, but he sensed that despite Nick's casual manner there was something troubling him, that he had something unpleasant to say and disliked having to say it.

"Well, Harry, now that you've seen the place, what do you think of it?"

"It's wonderful. It's so terrific here I can hardly believe it."

"Scarcely what you'd been led to expect, eh?"

"That's putting it mildly," Harry replied. "But to tell the truth, sir, I——"

"Nick."

"Yes. To be honest, Nick, I never really believed there was such a place."

Nick laughed. "And what about the *other* place, Harry? You didn't believe in that, either?"

"Not really. I don't know . . . I just couldn't ever seem to make up my mind one way or the other."

"Well, it's up there, all right," Nick said. "You've been here about four hours, I think."

"Yes, and what a four hours! I never had so much fun. I never enjoyed myself as much in all the thirty years I was alive as I have in the few hours I've been dead."

"You approve of our ladies, do you, Harry?"

"Who wouldn't? I mean, with the kind of ladies you have here—and with no clothes on and all."

"Ah, yes," Nick said. "And the gaming rooms?"

"I never saw anything like them. Not even in the movies."

"And the various—to use a euphemism—spectacles?"

"Oh, fabulous!" Harry said. "Absolutely fabulous." Harry paused, remembering what the secretary had told him. "I hope you won't think I'm being too forward, Nick," he said, "but that's a mighty handsome set of horns you have there."

"Why, thank you, Harry," Nick said, obviously pleased. "Actually, though, most of the credit should go to my special horn wax." He nodded toward a small round tin he was using as a paperweight. "It's a formula I developed myself—through more millennia than I care to remember."

"Very effective, indeed."

Nick smiled. "Still, Harry," he said, "as pleasant as our little place down here is, it does have a few unfortunate features."

"I can't imagine what they could be. From all I've seen so far, everybody is having a ball."

"Yes, that's true," Nick said. "But wouldn't you say it's a trifle warm?"

"Not enough to matter," Harry said. "I'd hardly noticed."

"Atmosphere, you know," Nick continued. "After

all, we do have a certain tradition to keep up. The brimstone, for instance—don't you find it annoying?"

"Not a bit," Harry said. "Oh, the fumes did bother my eyes a little, right at first. But I got used to it in no time. I hardly think of it."

"Glad to hear it." Nick fell silent for a moment, then said, "Harry . . ."

"Yes, sir? I mean—yes, Nick?"

"Harry, I'm afraid I have some bad news for you."

Harry swallowed. "Bad news?"

"Yes, Harry—very bad. You see, there's been a mistake. I'm not sure just where it occurred, but it did. We've only recently computerized the Personnel Section, you know, and so it may very well have been the fault of a machine. Or possibly someone in the Screening Section erred. And of course the Selection Committee isn't infallible, either. In any case, Harry, an almost unprecedented mistake has been made." He looked away, plainly ill at ease.

"Mistake?" Harry said.

Nick sighed. "Yes. There's no use in trying to tiptoe around it, I guess. The bald truth is that you don't qualify for admittance here."

Harry half rose from his chair. "What? I don't *qualify?*"

"I'm sorry, Harry. By rights, you should have gone up to the other place."

"But I'm already down here," Harry said. "I love it here. I just don't understand."

"You simply don't have the credentials, Harry," Nick said, reaching for a folder on his desk. "Here's your file. You weren't even a *naughty child,* for Pete's sake. In all your life, right up till you died a few hours ago, you never sinned at all. You never did anything wrong, Harry. You never even had an evil *thought.* I don't come across a life-history as spotless as yours once in a hundred years."

"But . . ." Harry began, and then compressed his lips and stared at the floor. It was all too true, he knew; he'd never sinned in his life.

"I hope you'll understand my position," Nick said. "I really have no choice in the matter."

"You're going to send me up there, you mean?"

Nick nodded sadly. "Much as I hate to do it, yes. You don't deserve to be here, Harry. You just haven't got what it takes. I'm sorry as can be, fella, but I'll have to send you upstairs."

Harry's shoulders slumped. "What's it like up there?" he asked dully.

"Oh, you'll like it fine," Nick said, trying to make his voice bright. "It's . . . well, very restful and all."

"Restful?"

"Yes, indeed," Nick said. "By the way, Harry, do you have an ear for music? A lovely instrument, the harp, and——"

"I couldn't carry a tune in a washtub," Harry said. "And besides, I've got ten thumbs. Do they really play —uh, *harps* up there?"

"Yes," Nick said, "they really do."

"And what else do they do?"

Nick shrugged apologetically. "Not much, I'm afraid, Harry. Of course, you'll have wings, so you can always flap around a bit."

"I see," Harry said. "Play the harp, and flap around."

"I admit the place doesn't swing too much," Nick said.

"Listen," Harry said suddenly. "Once I won twenty dollars in an office pool and didn't report it on my income tax!"

Nick's smile was kind. "Sorry, Harry."

Harry shook his head. "It's so ironic," he said. "Edna *wants* to go up there. She expects to. She——"

"Edna?"

"My wife."

"Oh, yes," Nick said, opening Harry's file again. "I have a poor memory for names, I'm afraid."

"It's just that *she wants* to go up there. She says she can hardly wait. And me—I'm actually going up, when all *I* want to do is stay down here."

"Hmmm," Nick said, studying the file. "Your wife seems to be quite a woman, Harry."

"Oh, she is. She is that, Nick."

"Nothing personal, of course," Nick said, "but judging from the file, she would appear to have given you a pretty hard time. Eh?"

"She's very strong-willed," Harry admitted.

"Indeed she is," Nick said. "She wouldn't let you smoke your pipe in the house, Harry?"

"No."

"Or drink? Not even a beer on your birthday?"

"No."

"Or go bowling with the boys now and then?"

"No."

"And made you turn your paycheck over to her every week?"

"Yes."

"And gave you an allowance of a dollar and a half a day for lunch money and bus fare?"

"Yes."

"What happened to the rest of your pay?"

"She had rather expensive tastes."

"So it would seem. And did she really make you sleep on a cot in the kitchen?"

"Yes, she did."

"Yet it says here that you lived in a two-bedroom apartment."

"There's a phone between her bedroom and the kitchen. She liked to have me in there so that I'd be handy in case she wanted anything during the night— a glass of water or something."

Nick closed the file and sat drumming his manicured claws softly on the desktop, his eyes thoughtful. "It's now 3:45 in your part of the country," he said at last. "You died in your sleep about four and a half hours ago."

"Yes," Harry said.

"Your wife would still be asleep, wouldn't she?"

"Yes."

"And no one up there knows you're dead?"

"No. But what——"

"Harry, you never did an evil thing in all the years of your life. If I were to let you go back topside for a few minutes, do you think you *could* do just one evil thing?"

"I—I could try," Harry said.

"Trying won't be good enough," Nick said. *"Could* you do just one evil thing, Harry? I'm asking you straight out. Yes or no?"

"I think I . . . Yes. Yes, I could, Nick I know I could."

"Good," Nick said, smiling. "Because if you can, I'll be able to keep you with me."

"You really mean it?" Harry said excitedly. "Golly, Nick, that's wonderful!"

"Poor Harry," Nick said. " *'Golly'*! You never even learned to swear, did you?" He laughed. "But no matter. I suppose you've divined—if you'll pardon the expression—what you'll have to do?"

"Uh . . . Well, I . . ."

"No, I suppose, being *you,* you wouldn't have," Nick said. "Well, Harry, it will all be very fast and very simple. And after it's over, you'll be able to come back here, a resident in good standing for eternity."

"I'll be qualified?"

"Fully."

"What must I do?" Harry asked.

"You'll wake up in your bed—in your cot, rather—in the kitchen, very much alive. There are knives in every kitchen, Harry. You'll take one of the knives and——"

Harry gasped.

"You said your wife *wanted* to go to that place up there, didn't you?"

"Yes, but——"

"So you'll be making her wish come true. You'll be doing a very good thing, Harry."

"In that sense, I suppose I would. But——"

"No buts, Harry; you would. At the same time, you'll be committing murder—and that's a very evil thing—but it'll qualify you for admittance here, which is where you want to be."

Harry felt excitement flooding through him. "By golly, Nick, you're right!" he said. "Edna and I—we'd both have exactly what we want."

"And I'd have what *I* want, too," Nick said. "I've taken quite a liking to you, Harry. I'd very much like to have you aboard."

"I just don't know how to thank you," Harry said.

Nick chuckled. "Please don't give it another thought. Shall we embark on our little mission at once, then?"

"Gosh, yes!" Harry said, jumping to his feet in his enthusiasm. "The sooner the better."

"Just one thing, Harry," Nick said as he reached toward his intercom. "Once you're topside, you'll have only five minutes. The regulations governing unusual procedures such as this are quite inflexible, I'm afraid. Five minutes, Harry. Not a second longer."

"That's more time than I'll need," Harry said. "Twice as much."

"Of course it is. I just wanted you to be informed." Nick depressed a key on the intercom. "Please arrange for Mr. Wilson's immediate return to his body," he directed his secretary. "And alert the Receiving Section to stand by for his readmission here."

"Yes, sir," the secretary's mellifluous voice said.

"Golly," Harry said, "this is almost too good to believe."

Nick stood up, shook Harry's hand, clapped him on the shoulder, and walked with him to the door.

"Good luck, Harry, old man," he said. "You'll be back with us before you know it. Don't worry."

When Harry returned to awareness, the luminous hands of the kitchen clock stood at exactly five minutes of four. There was snow on the windowsill, and a wintry moon shone through the window, cold and bleak and remote.

Harry rose from his cot swiftly, took a butcher

knife from the cabinet by the sink, and walked noise-lessly down the hall to his wife's bedroom.

Beside the bed, he paused for almost a full minute, waiting for his eyes to grow accustomed to the dark-ness. His wife lay motionless, snoring softly, a huge, shapeless mass beneath the electric blanket.

Harry grasped the edge of the blanket and gently inched it down to his wife's waist. Then he raised the knife above his head, judged his stance and the distance carefully, tightened his grip on the knife until his wrist ached, balanced on the balls of his feet for the plunge of the blade, took a deep breath—and froze.

He just stood there, poised for the thrust he could not make. Then, very slowly, he lowered the knife.

His palms were wet with sweat, despite the cold room, and he dried them on the front of his pajama jacket. There was a pain in his chest, and he realized he had been holding his breath. He sucked air into his lungs and braced his feet, trying to stop the trembling of his knees.

I've got to do it, he told himself. I've got to do this evil thing.

He raised the knife once again, and once again he set his mind and body for the single thrust that would qualify him for admittance to the place he so desper-ately longed to be. Again, it was like the first time. He stood as if paralyzed, the knife held high, while the seconds slipped away and the tremor in his knees spread throughout his body.

Down in the street a car went by, a broken cross link in a snow chain clanking against a fender well. From somewhere across the city a police siren keened suddenly, then was silent.

I can't do it, Harry thought. I simply can't do it.

Of course you can, a voice in another part of his mind said. *You must. Eternity's a long time, Harry. Do you want to spend it in a place where all you can do is play the harp and fly back and forth?*

No! Harry thought. No! I couldn't stand it—not

after I've seen what the other place was like. I just couldn't stand it.

Then kill her, the voice said. *Look at the clock on the bedtable. Your time's running out, Harry. Don't you want to go back down there with Nick? Down where all the naked ladies and the fabulous spectacles and all the other wonderful fun-things are?*

Yes! Oh, yes!

Then do it, the voice said. *If you want to spend eternity there, you'll have to qualify. You've only a few seconds left, Harry. Just raise the knife again— yes, that's right—and . . .*

Harry did, and then did it again, and again.

I've done it! he thought exultantly as he withdrew the knife from his wife's body. I've qualified! I'm going to hell!

"Congratulations, Mr. Wilson," the shapely secretary said with a smile as Harry entered the anteroom of Nick's office. "You see? You succeeded in spite of yourself."

"I was beginning to think I wouldn't be able to do it," Harry said. "I don't know what got into me."

The secretary laughed. "I do," she said. *"He* got into you, Mr. Wilson. As a matter of fact, he gets into a *lot* of people."

"He does?"

"Oh, my yes," she said. "He's waiting for you, Mr. Wilson. You're to go right in."

"Thank you," and Harry opened the door to the inner office.

Nick was standing beside his desk, grinning broadly. "Nice going, Harry. Welcome back."

"It's great to *be* back, I can tell you," Harry said happily. "But for a while there, I didn't think I was going to make it."

"You were superb, Harry. Magnificent. A truly splendid performance in every way."

"It's all so wonderful," Harry said. "I've never been

so happy. Is it okay if I go out and join in the fun now?"

"Well, no," Nick said. "All those happy sinners you saw gamboling about are merely awaiting final processing. They'll all soon be down in hell proper—where they belong."

"What?" Harry said. "They'll be where?"

"Down below," Nick said. "And in case you've wondered about my rather large clerical force, it's made up entirely of assistant Nicks, so to speak—beings very much like myself. The only exception is my pulchritudinous secretary, whom I keep around for reasons as excellent as they are obvious."

"I don't understand," Harry said.

Nick pressed a button on his desk. "Look behind you," he said.

Even as Harry turned, a large section of the floor suddenly slid back to reveal a yawning pit at his feet. He gasped, and cringed back, staring down at a scene of such unspeakable horror that he felt his legs begin to sag beneath him.

There, far below him, were the tortured souls in their multitudes, chained and naked, writhing in a churning sea of flame and molten rock. Bloodchilling shrieks of agony and terrible wails of despair rent the steaming air, and the sulphurous stench of brimstone mingled with the reek of burning flesh.

Harry whirled around, to find that Nick had come up behind him. The horned being was laughing so hard there were tears in his eyes.

"You tricked me!" Harry managed to say, his voice high-pitched with terror. "You were just playing a game with me all along!"

"Of course I was," Nick admitted.

"But why?"

"Why?" Nick said, his slitted yellow eyes twinkling merrily. "Why, just for the pure hell of it, Harry. We've got to have a little fun around here, after all. You wouldn't begrudge us a few laughs, now and then, would you?"

"What a fiendish thing to do!" Harry cried.

"It really is, isn't it?" Nick said and, laughing, he shoved Harry backward into the pit.

DEAD STOP ON THE ROAD SOUTH

Robert Colby

They had just left a swift span of interstate highway but now the route south toward Florida was continued on a narrow, two-lane road which would pass through a series of small towns. Determined to reach their usual stopping place between New York and Florida before midnight, Stan Sherwood ignored the reduced speed limit and poured gas into his luxurious new sedan.

Stan and his wife, Barbara, had been driving steadily since dawn. It was a familiar, monotonous trip and, always in a hurry to escape the winter, they generally paused only once for a few hours of sleep.

Stan Sherwood had been an account executive for a large New York stockbroker. His personal speculations were often far more daring than those of his clients, and at thirty-eight he had amassed a fortune large enough to drift for the rest of his life if he chose. He had sold all but a few blue-chip stocks, and was on the way to another fortune in Florida real estate.

Beside him, Barbara, thirty-one, mink-coated and attractive, though at times she looked deceptively haughty, poured coffee from a vacuum bottle. She offered him the cup.

"No thanks, honey. Way that stuff tastes, I'm sure it's the same batch of coffee they served up last year, slightly warmed over. All the roadside joints in these burgs share the same coffee grounds."

She chuckled. "They must share the same cook, too. All the food tastes alike."

"In this part of the country you don't call it food," he said. "Don't you read the signs? *Eats and gas.*

Gives it that homey touch. Just plain folks serving just plain eats and just plain gas."

"They don't season the gas, either?"

"Not really," he replied. "Sometimes they add a little water." She lighted a cigarette for him and he asked the time.

"Going on ten," she reported. "Sleepy?"

"Not sleepy. Tired."

"Want me to drive?"

"We'll have to stop for gas in a while. Then we'll switch."

They crossed a bridge and a sign advised a change of county. Another sign reminded that the night speed limit was fifty. He was doing a little better than sixty-five and again he ignored the warning.

Moments later, there was a flash of red in his rear-view and he swore softly as the patrol car pulled abreast and a cop waved him over. The money would be no problem, the ticket only an annoyance, but with the out-of-state tag they would haul him in to post bond or pay the fine. The way these jerk-water cops went about things it might be a slow process and, already exhausted, the delay would prevent them from making it to the luxury and rest of the best motel along the entire route.

"Probably cost us nearly an hour," he told Barbara as he braked and pulled to the side of the road.

"Maybe they'll just give you a warning," she suggested hopefully.

He snorted. "Never. They'll take a look at the car and another look at you in that mink and they'll double the fine. These hicks live on the blood of tourists zipping through their hayseed hamlets in big cars on the way to Florida."

"You sound like a professional cynic," she said. "No doubt it's just a job to them and they couldn't care less about where we live."

With a sigh, Stan cut the motor and waited. There were two cops and one of these, partner to the driver, got out and approached Stan's window with cocky-casual strides. He was big and tall and booted. Something in the cut of his uniform and his unbending posture gave him a Gestapo-like arrogance.

Stan poked the button and the electric window slid down to admit a draft of frigid air.

"Your driver's license, sir," the cop demanded.

Stan removed the license from his wallet and handed it over. The cop studied it briefly under a flashlight, returned it.

"We'll have to take you in to the station, Mr. Sherwood," he said, his mouth tight, his face a pale, sharp stone in shadow.

"Well," said Stan, producing a fifty dollar bill, "I'll admit that I was speeding, but we're mighty pressed for time. So why don't you just take this fifty and pay the fine for me, Officer. I'd be most grateful."

The cop glanced at the bill without touching it. His lips spread contemptuously. "Now, you know better than that, mister. Besides, I think you're gonna have a lot more to worry you than a little ole speedin' citation."

"Look, Officer," Stan replied, stuffing the bill into his wallet, "please don't threaten me. Just say what you mean."

"You'll find out what I mean soon enough." His eyes swept over the car, slid inside to Barbara. He motioned to his partner to drive on ahead, then climbed imperiously into the back of the sedan. "Get behind that patrol car," he ordered. "It'll lead you to the station."

Stan started the motor and followed the taillights of the retreating cruiser. No use arguing with a rube cop, he decided. Keep calm, speak to someone in higher authority.

"Why don't you tell us what it's all about," Barbara said waspishly, turning toward the cop, her face taut, angry. "You imply that we've committed some crime, when we were only speeding, as you know very well."

"Shut up," Stan said softly. "It's obviously a mistake, and I'll straighten it out with the officer in charge."

Shortly, they left the highway and rode a broken blacktop for a mile and a half before taking a dirt road to a gate which opened upon a squat frame building. There was a green globe above the door and a sign: *Sheriff's Substation*. The building was small and gray and somber.

Escorted by the two officers, they entered a rectangular room containing a couple of scarred desks behind a railing, some wooden chairs, an ancient typewriter and a filing cabinet.

The driver cop pressed a button which was on the wall just inside the door and then they waited, standing about uncomfortably behind the railing.

After what seemed time enough to assemble a regiment, a man entered from a door at the back of the room. He was buttoning the jacket of a sheriff's uniform and smoothing a great welter of coarse black hair with a knotty hand. He was a heavy man, with a large nose set in a square, rockjawed face. His deep brown eyes under bushy brows seemed to have been startled from sleep. They studied Stan and his mink-coated wife with roving speculation.

"Well, well, what you got here, Floyd?" he said cheerfully to the arresting officer, whose partner was slouched in a corner, smoking a cigarette.

"We got trouble, Sheriff," said Floyd, and stepped behind the rail.

The sheriff seated himself at a desk and they conferred inaudibly, a frown grooving the sheriff's homely features. Floyd passed him a slip from his notebook, in which he had been writing under the flash on the back seat of the Sherwoods' car. The sheriff searched the filing cabinet and came up with a square of paper which he placed on his desk beside the deputy's notations. For a moment he compared the two papers. He glanced up darkly.

"Speeding," he declared. "I got no use for speeders, none at all. This county, we go mighty hard on speeders. We fix it so they don't forget us in no hurry. That's a fact but, mister, you got a real good excuse—ain't that right?"

"No, sir," Stan said meekly. "I have no reasonable excuse and I'm sorry. I'd like to pay the fine."

"No reasonable excuse, huh? Well now, I disagree. When a man is drivin' a stolen car worth close to ten grand, he's got all the excuse in the world to be hustlin' down the road. 'Cause he's just naturally gonna be in a hurry to escape the law. And I call that plenty reasonable."

"Stolen car!" Stan said incredulously. "What stolen car? I bought that car in New York three months ago and I've got the registration to prove it's mine." He fumbled the ID from his wallet and thrust it across the rail.

The sheriff examined it, then glanced at the paper on his desk. He looked up. "Same car all right, accordin' to the hot-sheet."

"Then it's all a mistake, right?"

"Nope. Wrong! Way I see it, you and the woman swiped the car from this here Sherwood. Maybe it was some sort of con game, it don't say here, but anyway, you got the car from this guy, along with his wallet and papers."

"Fantastic!" Stan snapped. "Absolutely fantastic! *My* name is Sherwood, and this lady is *Mrs*. Sherwood."

"Yes," Barbara said indignantly, "I'm Mrs. Barbara Sherwood and this is my husband. Do we look like a couple of car thieves?"

"Well—I must admit," the sheriff retorted, "that even in that stolen mink you look pretty good to me, miss. But over to the state lockup for women we got a few dames just as classy." He snickered. "And not near as sassy." He grinned.

"I don't care for your sense of humor, Sheriff, whatever-your-name," Stan growled.

"Sheriff Clyde Hamlin, mister. And you better get used to my sense of humor 'cause you may be enjoyin' it for some time to come." He leaned back and lit a cigar in a smug, lazy motion.

"That right?" said Stan.

"Mmmmm," said Hamlin, nodding happily, forming a circle with his lips, pushing smoke at them across the railing. "Yup, that is the God's honest truth I'm tellin'."

"I'm accused of stealing my own car?"

Hamlin stared with narrowed eyes.

"What about my signature? I can sign my name exactly as it's signed on these papers in my wallet."

"Good con man is also a good forger. Ain't that so, Bart?" he said to the second officer. "You was a guard over to the state prison and you should know."

"Yes, sir, Sheriff," he answered. "Take my word for it."

"If it's your car," said the deputy, Floyd, "show us the title, or a bill of sale."

"D'you think I would carry papers like that around with me? They're in a safety deposit box."

"Too bad," the sheriff said. "They won't help you none there."

"I'd like to call my lawyer," Stan said.

Hamlin nodded. "Sure, you got a local man?"

"Of course not! I don't even know the name of the nearest town. I mean my lawyer in New York."

"We don't allow long distance calls."

"I'll pay for the call."

"Don't matter. It's a rule—and a rule is a rule. Any case, New York shyster won't do you no good. Likely he couldn't get here for a day or two. The court will appoint an attorney."

"All right," Stan said wearily. "How much to buy us out of this phony rap?"

The sheriff leaned forward sharply. "That sounds like a bribe to me. You got one charge of attempted bribery 'gainst you already. This officer tells me you tried to grease him with a fifty. I'd advise you to keep your mouth shut before you lose your whole leg in it, mister."

"I'd like to post bail," Stan said quietly.

Hamlin shook his head. "Can't do that tonight. Auto theft is a felony, in which case only the judge can set the amount of bail."

"And just when will the judge be available to set bail?"

"Can't say exactly. He's got a mighty stack of cases to handle, 'nough to fill a barn. With luck he might get around to it tomorrow, but I wouldn't take no bets."

"And meanwhile?" Stan said with forced control.

"Meanwhile, this place is kinda like a motel with bars. We got some nice rooms in back, all free. The chow ain't good, but it ain't bad, either. Step forward and empty your pockets on this here desk!"

Stan hesitated. Floyd clutched him by the arm and maneuvered him through a swinging gate to the desk. Beside his cash-heavy wallet, Stan placed his keys, a handkerchief, a book of traveler's checks amounting to fifteen hundred dollars, and his own personal checkbook. An expensive watch and a gold ring were also demanded of him.

The sheriff jammed a piece of paper into the typewriter. "Your name?" he questioned.

"Stanley Sherwood."

"Your *real* name?"

"Stanley Sherwood."

"John Doe," said the sheriff, typing.

"Your address?"

"Same as the one on my registration and driver's license."

"Address unknown," the sheriff mumbled, typing again.

"Occupation?"

"Stock and real estate investments."

Hamlin continued typing. He went over the items on the desk, listing them, counting the money and checks. He gave the paper to Stan, who read it in a haze of anger and frustration, certain he would awake from this sordid dream at any moment.

He glanced up at his wife, who stood gaping beyond the rail. Wide-eyed, she had doubled a black-gloved hand and was chewing her knuckles. She looked hopelessly inept and fragile. He felt pity for her and at the same time he resented her silly pose, wishing she would break the silence with an explosive scene in his defense.

"If it's all correct, sign it," Hamlin ordered, extending a pen.

Stan signed the paper and the sheriff stowed it away in a drawer of the desk. His eyes fastened upon Barbara. "You're next, miss," he said. When she stood rooted, Bart took her wrist and pulled her, stumbling, to the sheriff's desk.

"Keep your hands off my wife!" Stan barked.

"Make me," Bart said with a slit grin, one hand resting on the butt of his holstered revolver.

"Don't gamble I won't," Stan said evenly, his muscles tensing dangerously.

"Now don't race your motor," said the sheriff, removing the cigar from moist lips in a leisurely gesture. "You're just makin' noise but you ain't goin' nowhere." Again he eyed Barbara. "All right, little girlie, everything on the desk." When she stood dumbly, he plucked the pocketbook from her fingers. "You got a watch and a ring, let's have them too. Nothin' goes with you, law says. It's a nice warm cell and you won't need that fur, neither."

Although he had seen it coming, Stan had not believed that they would actually jail his wife. "She's no part of this, Sheriff," he thundered. "You're not going to put my wife in some dirty cell!"

"Call her your wife if you want. The law says she's an accomplice and she goes into a cell like anyone else."

"Listen, Hamlin," Stan threatened, leaning on the desk, "you and your hick cops just try railroading *my* wife into jail on this trumped-up charge and when I get out I'll come back and spill your fat carcass all over this county!"

The sheriff casually took the cigar from his mouth, studied the glowing tip, then jammed it savagely against Stan's cheek, grasping him by the hair and grinding the ash deeply into his flesh with a twisting motion.

"I ain't sure you'll *ever* get out now," he said when Stan's scream faded to a soft moan, a palm held over his agonized cheek.

The sheriff opened Barbara's pocketbook and turned it upside down on his desk, where half a dozen items clattered, a lipstick rolling to the floor. Standing quickly, he caught her coat by the collar and yanked it from her. He jerked a glove from her hand and was working with demented energy to separate the big diamond from a reluctant finger when Stan shoved him off and punched him solidly in the mouth, giving a hundred eighty pounds to the blow, plus the added steam of his fury.

Hamlin crashed to the floor in a sprawling heap. He climbed to his feet awkwardly, blood washing the fingers he held to his mouth. When he dropped the hand to his holster, he revealed a jagged gap of broken teeth.

He brought the gun up swiftly and fired. The little flame seemed to spurt directly at the center of Stan's forehead, but the shot was wildly aimed and only gouged a tiny notch from his left ear.

Floyd chopped the sheriff's wrist before he could squeeze off the carefully aimed second shot. Bart clubbed Stan from behind and darkness fell.

When Stan regained consciousness, he was lying on the bottom bunk in a cell so narrow it seemed almost possible to reach out and touch the opposite wall. Apparently the cell was windowless, though there was an air duct in the ceiling beside a naked globe.

A solid steel door sealed the room. It contained a slot large enough to deliver food and observe the prisoners. Against the back wall there was a large, covered bucket which he guessed was a concession to sanitation.

He surveyed these arrangements with only a small movement of his head. He felt somewhat as if he had awakened from a monumental hangover. His head throbbed and there was a thin bandage taped to his ear. His cheek was sore to the touch and had begun to blister. His overcoat and gloves had been taken but otherwise he was dressed as before. The room was uncomfortably warm, the stale air tainted by the sharp odor of disinfectant.

Wondering now if there might be a companion prisoner, he climbed gingerly to his feet. No, the top bunk was vacant. He searched his pockets but they were all empty. Wrenching out of his suitcoat, he glanced about woefully. It was a strange cell, little more than a large coffin. Were they holding Barbara in a similar tomb? The thought depressed him unbearably. Further, he was stricken by a frightening sense of claustrophobia.

The only light, from beyond the door and cut to the size of its window, barely lifted the cell from darkness. How much time had passed? In such a place you couldn't tell night from day.

He went to the door and peered out through the chest-high slot. He viewed a narrow corridor spaced with three other doors, all identical. The cells were in a row, except for one which stood by itself at the right extreme of the brief passageway, crossing it. Where the corridor terminated to the left, a guard sat cross-legged on a wooden chair, smoking a cigarette. A shotgun rested against the wall beside him.

Stan managed to put his head through the opening and call to the guard, who ambled over with the cigarette fixed to his mouth. He was young and lanky. He had a slouching posture and a lean, farmboy's face.

"Yeah?" he said. "What's the beef?" The cigarette bobbed between blade-thin lips.

"What time is it?" Stan asked him.

The guard examined his watch. "Ten past eleven."

"Night?"

"Sure, what else? You ain't been out much more'n a half hour. You feelin' okay?"

"Well, I'm alive, at least."

"You're lucky, friend. The sheriff and his goons play rough." He plucked the butt from his mouth and ground it under foot. "Man, you sure belted him a good one right in the kisser," he said delightedly. "He'll be huntin' up a coupla teeth for hisself."

"Sounds like you don't care much for the sheriff."

"Hamlin?" He smiled a crooked smile. "Hate his guts. Got plenty reason to, would take a year to tell. Listen, I don't hold with what he done to you people. Just remember that if the time ever comes when you get outta here."

"When do you think that'll be?"

"Huh!" he snorted. "No tellin'. Way you punched him out, you might rot in here for a month or more till he cools enough even to get his mind onto it."

"And my wife?"

"Same."

"No! He can't do it! The law is clear! The law states that——"

"Clyde Hamlin is the law—his own law. 'Round here anyway."

"There are people above him we can reach."

"When? You'll have a beard down to your belly. 'Sides, he'll cover his tracks and his deputies'll swear to anythin' he builds up against you people."

"We'll see about that. What's your name?"

"Sam."

"Can you help us, Sam?"

"Don't see how."

"You could get word to someone for us."

"Nah. He'd find out and bust my head in. Can't risk it."

"I'd make it worth your while, Sam."

"A dead man ain't got no use for dough. You don't cross Hamlin. He's a nut. Outta his skull. Somethin' happened to him a while back, made him that way."

"What?"

"Tell you sometime, maybe. I gotta move on."

"You can't help us, then?"

Sam was silent, his bleak, bony features groping painfully with his thoughts. "Might be I could find some way to help," he said. "But not with the law."

"What then?"

"Don't know. Lemme think on it a bit."

"Where's my wife now, Sam?"

He pointed. "Down to the end. They got a special cell for women. She really your wife?"

"Yes. Is the cell like this one?"

"Pretty much. All them tin boxes're alike. One she's in is bigger. Holds four dames, five wormed in when business is good and it gets loaded up with customers."

Stan moaned. "She never saw the inside of a jail, let alone one like this."

"Supposed to be temporary," Sam said. "Just over-night stuff. They was gonna build a good one, never got around to it. You want a weed?"

"What?"

"A butt."

"Please. I could use one."

Sam produced a cigarette and held a match for him. As an afterthought, he handed over the rest of the pack. "Got plenty more," he said. "You wanna light, just holler. Prisoners ain't allowed no matches." He went away.

Beyond the door to the jail section, in the reception area, a tall, graying man in his sixties, neatly dressed and reflecting an air of moneyed dignity, was being confronted by Sheriff Hamlin and his patrol officers, Floyd and Bart.

"This is an outrageous complaint!" the man said forcefully, though his voice trembled with emotion. "It's completely false and unjustified. You have no right to hold me another minute! What evidence do you have? Where's your witness?"

"Don't tell *me* what I can do," said Sheriff Hamlin, who was again behind his desk, scowling and nursing a badly swollen, discolored lip which at least had the advantage of concealing the recent embarrassment to his front teeth. "We get an APB to pick up a hit-run driver who slaughters some innocent woman crossin' a street in a town sixty miles north, we damn well are gonna grab that man and hold 'im till the law in that town sends people to return him to justice.

"Yessir, if it takes till doomsday, you'll be here when they come. The burden of proof is on them people. Evidence I don't need, beyond what's on this here piece of paper." He glanced down and began to read: "'A 1968 sedan, color, light-green, with whitewall tires. Bears AAA emblem on rear bumper, the front right fender is dented.' That sound like your auto?"

"Yes, but that fender was damaged when a man backed out of——"

"'Witness identifies license number as follows,'" Hamlin continued. "'Tag number ID-82347.' Now how 'bout it, mister? That plate go with your car? And is the car registered in your name—Howard W. Stoneman?"

"Yes, but——"

"And would you be described as," glancing down at the paper again, "'a male Caucasian sixty some years, gray hair, slim build, appears to be tall . . .' Sound like you?"

"Yes, but I tell you it's a mistake! I never in my life——"

"That's enough, Stoneman. Step forward to this here desk and empty your pockets. C'mon, snap it up! Floyd, is this man nailed to the floor? Bring 'im here to me!"

Three days passed and, presumably, nights also, though one could not be distinguished from the other in the changeless confinement of the tiny cell.

On the night following his arrest, Stan Sherwood was given a reluctant companion to warm the top bunk. Dennis Kinard was a small, quiet man of fifty-two, unassuming behind steel-rimmed glasses, though he was vice-president of a national food products corporation. Like Stan, he had been traveling south to Florida, driving with his wife in a car which was practically fresh from the showroom floor.

He had been exceeding the speed limit when arrested. Later, an open bottle of Scotch was found in the car. After his wife had been trapped into admitting that she had taken her turn at the wheel, the bottle was produced and they were both held on the ridiculous charge of drunk driving. They were in custody until the judge could "find time" to fix bail.

"Naturally," Kinard reasoned, "it's a frameup, some kind of swindle I haven't yet figured. Either that, or this peanut-town sheriff is a maniac with some sort of grudge against the world, especially the world of people who have a little stature and a degree of wealth.

"I don't know what other poor suckers they've got lumped in this sardine can, but I'd be willing to wager my grandfather's gold pocketwatch that they own shiny new cars the likes of which are rarely seen in these parts, except breezing through town on the way south."

"Well, I can't predict how or when the game will end," replied Stan. "But the guard, who appears a minor friend in the enemy camp, implies that Hamlin is a psycho who might be taking vengeance for something done to him in the past."

"When I get out," Kinard promised, "that man will hold office in a cell of his own, even if I have to go before the governor himself!"

Since the arrival of Kinard, Sam, the guard, refused to discuss further his tentative offer of help. "I'm workin' on it," was all he would say in a whisper when he got Stan alone by the door. "Meantime, you don't tell nobody. You don't say nothin' to your mate there, understand?"

On the morning of the fourth day, with Stan in a frenzy of rage and frustration, Sam unlocked the door and took Dennis Kinard off to the "showers," winking at Stan behind Kinard's back. Stan did not understand the wink until it came his turn for the welcome cleansing.

The "showers" was a tiny cubicle at the end of the corridor. It was composed of a single, tin-stall shower, a wash basin and a mirror. Below the mirror on a shelf was an assortment of shaving equipment.

Sitting on a stool, cradling his shotgun, Sam delayed until Stan had bathed and was beginning to shave before he spoke.

"I been savin' you for the last," he said. "This way we can chew a bit longer without nobody breakin' it up. Now, first, I'm gonna tell you straight out about this here Sheriff Hamlin. Like I tole you, he's a nut. How he come to be that way is like this. Five, six months back he had hisself a daughter. Pretty little thing, goin' on nine, she was. The mama, she done died long ago.

"Well, sir, the sheriff, he lives right smack onto the edge of the highway, this side of town—which is near to three miles south once you get to the main road. One day this city fella and his woman come speedin' down the highway all boozed up and goin' ninety to the wind in one of them sparky New York cars longer than Mr. Peabody's hearse. Speed limit says thirty, mind you, but they didn't pay it no heed."

"They hit his little girl, I suppose," said Stan, turning from the mirror with a lathered face.

"Sure, don't take no brain to see that. Clobbered her so hard she was squashed like a bug against the grill, then kept right on agoin' and never did get caught up. Truck driver seen the whole thing but he can't make the plate at that speed. Car just lost itself like smoke in a storm."

"How'd they know the people were drunk?" Stan questioned, yanking at his four-day beard with the razor but eyeing Stan in the mirror.

"Anyone flyin' that speed in a thirty-mile zone has just *got* to be stone drunk," Sam said doggedly.

"So now Hamlin makes whipping boys out of rich

tourists who roll by in big, classy cars; that it, Sam?"

"How's that?"

"He takes revenge by arresting people like us on any old pumped-up charge he can find."

"Yeah, that's it. Longer he holds 'em, better he likes it, too."

"How does he get away with it?"

"Well, Clyde Hamlin is nuts, maybe, but he's sharper'n that razor. You could cut yourself on his brain."

"I'm sorry about his little girl," said Stan. "But that doesn't mean I excuse him." He washed the lather from his face and turned, mopping his skin with a paper towel. "Are you going to help us, Sam?"

"Might. Depends."

"Depends on what?"

"Depends on how well you scratch my back 'fore I scratch yours."

"Don't tell me you're on the take, Sam. That makes you almost as bad as Hamlin and his boys." Stan pulled on his soiled shirt and fingered the buttons. He was smiling a little, not really offended or surprised.

"No, sir, you can't put me in the same sty with Hamlin and his boys." Sam pinched his angular chin. "But I ain't much for pure charity, neither. Not the way this thing has got to be done."

"How, Sam?"

"Well, since I can't pigeon to the law upstairs and it won't do no good nohow, the only way is to bust you people out."

"You could do that?"

"Late at night, when Hamlin is asleep and his goons're on patrol."

"Now you're talking, Sam!"

"Yeah, but course they'd know I done it. Couldn't be nobody else. One guard, that's me. Sleep in a little crib up front, this side of the cell block door. Sleep or no sleep, I'm always on call. Day off, Bart takes over— oletime guard hisself. I got no home, was glad to find even this hole to crawl into."

Stan tucked his shirt into his pants thoughtfully. "So, if they will know you let us go, what then?"

"That would blow it sky-high for me. Here lies Sam, like this—" He made a slit-throat gesture.

"Well, you must have the answer, Sam, or we wouldn't be talking, would we?"

"Only one answer. When I bust you folks out, I go along with you. Maybe just to the next state. Or maybe clear down to Florida. Yeah, that would be a gas. Summer sun and coconuts, pretty gals, 'n sand between the toes." His rustic features exploded in a toothy grin.

"Okay, Sam, you've got a deal."

"Not so fast, friend. Slow down so I can catch the brass ring. I'll need more'n a little ole ride south. I'll need a stake. A big stake. Good job gone, no place to duck in outta the rain, no steady eats to warm the belly. Now what I always wanted was to hitch up a little business of my own. Maybe a hash house, even a little old burger stand."

"I hear you, Sam, but you're far away. How much?"

"Well, I reckon ten grand would do it up sweet."

"Ten thousand! Sam, you're pulling my leg. Come down out of the clouds. Land somewhere close, will you?"

Sam lit a cigarette and inhaled deeply. "Ten grand," he said. "Take it or leave it. Listen, to me it's a chance in a lifetime. For you, just a fly in the soup. Big man like you, what's ten grand?" He stood. "Think on it, if you want. Ten grand against what? A coupla months, maybe six in this stinkin' can. I reckon more like six, to pay for the sheriff's busted teeth. Might be you could take it, big man. But not your woman. Another week and she'll climb the walls."

Stan nodded gravely. It was true. Barbara would not be able to endure such an experience. She would be broken by it. And it wasn't as if he couldn't afford the money . . . "But I don't have that kind of money with me," he complained. "Where would I get it?"

"You write a check," said Sam, composing dramatically, a dreamy smile hovering about his thin lips. "And you make it out to me, Sam Packer. I take it to a bank where I got a bitsy account. I deposit the check and we wait. When it clears on through, I yank out all the dough, and then the three of us zoom off in your sparky gold car." He made a zooming motion with a sweep of his hand.

"It could take a good three or four days before a check on my bank would clear."

"Yeah, but I can have it rushed, special."

"And where would I get the check, Sam? My checkbook was impounded with everything else."

"All that stuff is in a locker," Sam said. "I can get my hands on the key."

"Can you also get your hands on the rest of our property? Traveler's checks, my wallet, watches, rings and coats?"

"For ten grand, why not?"

"And the car keys?"

"First thing, the keys. We ain't goin' nowhere without we got wheels!"

"How do I know I can trust you after you get the money?"

"What you want, a IOU? You got anyone else you can trust in this joint?"

"All right, Sam. But I'm warning you——"

"Don't gimme no warnin' or the deal is off, pal."

"How soon do we get started with this?"

"Tonight, late. I'll come get you outta the cell. I'll take you to my bin to put your handle on the check. We'll do it when that Kinard fella is alseep. He might sing to Bart when it's his guard trick. Bart would carry it to Hamlin. Don't trust nobody, hear? You tell Kinard and you're a loser."

Stan nodded. "Can you let me see my wife for a minute?"

"Nope. Start a riot. Them other dames'd wanna chew with their men, same way. But I'll try to sneak word to her." With the barrel of the shotgun he gestured toward the door. "You ready? Let's go."

It was after two A.M. by Sam's watch when Sam came for him, Stan discovered later. As Kinard's polite snore testified to sleep, Sam hissed at the cell door, opened it. They stepped softly down the corridor to his oversized closet of a room. It surrounded a cot, a miniature desk and a chair. A uniform and other clothing hung on wall pegs.

Sam laid the shotgun on his cot and opened a drawer of his desk. "Got the checkbook," he said, his hand searching inside the drawer. "I'll stick it in the locker again tonight and they won't never know the difference . . . Somewhere in here I got a pen," he muttered.

Stan had been eyeing the shotgun. It was within easy reach and Sam's back was turned. It was a frightening decision to make in a matter of seconds. If the cops were about, there might be a gunfight and someone could get hurt, including Barbara after he rescued her. On the other hand, if Sam crossed him . . .

Stan snatched the gun and leveled it. "Turn around, Sam. And be careful how you do it."

Sam froze in place for an instant before he peered over his shoulder and came about slowly. "That's the kinda faith you got in me, huh?" He said it with a puzzled shake of his head. "I thought we was friends."

"I never bought a friend who didn't sell me out, Sam. It isn't the money. Money can be replaced. I'm thinking of my wife. I want her out, and I'd rather gamble on this gun than on you. At least it's quicker."

Sam lit a cigarette without asking permission and leaned back against the desk. He was a cool one, all right. Even behind the gun, Stan felt overpowered by his confidence. "I want the keys, Sam. To the cells, my car, and the locker."

Sam exhaled smoke. "You gonna tie me up or beat me down?"

"Neither. I'm going to poke this gun in your back while you help me."

"Suppose I won't give you the keys? Suppose I was to jump you right now for the gun? Would you blast me?"

"No, that would be noisy, Sam. I'd just quietly break a few bones in your head."

Sam smiled easily. "Well, I was just testin' you to see what you was made of. C'mon, let's get to work on that check. The gun ain't loaded." He turned and this time brought the checkbook and a pen from the desk drawer.

It was no lie. Stan found the gun empty. He tossed it to the cot disgustedly.

"Wouldn't keep no loaded gun near to my own mama," Sam sneered. " 'Sides, you didn't have no chance. Had my hand on a button under the desk, sounds an alarm that could wake a stiff in the next county. No hard feelin's, I like your guts. Now sit down there and make up that check to old Sam Packer."

Stan shrugged. He sank into the chair and wrote the check.

"Time's runnin' out," said Sam, tucking the check into a pocket. "C'mon, back to the cage, big bird."

Another day limped by, spaced only with the serving of meals which were neither good nor bad, merely tasteless. Logically, night would follow dinner, though there was no other mark of its coming but for Sam's watch and the erasure of cell lights at nine.

The day had been like all the others. Hamlin had not once appeared, even to gloat. Nor had his deputies, Floyd and Bart, been seen, though in the first two nights they had occasionally passed by the cell door, escorting well-groomed, harried prisoners of both sexes.

Following blackout, Stan fell asleep at once. He awoke after what seemed hours later, though morning had not yet been signaled by the harsh glare of overhead light. Restless, he lay on his back, staring inward at the tangled web of his thoughts. Oddly, when he heard the sound, he was involved with the absurd problem of trying to remember the precise color of Barbara's eyes. Was it possible that he really didn't know?

The sound was created by the stealthy opening of the cell door. He glanced up in time to see Kinard make a slithering entrance as Sam departed, locking the door with no more than a feeble snick of metal-on-metal.

Stan bounced off the bunk. Startled, Kinard paused abruptly, recoiling.

"Where you been?" Stan murmured, though he knew all too well.

"I—I had a powwow with Sam," Kinard low-voiced back. "I wanted him to get word out we were being held without process."

"Yeah? What'd he say?"

"Said no dice. Too big a risk."

"And that was when you wrote the check, huh?"

"What check?"

"You're a nice guy, Dennis, but you're also a lousy liar."

As if in confession, Dennis sat wearily on Stan's bunk and began to dry-wash his hands.

"When did you get the pitch? When he took you to the shower?"

In the gloom, Kinard's head bobbed affirmatively.

"And then he told you to keep your mouth shut to me or he'd slam the gate. Right?"

Kinard turned with a sad little smile of resignation. "I see you went the same route," he muttered.

"We've been taken!" Stan said, his voice rising recklessly. "Taken right along with every other sucker they scooped off the road into this sweatbox!"

"Yeah," said Kinard. "That does seem to be the way it is. What do we do now?"

"What do we do? What *can* we do? We sit and wait for them to deal the next card."

"Eventually they'll have to let us go," Kinard said weakly. "Won't they?"

" 'Eventually' could be six months. And when you

come right down to it, why would they let us go at any time, under any circumstance you could name? We know too much and we're too many to be denied. Also, there'd be evidence in the form of canceled checks. Even the fact that we've been missing backs our story. By now, we're those people who mysteriously disappeared on the road south. They'll be combing the country for us."

"Still," Kinard said, "they don't really have any other choice but to let us go. Either they release us or they——"

"Or they what, Dennis? You're a crooked cop involved in a game of extortion so dirty you could be sent up for life if a sharp D.A. can build this into a kidnap-and-hold-for-ransom sort of crime. It certainly comes down to kidnapping—we simply paid our own ransom. All right, so what do you do with these so-called honest and reliable citizens who will pop up to accuse you if you turn them loose?"

"Well," Kinard replied, his horrified expression apparent even in the dusky cell, "I—I'd rather not answer that question, if you don't mind."

"You already have," Stan told him.

The next five days were the more terrifying because they passed in an electric vacuum of insinuation, unrelieved by a single hint of what was to come. For a day and a night, Sam vanished and was replaced by Bart. Then it was four days of Silent Sam, for he answered no questions and made no response to the accusations hurled at him by a half-dozen voices echoing up and down the corridor.

He poked food on plastic trays through the slots without a word, his face a stony etching in frame for a moment before it slid from sight, not to be seen again until the next meal.

Then, on the fifth day since Stan discovered the plot, Sam did not appear with the evening meal. Even when the cell lights winked out, not a tray had been delivered. Nor was Sam to be seen at his usual perch at the end of the corridor, shotgun leaning against the wall beside him as he smoked an endless chain of cigarettes.

Stan exchanged speculations with Kinard, both shouted from the cell door and were answered only by calls from other cells, one of them identified as belonging to Barbara, fear-choked and hysterical. At last all sounds died an unnatural death and there was nothing but the distant throb of what Stan had recently decided was a gasoline-powered generator.

When even that sound halted abruptly, all lights went out. There was a period of wall-pounding, door-rattling panic among the prisoners, followed by a still more startling silence.

"Don't you get it?" said Stan to Kinard, who was foolishly shouldering the cell door. "They've gone. They've all gone."

"You mean," said Kinard in an awed tone, "they've just gone off and left us locked up to starve and die?"

"Exactly," said Stan, experiencing a deep melancholy. With Barbara only a few feet removed down the corridor, he might never reach her. He stepped to the door beside Kinard and shouted, "Don't panic, Barbara! Keep calm. We'll find a way out!"

There was no reply but he heard a muffled sob. Wretched, he left the door and sprawled upon his bunk. Kinard came to sit woodenly at his feet. After a minute he sniffed and said, "Do you smell smoke?"

Stan lifted his head and took a breath. "No, same stale air, but no smoke. The only thing on fire is your imagination."

"Perhaps," said Kinard. "Just the same, I did smell smoke and I wouldn't put it past them. Burn us to ashes, make it seem an accidental fire. Don't you see, it's the perfect answer!" His voice rose in tremulous alarm.

Stan was forced to take another sniff of air. Now was it *his* imagination, or did he also smell smoke?

"Smoke or not," he said, "don't go yelling 'fire.' These people would kill each other trying to break out."

"It's getting colder," Kinard grumbled. "They cut the heat so we'd freeze to death, and perhaps it didn't occur to you, Stan, but we're all gonna die in darkness. Whatever happens, we'll never know night from day."

"Ah, shut up, Kinard. You're getting on my nerves."

Folding his arms across himself to keep warm, Stan closed his eyes. Surprisingly, he slept. How long? Was it a minute or an hour? Something had awakened him, a sound he couldn't place. Then there was a distinct jangle of metal on the cell floor which he recognized instantly. He bounced up, colliding with Kinard, who was descending from the top bunk.

He stooped and felt around the floor. He came up with a large key in his fist. Pushing his arm through the door window and groping down, he was able to insert the key and twist. The cell door opened.

"It's over, Dennis," he said quietly. "We're free."

He retrieved the key and, clutching Kinard by the arm, maneuvered up the corridor toward the front of the building. "We've got to find a light of some kind," he said at the connecting door between cellblock and office. "Even a match would help."

He found the door unlocked and shoved it open. They were greeted by the soft glow of a kerosine lantern atop Hamlin's desk. It cast flickering shadows about the empty room.

"Nice touch," Kinard muttered. "At the last second they went all soft and poured the milk of human kindness."

"Probably," Stan sneered, "it was Sam on the run. He just forgot his little old lantern, that's all."

They found nothing in the desks, not a scrap of paper in the filing cabinet. A heavy locker stood open, vacant, but on a table, coats and gloves had been piled. Even Barbara's expensive mink, by a fathomless quirk of human nature, had been left behind.

Stan went outside and peered into the darkness. The area was remote, surrounded by woods. In the distance, he could see a crumbling barn and a broken shack. He circled the building and returned. "It's nothing but a deserted farm," he reported. "Bunch of phony cops. They got away with everything—cars and all. We're on foot."

"Never mind," Kinard replied.

"We're free!" He sounded almost happy.

Stan caught up the lantern. "C'mon, Dennis, let's go turn the captives loose!"

They stood beneath the cold glitter of stars, six men and five women grouped together in the winter darkness, Stan holding the lantern and hugging Barbara against him as they stared at the shadowy substation. The building appeared small and bleak and abandoned.

"We ought to burn it down," said Howard Stoneman, the falsely accused hit-run driver.

"No," Stan objected, "we'd only be burning evidence. And we'd be like the very animals we'll be hunting."

"Police'll handle this," Dennis said, "if we can find a real cop within a hundred miles."

"How far is it to town?" asked Stoneman.

"Sam said three miles, once we reach the highway," Stan replied. "If he wasn't lying, it should be about four miles and a half from this point."

"A miserable hike in this weather," Kinard groaned to himself.

"I'll never make it in high heels," a woman whined.

"You'll make it if I have to carry you the whole way," a man answered.

"Well, then, let's get moving," said Stan.

Inside the ancient barn the bogus Sheriff Hamlin and his three accomplices, Floyd, Bart and Sam, stood in darkness, squinting out through the cracked, decaying boards. Their uniforms had been replaced by the overalls and jackets they wore when "police" operations were suspended. Presently, Hamlin was watching the receding glimmer of the lantern and beside him, greedy Sam was asking about the take.

"I got it all figured in my head," Hamlin announced. "Sixty grand from the six checks Sam got cleared through the bank, fifty-eight hundred cash if you include the traveler's checks we can forge. Watches, rings and assorted other loot come to about five big ones when you knock it down to what a fence will give us for the stuff.

"All told, less the rent on this beat-up farm, better than seventy grand, I'd say. Took nine days, so that's right on to eight grand a day."

"Man, them's swee-eet pickin's!" Sam exclaimed joyously.

"Too bad we can't unload them big, shiny heaps," Floyd grumbled. "That would bring it close to a hundred grand, I reckon."

"Too risky," Hamlin said. "It's not our line, hot cars."

"Sure hate to just leave 'em here in the barn," said Bart woefully. "They'll come back and find 'em, sure enough."

"Only wanted to give us a little extra time by keepin' them suckers afoot, first place," Hamlin muttered. He stared out into the darkness where the lantern shimmered once more and vanished around a bend in the road.

"Okay," he said. "They're outta sight and you could bet your last buck it'll take at least a couple hours 'fore they can shoo the law down here from that three-cop town. By then we'll be in the next state. So hop to it—let's roll it!"

The barn door was heaved wide, and Floyd drove out the fake patrol car, stripped of its markings. Sam closed the barn door and hopped in with the others. Then Floyd headed toward the sham substation where Hamlin ordered a halt. Sam went inside with a flashlight. Shortly he returned.

"Clean as a hound's tooth," he reported. "We didn't leave a clue nowhere." He paused. "That there is a nice, cozy little jail we done builded up. Darn shame —all that work for nothin'."

Hamlin snorted. "You call seventy grand nothin'? 'Sides, we can fake up any little ole house into another jail.

"C'mon, roll it, Floyd! Plenty more hayseed counties and city suckers just waitin' to be plucked."

RUSTY ROSE

Edward Hoch

Captain Leopold was staring out of his office window, watching the haphazard assortment of cars in the police parking lot behind the building. "Know what I'm thinking, Fletcher?" he asked over his shoulder.

"That the window needs washing?" Sergeant Fletcher replied without looking up from the afternoon newspaper.

"That, too. But I was thinking about all those cars, and all the people who drive them. I was thinking that man isn't an individual any more when he crowds into parking lots and fills the highways with these iron monsters, so identical except for their color."

Fletcher came over to stand beside him. "So what? I suppose cowboys' horses were pretty identical, too, except for their color."

"That was different, though, Fletcher. The horse. . . ."

"Never mind now, Captain," Fletcher said with a smile. "There she is, waiting for you."

Leopold followed his gaze until he picked out the familiar red rose topping the antenna of a low-slung French sports car. He hated to admit, even to himself, that he'd been watching for her. He was too old to admit anything.

"Take care of things, Fletcher. I'll see you in the morning."

"Right, Captain." Fletcher smiled and went back to his newspaper.

The rose was artificial, but the girl was very real. Her name was Nina Blake, and Leopold had known her for three years. She was a straight-haired blonde with long legs and an exceptional smile, a girl everyone liked and everyone remembered. He'd met her during tragic days, while investigating the killing of her father. The case had never been solved, but later, after time had begun to heal the sores of grief, they'd grown into casual acquaintances, then close friends, and now perhaps something more. Leopold's marriage had not worked out and, at forty-four, he was beginning to consider himself a lonely, middle-aged man with nothing to string the days together but the cynical demands of his job.

Nina Blake was still under thirty, and she bore her father's proud name well. Hamilton Blake had been a world-famous author and something of an inspirational philosopher. He had written a newspaper column and annual best-selling books on the value of hope as a virtue. If his readers were mainly the elderly and the infirm, they still took heart from his regular messages. Some said he hadn't an enemy in the world, but he'd found one that night someone hurled him from the window of his tenth floor apartment. The police theory was that he'd returned home to discover a sneak thief at work, but the disorder of the apartment had an almost studied plan about it that had always bothered Leopold. His friendship with the dead man's daughter had begun originally as an attempt to enter her circle of friends, to find, perhaps, some person who might have reason to kill a man who had no enemies. But gradually the file on Hamilton Blake had sifted deeper into the unsolved file, and Leopold found that he enjoyed Nina's company for other reasons.

"Busy day?" she greeted him, kicking open the door on his side with one long leg. She was wearing a bathing suit under her beach jacket, and her body was tanned a deep golden color that contrasted nicely with the light blonde of her hair. "Climb in."

"I will, thanks. Still enjoying your vacation?"

She shifted gears and eased the little sports car into the flow of rush hour traffic. "This is the last of it. Frank called and wants me to go in to work tomorrow."

"Oh?" Leopold's knees were cramped in the little car, but he never complained.

"Lots of orders to be shipped with the Fourth of July coming up. More than he expected." Nina Blake was secretary to the president of the Patriot Fireworks Company, a firm that had never ceased to fascinate Leopold.

"Still, you should get your full vacation."

"No hurry. I can take it later. I have to stop and see Frank for a minute now, about an order. Then I'll change and we can go to dinner. All right?"

"Fine." He rested his hands on his cramped knees, studying a tiny wart he hadn't noticed before.

By the time they reached the office and warehouse of Patriot Fireworks, the homebound rush had begun to thin out. Nina whisked the little car under a massive overhead door and came to a stop at the loading dock at the rear of the building. "I'll only be a few minutes," she said; then added with a smile, "Get out and stretch your legs."

Leopold went up the steps to the loading dock and through the little door to the shipping room. Nothing could be sent by mail, and the protected cartons that awaited the following morning's trucks bore such intriguing markings as *Golden Wheel, Butterfly,* and *Grand Finale Aerial.* Mostly they were bound for ball parks or amusement parks or suburban shopping centers in the northeast, where customers would be lured to weekend events by the promise of noise and spectacle.

Nina returned in a moment, tanned legs flashing beneath her beachcoat. Frank Oates followed her, looking tired and just a little bit disappointed to see

Leopold. "Hello, Captain. How's the crime rate these days?"

"Growing." Leopold didn't dislike the man, but he felt a little sorry for him. The fireworks business seemed to be Frank Oates's only claim to an exciting life. Nina Blake had worked for him nearly five years, ever since she came back from Manhattan after a disillusioning try at modeling.

"I guess the hot weather is good for both our businesses," Oates said with a chuckle. "Have a good time, you two."

Leopold nodded and mumbled something under his breath. He resented the fatherly attitude from someone so close to his own age. After all, he wasn't really going out on a date with Nina. Or was he?

They dined that night in a little place down by the water, watching the long inboards with their sleek lines and shining decks. Summer had come once more to the north shore of the Sound, and Leopold was enjoying it.

"Happy?" Nina asked.

"Why shouldn't I be? You make a man feel young again."

She squeezed his hand across the table and then reached for her purse. "I hate even to bring this up, because it's too much like business."

"What's that?"

"About my father, but it's always been there, hasn't it? Between us? In the beginning I thought that was the only reason you saw so much of me."

"Your father's murder was a shocking crime. I don't think we should ever let the case rest."

She nodded, but it seemed to bother her. "Three years is a long time. Do you think the killer is still around?"

Leopold shrugged. "Some people think it was a sneak thief. If so, he'd have been far away within twenty-four hours. I had other ideas, as you know."

"I know. You thought it was one of his friends, someone he knew."

"There was no sign of the door being forced, and the ransacking of the apartment had a phony look to it."

"He didn't have an enemy in the whole wide world," Nina said.

"I've heard that before. None of us have enemies, only rivals." He glanced down at her purse. "What was it you started to show me?"

"A letter. It came yesterday. Remember a man named Sam Xavier?"

"I remember him," Leopold said, a bit distastefully. Sam Xavier had been a sportswriter on the local newspaper until he was fired during a scandal over bribery of college basketball players. He'd drifted into fight promotion, but only a few days earlier Leopold had heard he'd lost his license. "He's not doing so well these days."

"I think he wants money from me. Read this."

Leopold took the letter and scanned it. *"Dear Miss Blake: I know who killed your father, and I have a letter in my possession that will prove it. All yours for five thousand dollars. Let's talk about it. Friday at your office. After hours—say nine o'clock. Regards, Sam Xavier."*

"What do you think?" she asked.

"It's a shakedown. He's out of work and needs the cash. I wouldn't trust Sam Xavier any farther than I could throw him." Leopold resented the letter. He'd worked on the case too long to be cheated out of a solution by some two-bit con man looking for easy money.

"He might know something," she said. "It wouldn't do any harm to talk with him."

"He was around that night," Leopold admitted. "I remember him being with the reporters covering the case."

"Tomorrow's Friday. I should see him."

He sighed and reached for her hand. "Let me do some checking tomorrow. I'll phone you. You're working all day?"

She nodded. "Frank's half out of his mind."

Leopold signaled for the check. "Why do you stay there? You could live off your father's royalties."

"Too much ambition, I guess. I have to be doing something."

"I don't like Frank Oates."

She smiled then, showing a youthful dimple. "You don't like any men who make a pass at me."

"Oates made a pass? That creep?"

"So? There are worse creeps."

"Now you're kidding me. Come on."

They drove for a long time, following the curve of the Sound, watching the darkness sweep over the water from the east, seeing the tiny colored dots that were the running lights of the boats.

"Have you spent much time on the water?" she asked him once.

"I once caught a murderer out there," he told her.

"How romantic!"

"My life never had much romance in it."

They were in her car because she liked to drive with the top down in the summer. She switched on the radio and found some quiet music. "Tell me about your wife," she said.

"I'd rather not."

The music faded and sputtered. "I'll have to get this radio fixed. It doesn't have the power anymore."

"Never mind," he said. He reached over and switched it off.

"Look! Fireworks!"

They were straight ahead, far in the distance, adding a spark of something to the mood of the night.

"No great thrill for you."

"They're always a thrill for me. Everything is." She was silent for a time, then she said, "That letter from Sam Xavier—it makes me feel like I'm on the verge of some great discovery."

"Don't get your hopes up."

"But I have to. Don't you see?"

"Does it matter so much, now, who killed your father?"

"He was a great man and people loved him, people he'd never met but who read his column and books. Of course it matters." She turned to look at him. "It matters to you, doesn't it?"

"It matters to me for a different reason. I'm a detective."

Overhead, the stars were beginning to come out.

In the morning Leopold went down to the newspaper and asked for a man named Jimmy McDonald. Three years ago, on the night Hamilton Blake was killed, Jimmy McDonald had been assigned to the city desk. He'd gone to Hamilton Blake's apartment for an interview, and had been the first one on the scene. Jimmy was a short, friendly man with thinning brown hair. Leopold had always liked him.

"Remember the night Hamilton Blake was killed?" Leopold asked him over coffee.

"Sure I remember."

"You went up to his apartment, just after it happened. Was Sam Xavier around?"

"Sam? Sure, he was around. He was always around, those days."

Leopold sipped his coffee. It was too hot and too bitter. "Do you remember anything unusual about Sam that night?"

"No."

"He didn't say anything to you?"

Jimmy McDonald thought about it a moment. "Nothing special."

"Have you seen him lately?"

"Not for a month. The state took away his license to promote fights. I hear he's strapped financially."

Leopold nodded. "If you think of anything, anything about that night, call me."

The short man gave him an odd look, out of the corner of his eyes. "Sure, Captain."

Leopold went back to his office, feeling uneasy. He telephoned Sam Xavier's apartment, but got no answer. The address was near the Patriot Fireworks Company, which explained why he'd suggested meeting Nina at her office. He'd be coming from the apartment with his mysterious letter.

Leopold paced his office for an hour, growled at Fletcher when he poked his head in, and finally went off to the basement files to dig out the reports on Hamilton Blake's murder. Reading them was something like going over an old school book, or a forgotten photo album. There was Nina, the first time he'd met her, and the reporters, and Hamilton Blake's body crushed into the pavement.

He flipped through the typewritten pages, occasionally smiling at some patrolman's half-literate descriptions. Then he paused at a familiar name—Bob Dante. He'd been engaged to Nina at the time of her father's death. Leopold made a note to look up Mr. Dante. The case was coming to life again, thanks to Sam Xavier.

Nina was waiting for Leopold in the parking lot at five, the rose on her antenna poking up from the midst of the cars like a beacon for lost travelers. "Hello," he said. "I'm afraid we'd better skip dinner tonight. I'm working on something."

"Oh?"

"Your father's case again. I've been talking to people."

"If I pay Xavier the money, maybe we'll have the answer."

"I don't want you to pay him. I don't even want you to meet him. I'll be there at nine to talk to him. You stay away."

"But . . ."

"Promise?"

"All right."

"I'll phone you as soon as it's over. I don't want you playing games with Sam Xavier."

"I can take care of myself." She flipped open the

glove compartment to show him the little automatic he'd brought her last Christmas. "Remember this?"

"Stay away from there!"

"All right," she repeated. "But call me."

Leopold watched her drive away. Then he went inside and tried to phone Xavier again. There was still no answer. He smoked a cigarette down to the filter and then went out for a quick sandwich.

At seven-thirty he began to grow impatient. He looked up Bob Dante's address in the phone book and discovered he lived in the suburbs. It was too far to drive and be back by nine. Finally, Leopold went back to the office and looked through some of the day's routine that he had neglected. He phoned Nina at her place and was annoyed and a bit disturbed when she failed to answer.

At eight-thirty he went back to his car and headed toward the Patriot Fireworks Company. The sun was still visible, low in the western sky, and the heat of the day still clung to the streets. He did not drive fast, not wanting to get there much before nine. By the time he turned down the street, dusk was beginning to cloud the brightness of the evening. He saw the familiar building and saw the unfamiliar car parked in front. It didn't belong to Frank Oates or Nina, and he was sure none of the employees would be working this late on a weekend. Sam Xavier had arrived early.

There was a glow, a sputtering, from the shipping room. Leopold knew in an instant what it was. He flicked on his two-way radio. "This is Captain Leopold, reporting a fire at the Patriot Fireworks Company. Send all emergency vehicles. Also contact Sergeant Fletcher and the arson squad. Hurry!"

Then he was out of the car and running. He'd reached the loading dock before the first awful blast sent rockets and sparklers buzzing about his head. He grabbed an extinguisher from the platform and played it on the worst of the flames, hoping they hadn't got too much of a start.

He edged into the shipping room, and saw at once

the crumpled body on the floor. He made for it, stamping out the licking flames. The deafening roar of a box of giant firecrackers shook the building as he turned over the body and looked into the staring dead eyes of Sam Xavier.

In the distance he could already hear the sirens, but a glance at the advancing flames told him they'd be too late to save any evidence. He dropped the fire extinguisher and lifted Xavier's body to his shoulders.

By the time he'd reached the street with his burden, the rubber-clad firemen were already turning their hoses on the building. He laid Xavier's body carefully on the grass, and then dropped next to it to still the throbbing of his overworked heart.

From somewhere Fletcher came on the run. "What happened?" he asked.

"Sam Xavier. Somebody pumped a few bullets into him, and then set fire to the place to cover the traces. See if you can find anything around the loading docks before the firemen tramp it up too much."

Leopold fumbled for a cigarette and watched Fletcher run off toward the building, his slim figure outlined by the orange smoke and frequent showers of sparks. The grass was damp beneath him, and presently he stood up. He patted Sam Xavier's pockets gently in preliminary examination, wondering about the letter. But if he'd had it with him, it seemed to be gone now.

The fire chief came over, and Leopold gave his report. Then he saw Fletcher coming back, a troubled expression on his face.

"Looks like the fire's under control," Leopold said. "They saved the main building. Find anything?"

Fletcher looked grim. "Just this." He opened his hand and held out a smudged artificial rose, like the one from the antenna of Nina's car.

Leopold didn't phone Nina that night. The hours until dawn were mainly filled with reports and the beginnings of a hundred threads of investigation. Even in the morning, after a few hours' restless sleep, he could only phone her a few reassuring words.

"You've heard about it?"

"Of course. I wondered why you didn't call."

He sighed into the telephone and asked his question. "Nina, you weren't there last night, were you?"

"No."

"All right."

"You told me not to go. You believe me, don't you?"

"I believe you. Look, I'm sending Fletcher down for you. We'll need to ask you some questions."

"I can come by myself."

"He has to look at your car. It's just routine."

"All right," she said finally.

"Nina . . ."

"What?"

"He was killed with a .25 pistol—like the one in your glove compartment."

"I told you I wasn't there."

"I'll see you soon," he said, and hung up.

In a little while Fletcher came in, looking tired. He'd been with the lab people since eight o'clock. "They're working on it," he said. "Just another case to them."

"What about the rose?" Leopold managed to ask.

"The spots were rust. They match the rust on the bottom of the corrugated door. She drove under it, and the flower got knocked off."

Leopold shook his head. "That's a loading dock. There has to be enough leeway for trucks to get in."

"It was half-closed during the fire."

"Look, go out and pick up Nina. You can check the car while you're there. And bring in the gun from the glove compartment."

Fletcher looked away. "Are we arresting her?"

"Of course not! It's just routine. Remember, she's the reason Xavier was there."

Fletcher shuffled his feet like a small boy. "Captain . . ."

"No comments. Not this morning. Just pick her up."

"All right." At the door he paused, "Frank Oates is outside. Want to see him now?"

"Yes. Send him in."

Oates was far from happy. His face seemed locked into a frown that didn't relax when he saw Leopold.

"Were you responsible for what happened last night?" he asked. "My business half-ruined at the peak of the season!"

"I wasn't responsible," Leopold told him. "I discovered the fire and turned in the alarm. The whole place could have gone up; the whole neighborhood."

"Why would anybody do it to me?"

"It was done to Sam Xavier. To try and cover up the murder."

"Who killed him?"

"We don't know, Mr. Oates."

"But you'll find out?"

"We'll find out. You're insured, aren't you?"

"You know how high the rates are for my business? I can barely afford to insure the building."

"I want to ask you a few questions about that building," Leopold said. "How could Xavier have gotten in?"

Oates shrugged. "Somebody let him in. The alarm would have rung if he broke in."

"How about the shipping room door?"

"The big overhead door? That would be partly open. We roll it down about halfway at four-thirty, but it doesn't get locked until the watchman checks the place at eleven."

"Why is that?"

"We close it halfway so trucks can't get in to make deliveries or pickups. The shipping room people go home at four-thirty. But we leave it open enough for cars to get under. I often park in there when I'm working nights."

"Were you working last night?"

"No. Nina had told me she might come down."

"So the overhead door was open halfway? Where was this watchman?"

"It's a private patrol, actually. He makes his first check around eleven."

"To your knowledge, no one was in the building shortly before nine?"

"Not unless it was Nina."

Leopold didn't like that answer, but he was stuck with it. "What about Sam Xavier? Did you know him?"

"Not really. He bought some fireworks from me once, when he was promoting an outdoor fight at a shopping center."

"Had you heard from him lately?"

"He phoned once while Nina was on vacation, looking for her."

"Oh? Did he say what he wanted?"

"No."

"You weren't curious?"

Oates shrugged and almost leered. "I figured he was a boyfriend."

Leopold might have reached across the desk and punched him then, but he'd learned long ago to control his emotions. The thing was difficult enough already, without giving Frank Oates reason to gloat.

"All right," he told the man. "Just one more thing —where were you between eight and nine last night?"

"If you think I tried to burn down my own place . . ."

"Where were you?"

"At home. Alone. The neighbors might have seen me working around the yard. I don't know."

Leopold got to his feet. "Thank you for coming down. I may have more questions later."

Frank Oates mumbled something and went out. Leopold stood staring at the door for a moment and then went over to the window. He knew he was waiting for Fletcher to return with Nina, but he couldn't really admit it. Instead he simply stared down at the parking lot and wondered what the temperature was.

"Yes, that's the flower from my antenna," Nina said quietly. "I noticed it was missing."

Leopold asked, "Where did you lose it?"

"I don't know."

He frowned and tried shuffling some papers. It was difficult, the most difficult interrogation he'd ever conducted. She was more than just a person to him, and he'd never realized it so much as in that moment. He knew he should have turned the questioning over to Fletcher or one of the others, but that would have been an admission that she was a suspect, something he was not yet prepared to do.

"Sergeant Fletcher says the gun is missing from your glove compartment. What about that?"

"I don't know."

He sighed and leaned forward, resting his elbows on the desk. "Nina, Nina! Talk to me! Were you there last night?"

"I already told you I wasn't."

"And I believe you! But somebody met him there, and killed him." He leaned back for a moment in silence. "I think it was the same person who killed your father three years ago. Don't you want to help find him?"

"Of course I do! You know that."

"You loved your father very much, didn't you?"

She nodded, and there was a hint of tears at the memory. "He was a great man. He inspired so many people."

Leopold nodded. "That's why I know you'd never have killed Sam Xavier to protect your father's murderer. But somebody did, and no doubt destroyed that letter Xavier mentioned."

He pondered it a while longer and finally sent her home. He was not yet ready to face the problems of her rose and the missing gun. Someone had been there before the scheduled nine o'clock meeting. Someone who . . .

He started pacing the office, his mind not quite over

the edge of a half-formed idea. "Fletcher, come in here."

The sergeant glanced at the empty chair. "You sent her home?"

"Of course. What else could I do?"

"Captain, if we find that gun and it's hers . . ."

"It won't be." But he remembered too well that the gun had been in her glove compartment the previous afternoon. Something had happened to it. "Don't you approve of the way I'm handling the case?"

"You should take yourself off it, Captain. I say that as a friend."

Leopold rubbed a hand over his eyes. "Look, I didn't call you in here for that sort of advice."

"I'm sorry."

"There's something on the verge of my mind, and I want to talk it out. Will you listen?" Fletcher nodded and settled into the chair still warm with Nina's presence. Leopold hurried on. "Xavier's appointment with Nina was for nine o'clock, but he must have gotten there about eight-thirty. Now assuming that he told no one else of the meeting, we have a somewhat fantastic coincidence. He arrived early, and the very person he feared, apparently the killer of Hamilton Blake, also arrived at that time."

But Fletcher was shaking his head. "No coincidence. Somebody could have followed him there, some gambler with a long memory."

"I don't think so, Fletcher. The crime was a spur-of-the-moment thing. A small-caliber gun, the fire afterwards—that's not a gang killing. We have a motive and it's a darn good one. Xavier's luck turned bad and he needed some cash, so he dug out this old letter about Hamilton Blake's killing. He wrote to Nina and maybe to the killer as well . . . Sure, that's it. He set up an appointment with the killer for eight-thirty, hoping for a double bag of blackmail. He'd sell the letter to the killer at eight-thirty, and then to Nina at nine."

"Who?" Fletcher asked.

Leopold shrugged. "Maybe Frank Oates. It was his place."

"You think he'd try to burn down his own factory?"

"He would, to cover a murder."

"Maybe," Fletcher conceded, "but I'll still look for the gun."

Leopold fingered the rose on his desk, looking again at the tiny fleck of rust. "Did you ever know there used to be a god of rust, Fletcher? They called him Robigus, and people worshipped him, a long time ago."

"That overhead door was halfway down, Captain."

"But I drove under it the night before in her car, and the flower cleared it. She wasn't there, Fletcher."

"All right," he said, but Leopold could see he wasn't satisfied. At the door he turned and said, "I almost forgot, Captain. That reporter, Jimmy McDonald, phoned. He wants to see you. Says it's important."

"Thanks, Fletcher. Keep at it."

Leopold thought of phoning the newspaper, but then decided he needed some fresh air. He walked over to the familiar editorial rooms and sought out the little reporter. The place was a bustle of approaching deadline, and he had to wait while McDonald finished taking down a story over the phone.

Finally the man put down his pencil and came over. "Want to go up for more coffee, Captain?"

"You've got something for me?"

"I've got something."

Over the coffee he told Leopold what it was. "Now that Sam Xavier's dead, I guess I can tell you. Maybe, somehow, it'll help you find that guy who killed him. Anyway, that night old Blake was killed, when I got to his apartment, Xavier was already there."

Leopold sipped his coffee, feeling the edge of the fiber cup against his lips. "You think he killed Blake?"

"No, nothing like that; but he asked me to say that I was the first one on the scene, so I did. The place was a mess and we didn't touch anything, but later I got the impression that Sam might have found something, some sort of clue to the killer's identity."

"Did he ever say that?"

Jimmy McDonald looked uncomfortable. "Once. Once, after a few drinks, he told me he had a letter. He called it his unemployment insurance. He said he could get a lot of money for it."

"Did he ever say who the killer was?" Leopold asked, holding his breath.

McDonald frowned. "Not really. I asked him that same night, and he said the killer was a poet. I think he said a religious poet. He was drunk and he didn't mean it literally. I think he was referring to the killer's name."

Leopold said nothing, but behind his veiled eyes he was thinking it was about time he had a talk with Bob Dante. After leaving McDonald, be stopped in a phone booth and called Fletcher. "Anything new?"

"I've been trying to reach you, Captain. We've found the gun."

"Where?"

"In a sewer a block away from the murder scene. It's Nina Blake's, and it's been fired recently. Ballistics is working on it now, but I'm sure it's the weapon."

"All right, I'll check in later."

"Captain, should I pick her up?"

"No."

"They'll have your neck upstairs."

"It's my neck, Fletcher." He hung up and went back to the car. On the western horizon, storm clouds were beginning to gather over the trees.

Bob Dante lived with his wife and new baby in a quiet suburban area. The backyard of his home sloped gently toward the distant bay, and when Leopold found him he was on his knees among the roses at the end of the yard. In the distance, on the deep blue water, a score of pleasure boats shifted positions like tiny chess pieces seen from afar.

"I didn't know you were a gardener," Leopold said.

"Oh?" Dante got to his feet, slim and handsome and very confident. "Captain Leopold, isn't it? You worked on the Blake case."

"That's right; and now I'm working on the killing of Sam Xavier. You may have read about it in the morning papers."

Bob Dante nodded. "I used to see him around town." He motioned out toward the bay. "Looks like we might be in for a storm. They always seem to come on weekends during the summer."

"You've got quite a view here, and a nice garden."

"Thanks."

Leopold took out his cigarettes. "Ever see Nina Blake anymore?"

"I'm married and a father now. I haven't seen Nina in a couple of years."

"You liked her, didn't you?"

Bob Dante looked up from his roses. "You might say that. I was engaged to marry her."

"Why did you break it off?"

"She broke it, not I. I don't know; personality differences, I suppose, or maybe she just didn't like being married to a struggling young lawyer."

"You knew her father?" Leopold asked, his memory vague.

"Hamilton Blake was one of the finest men who ever lived. I don't think the world will ever really know how many millions of people found the will to go on—to *hope*—after reading his books and columns. He was a close friend of mine, and he introduced me to his daughter."

"I remember now. You handled some of his legal business."

Bob Dante nodded. "I drew up his last will for him, leaving his money to Nina and certain charities. Perhaps you don't know just how brave Hamilton Blake was. He was in constant pain during those last months of his life." He almost smiled at Leopold's sudden frown. "I suppose you came to question me, to consider me a suspect again, but you see, Captain Leopold, I am the one person in the world who wouldn't have killed Hamilton Blake. I am the one person to whom he confided that he had only a few months left to live."

Leopold turned his eyes toward the sky. "It's starting to rain," he said quietly.

The rain stopped, just at sundown.

"You look tired," she said.

"I am tired. It's been a long day."

"Do you have the killer yet?"

"I have the killer," he said, not looking at her.

"Who?"

"You, Nina. You killed Sam Xavier."

"You think so?"

Leopold felt a grinding pain between his eyes. "I know so, Nina. You phoned him and moved the appointment up a half-hour, so you could see him before I arrived. When he showed you the letter, you shot him and destroyed it, and then set fire to the place. It's your gun that killed him, and the rose was from your antenna. That rose fooled me for a while, because we drove under the door without hitting it the previous night. But then I remembered the poor reception on your radio. You raised the antenna, didn't you, and knocked the rose off it when you drove under the door to meet Xavier?"

"Why would I kill him? To protect my father's murderer?"

"Yes."

"That's insane!"

He was staring out the window at the wet streets, trying to see as far away as yesterday. "I'll see that you get a good lawyer," he told her.

"I had no reason to kill him!"

"You had the best reason in the world. Sam Xavier was the first one into your father's apartment that night. What he found wouldn't be good for future blackmail, so he wrecked the apartment, to make it look like a struggle. He had only a few minutes before

Jimmy McDonald arrived, and the job he did was a bit too phony, but it fooled most people. Now, three years later, he produced the letter and came to you for money—not to reveal the killer's name, but to hide it. Xavier said one night after a few drinks that the killer was a religious poet. He wasn't referring to the Italian poet Dante, but to the English poet Blake."

"You think I killed my father?"

He could almost see it now, as darkness settled slowly over the city. A girl with long golden legs and a smile just for him, waiting in that car with the funny rose on its antenna. "Of course not," he said. "But what kind of letter would Xavier be most likely to find at a death scene? What would we have thought if he hadn't messed up the apartment? Your father was in pain, and all the hope he'd given others wasn't enough to sustain him. You killed Sam Xavier to protect your father's memory—so nobody would ever know that Hamilton Blake committed suicide."

HENRY LOWDEN ALIAS HENRY TAYLOR

Helen Nielsen

As the train neared Kirkland, the land leveled out and took on the look of river country. It was a long time since Henry Lowden had been so far downstate. The coming brought memories of Sunday School picnics with ripe watermelons and bottled pop kept cool in gunny sacks plunged into the water; of girls' laughter and the plop of a baseball in a catcher's mitt, and of all the other rich remembrances that hadn't been so far behind Arnold Mathias when he died with a bullet in his back.

When he thought of that, Henry Lowden could feel the weight of the snubnosed .38 hugging his ribs. It wasn't as if he had never killed a man before. A convict who attempts to break out of prison asks for death; and a man whose job is seeing to it that convicts don't break out of prison has to do that job as mechanically as the engineer who was now slowing the train for the Kirkland stop. What troubled Henry Lowden about having fired the shot that killed Mathias was the thing he knew about him. Arnold Mathias hadn't belonged in prison. He was an innocent man.

Ripe watermelons, girls' laughter, the plop of a baseball in a mitt . . . Memories faded as the train came to a stop. Henry Lowden looked at his wristwatch: 2:10 P.M. Only twenty minutes late, and still time to do what must be done. He stood up and took down a small black suitcase from the rack above the seat. He held it firmly as he descended from the train; for it, like the gun whose weight he felt under his coat, was important. The state didn't know it yet, but the case of Arnold Mathias wasn't closed.

Lowden was the sole passenger to alight from the train. It was July, hot, clear sky and sultry air, with the dust long undisturbed on the wide leaves of the burdock weeds skirting the station platform, and the sun raising sudden streams of perspiration on his grave, forty-year-old face. He left the sun quickly and stepped inside the station house. The waiting room seemed as devoid of life as the platform had been, until his ears caught a sound from the baggage room. He walked to the doorway. An elderly man in shirtsleeves and baggy trousers was shoving a large crate across the floor. He paused at the sight of the newcomer.

"Are you the station master?" Lowden asked.

The old man gave the crate a final shove with his foot.

"Fragile," he muttered. "How can anything so danged big be fragile?" Then, remembering the question, "I reckon you could call me that. Station master, ticket seller, baggage clerk. Anything to be done around here, I'm the one to do it."

"Can you tell me where to get a taxi?"

The old man scratched his graying head. "I do believe I've seen one or two uptown," he answered. "No-

body comes to Kirkland as a rule except those that
have family to fetch them. You're the first stranger
I've seen come in on the train since old State Senator
Dawes died and all his kin come to see what he left
in his will." He eased through the doorway and shuffled across the room to a small office with a grilled
window. "Got a telephone book in here somewhere,"
he added. "Whereabouts did you want to go in the
taxi?"

"The Grand Hotel on Maple Avenue," Lowden
said.

The old man stopped searching the clutter on a
rolltop desk and peered quizzically through the grill.
"How long since you was in Kirkland, mister?" he
asked.

"This is the first time. A friend who used to live
here told me about the Grand."

"Then your friend must not have lived here for at
least two years. The Grand Hotel on Maple Avenue
burned to the ground two years ago last March."

"Is there another hotel?"

"There sure is. There's the Grand———"

"But you just said———"

"The new Grand. They rebuilt on Center Street,
two blocks north of the post office. You can't miss it.
Six blocks straight ahead as you leave the station. But
I can go on looking for that telephone book———"

"Never mind," Lowden said, "I'll walk." He started
to turn away; then paused. "Are you sure there's been
no one you didn't recognize come off the train in the
past two days?"

"No, sir! Not since old Senator Dawes died, and he
didn't leave hardly enough to bury himself. Served
them right!" The old man chuckled over the joke on
Senator Dawes's greedy relatives, and then sobered
as his eyes were drawn to the touch of green being
slipped under the grill of the ticket window. He took
it up in his hands, tenderly.

"It's yours if you can remember to do one thing for
me," Lowden said. "If any stranger—anyone you

can't identify—does come in on the train before I leave Kirkland, you're to call the Grand Hotel and ask for Henry Taylor. That's my name—Henry Taylor. If I'm out, leave the message with the room clerk. Understand?"

There was a great deal of understanding in a twenty dollar bill.

"Henry Taylor," the old man repeated.

"Maybe you should write it down."

"No, sir! I never forget a name. A name or a face. Don't you worry about that, Mr. Taylor."

"And you needn't mention this to anyone."

"Not anyone, Mr. Taylor. Not a soul!"

Any stranger to Kirkland would have recognized Center Street on sight, because of its location. The narrow artery Henry Lowden had taken—neatly divided into blocks of unassuming frame bungalows shaded by oaks—emerged onto a wide circle of green containing more oaks and a bronze union soldier charging south. Threading out from the circle, twin rows of stern red brick and gray stone business houses faced one another like scowling adversaries across an asphalt aisle. The new Grand Hotel differed from its unimaginative brethren only in the concession to modernity of a stainless steel-edged canopy and a pair of plate-glass doors. Henry Lowden went inside. The small foyer was dotted with simulated leather chairs holding occupants who, reassuringly, evinced only mild curiosity as he made his way to the desk and requested a room.

There were questions.

"Name?"

"Henry Taylor."

"Home address?"

Lowden hesitated. "Chicago."

"Business?"

Lowden smiled wryly. "Historian," he said.

"Historian," the clerk repeated soberly. "I don't believe we've had a historian staying here before."

"That's odd," Lowden said. "It seems that big flood control dam down at the basin would lure every sort of tourist."

"I beg pardon?"

"Three years ago this town was humming. The payroll, locally, ran over a million dollars."

The room clerk was a boyish lad who had only shaved a few times.

"I guess I don't remember," he said.

"Many things are forgotten in three years," Lowden remarked. He glanced at the wall clock above the clerk's head. It was almost two-thirty. "Here," he added, depositing the small black suitcase on the desk, "send this up to my room. I have to get to a bank before it closes."

"Don't you want to see the room?" the clerk queried.

"Does it have a bed?"

"Why, yes. Of course."

"Then I don't need to see it. Tell the boy to take good care of the bag."

Tossing a fifty-cent piece on the counter, Lowden turned and walked back to the street. Outside, he stepped into the first doorway beyond the hotel and waited until he was certain no one had followed him out of the hotel, and then proceeded toward the circle of green which was always called the square. There was only one bank in Kirkland—the Farmer's and Merchant's on the southeast corner of the square. It was a two-story, gray stone building with a high arched doorway and a cornerstone dated 1898. Gold lettering on one window advertised the impressive assets within, a figure Henry Lowden studied while straightening a few wrinkles out of his coat and giving a reassuring pat to the area of the shoulder holster. He then went inside.

In 1898, banks were designed with high ceilings, marble floors, and piano-mahogany furnishings. Six people were within range of vision: three tellers, one secretary, female, behind a waist-high counter to the left, a farmer at one of the teller's windows and a small boy on tiptoe playing with a pen at one of the customers' desks. No bank guard was in sight; but at the end of the room, behind a brass-barred entry, stood the huge circle of the vault.

Henry Lowden turned to his left.

"I'd like to see someone about opening a new account," he said.

A nameplate on the secretary's desk informed him that it was Miss Foster who looked up with tortoise-shell rimmed eyes.

"Mr. Kern handles new accounts. Won't you wait?"

Mr. Sam Kern—Vice President was the nameplate on a deserted desk. Behind it was a mahogany door lettered: Wm. O. Spengler—President.

"Mr. Spengler will do nicely," Henry Lowden said.

"Mr. Spengler is in conference with Mr. Kern—"

Before further enlightenment on this impass could come, the mahogany door swung open, violently, and the loud, rasping voice of an old man shattered conversation.

"If I didn't keep check on you, William, you'd have my bank in receivership! No, I won't have you handling my chair! You take me out, Sam. Should have left you in charge of the bank instead of my idiot son-in-law!"

The occupant of the wheelchair was the last remaining fragment of a man, white hair, piercing eyes, a face withered with age until the skin stretched like parchment over the sharp bones.

"Out to the street, Sam," he ordered. "Ralph is waiting with the car. Don't you jostle me now. I've got a bad heart and can't stand being jostled. Open that gate, young lady——"

The stream of orders being issued from the wheelchair ceased abruptly as Henry Lowden reached out and opened the small gate in the counter. The piercing eyes looked upward.

"You're not an employee," the fragment snapped.

"That's right," Henry Lowden said, "I'm not."

"Couldn't be an employee. Too wide awake. You're a customer."

"I hope to be," Henry Lowden said.

"A new account? William—" The old man twisted about in the wheelchair. "Come out here and take care of this man! Fifty-five years I was president of this bank, and I never failed to shake hands with every new customer. That's one thing folks could say for Josiah Wingate. Sam, roll me over to that desk where the boy is. Boy, you're getting off to a fine start. Here's a silver dollar for you. Ask your Daddy to put it in the Kirkland Farmer's and Merchant's Bank and watch it grow. All right, Sam. Don't dawdle! Roll me out to the car!"

Sam Kern, the chair, and its vociferous occupant rolled out of sight, leaving behind a bewildered boy with a silver coin, promptly deposited in a trouser pocket. Henry Lowden turned back to Miss Foster, but now the doorway behind her was filled by someone who could only by William, William Spengler. Tall, graying, an expression of smoldering fury darkening his face, he became aware of Lowden and smothered the fury.

"Miss Foster, is this gentleman here to see me?"

"Why—yes, Mr. Spengler. Unless Mr. Kern——"

"Mr. Kern is busy. Don't keep the gentleman waiting."

The office of W. O. Spengler—President was as dated as the rest of the building; mahogany paneling, a massive desk, tall leather chairs. Spengler had gone to the window and stood peering down at the street below, his hands making fists at his side. Over his shoulder, Henry Taylor caught a glimpse of the invalid's chair being folded into the back seat of a limousine. When Spengler turned about and caught him watching, Henry Lowden smiled.

"They get difficult as they grow older," he observed.

"Yes, they do," Spengler said. "I have to humor him. Not only is he my father-in-law, but he founded this bank. He can't seem to adjust to retirement. Won't you sit down, Mr.——"

"Taylor," he said, as he sat down in one of the leather chairs. "Henry Taylor. I have a letter of credit——" He reached under his coat, felt the cold steel in his holster, and then found the inner pocket—"from my bank in Chicago," he added. "I wish to transfer some funds to this bank while I'm here doing research."

"Research?" Spengler returned to his desk and accepted the letter. "In what field, Mr. Taylor? Perhaps I can be of assistance."

"I'm sure you can," Lowden said. "It's for a book I'm doing on the subject of unsolved crimes."

William Spengler had a peculiar face. One emotion could overlap another like a double exposure. What was left of the fury folded into an alerted curiosity which finally became articulate.

"And you have come to Kirkland to do research for such a project?"

"I'm surprised that I'm the first," Lowden said. "You read the newspapers, don't you?"

"I have little time——"

"But you must know that Arnold Mathias is dead. He was shot down by a guard while attempting to break out of State Prison two days ago. His cellmate escaped, but Mathias was killed.

"Yes," Spengler reflected. "I did hear a newscast——"

"And this is the Kirkland Farmer's and Merchant's Bank where Arnold Mathias was employed in December of 1956."

William Spengler was no longer interested in the letter of credit. His eyes were almost as sharp as those of his father-in-law, and they were fixed on the face of the man who called himself Henry Taylor.

"You didn't have to come to Kirkland to learn that," he said.

"No, I didn't. But there are some things I did have

to come here to learn. Let's recapitulate. Mathias was a trusted employee——"

"Hired by my father-in-law the year before he retired." Spengler added, "And against my advice."

"Because Mathias had a record?"

"A juvenile record. Let's not make it sound worse than it was, Mr. Taylor. My father-in-law has a philanthropic streak where young people are concerned. You saw him just now with the boy out front. Mathias had come from a broken home—the usual sad story. Mr. Wingate wanted to give him a chance. I wanted to protect the bank."

"But you kept him on after you succeeded Mr. Wingate."

"There was no reason not to keep him on. He was a willing worker, seemingly honest. Then, in '56, the Dyer Construction Company transferred $500,000 in cash from their St. Louis bank to meet the local payroll on the dam project. We kept it in the vault. Only Mr. Kern and myself had keys, and only Mr. Kern and myself handled the payroll. But Arnold took to working late. I never suspected the reason until after the theft. You know the story, Mr. Taylor. Arnold took $200,000 from that vault."

"He never admitted taking it."

"But he was convicted in a court of law. I hired Ira Casey to defend him—the best defense attorney in the state. He was convicted, nevertheless."

"On a plea of not guilty," Lowden said. "Do you know what Mathias was doing at State Prison, Mr. Spengler? He'd gotten hold of a set of court records of that trial, and he'd gone over every word of testimony again and again until he found something he was looking for. He marked it off and then drew some maps. Maps of this bank."

Spengler's face was interesting to watch. It was as if an unseen hand had wiped away all expression. But his voice had a cutting edge.

"How do you know all this?" he demanded.

Henry Lowden smiled. "Now, I couldn't tell you

that, Mr. Spengler. A writer can't reveal his sources of information. They might dry up."

"Then why should I believe you?"

"Because I'm in possession of those court records —and the maps. I was hoping you might find time to go over them with me—that is, if you really are interested in my book."

Spengler was silent for several seconds. One hand reached down and pulled at the long desk drawer in front of him. He seemed about to take something out of it; then changed his mind.

"Do you think there's a market for such a book, Mr. Henry?" he asked.

"Taylor," Henry Lowden corrected. "Mr. Taylor. Yes, I'm sure there is. Consider the fact that the theft occurred on the afternoon you were called home because your wife was dying—that gives the story emotional appeal. And then there was Mr. Kern's early departure because his only son was playing his first varsity basketball game forty miles away, and he had to drive over icy roads to watch him play. That gives the story family appeal. But what makes it most interesting, and what has bewildered the authorities for two and a half years, is the fact that—even if Mathias did commit the crime for which he was convicted— no trace has ever been found of the $200,000. What's the trouble, Mr. Spengler? Is something wrong with my letter of credit?"

William Spengler had closed the desk drawer and picked up the letter of credit. He came to his feet.

"I'll see if Mr. Kern is back," he said. Then, as he started toward the door, he looked back and added: "Mr. Taylor, perhaps you will have dinner with me in my home tonight."

"That's very kind of you," Henry Lowden said. "Very kind indeed."

"And perhaps you will bring those court records and maps so we can study them together."

"Now, that's more than kind. I was sure you would be cooperative, Mr. Spengler."

When Spengler left the room, Henry Lowden went quickly from his chair to the opposite side of the desk. He opened the long drawer to find what had held Spengler's interest. It was a newspaper two days old, folded to a feature story—

ARNOLD MATHIAS
SLAIN

Arnold Mathias, 24, convicted of stealing $200,000 from the Kirkwood Farmer's and Merchant's Bank in 1956, was shot and killed early this morning while attempting to escape from State Prison. H. T. Lowden, the guard who shot Mathias, stated that Mathias had always insisted he was framed.

"I don't know why he broke for it," Lowden told reporters. "I believed in his innocence, too."

A cellmate, Thomas Henry, 40, made good his escape in a laundry truck . . .

The man who called himself Henry Taylor read no further. He closed the drawer quietly.

It was very old brandy. It lay golden amber in the bottom of the snifter, moving in lazy circles as Henry Lowden gently shook the glass. The dinner had been as heavy and unimaginative as the square-faced housekeeper who prepared and served it, but within William Spengler's study the atmosphere changed. The architecture was still Midwestern Victorian, and the furnishings slightly rural English, but above an ugly mantlepiece hung a surprisingly good French painting. In William Spengler's house—to be more exact, Josiah Wingate's house—the painting was as conspicuous as a carrousel in a mausoleum.

Spengler didn't touch his brandy. His eyes were fixed on the small black suitcase at Henry Taylor's feet.

"It's a pity Mathias attempted to escape," he remarked. "He might have been up for parole soon."

"Parole boards are notoriously slow in this state," Henry Lowden mused, "and Mathias had no friends to prod from the outside."

"That's not true! I hired Ira Casey——"

"Who was a college classmate of yours and friend of almost thirty years standing."

"What's wrong with that?"

"Nothing. I would say it was very convenient. I would have considered myself lucky to have such a friend if $200,000 had disappeared from my bank."

"I hired Casey to defend Mathias!" Spengler protested.

"And the Kirkland Farmer's and Merchant's Bank," Lowden added quietly. "This is excellent brandy, Mr. Spengler. I don't suppose you buy this in Kirkland."

"I'm not chained to Kirkland! I get out occasionally."

"Out," Lowden repeated. "That's an apt word. It's what Mathias wanted—and a chance to clear his name."

"Or to recover the $200,000 from wherever he had it hidden," Spengler said.

Henry Lowden drained the contents of the brandy snifter and lifted his eyes to meet Spengler's. There was a speculative smile in them.

"But where could he have hidden it, Mr. Spengler? That's what makes this case so interesting. Two hundred thousand dollars is a difficult sum to dispose of —or to acquire unobtrusively—in a town as small as Kirkland. Let's assume that Mathias did take the money, but wasn't convicted. What could he have done? He couldn't use it locally without creating suspicion. He was a bank teller on a fixed income, just as Sam Kern is a bank official on a fixed income."

"And just as I am a bank president on a fixed income," Spengler interposed.

"That's my point. The man who took that money from the vault would have had to do one of three things. He could have left town—which, obviously, he didn't. None of the three men who were in the vault the day the money was taken went anywhere —except, one of them, to prison."

"The three men," Spengler repeated.

"Mathias, Kern and yourself, Mr. Spengler. It's all here in the court records." Lowden took up the suit-case and carried it to Spengler's desk. He opened it and took out a sheaf of papers. "It was the last Friday before Christmas," he continued. "The bank closed at three. The tellers, Mathias, Peterson——"

"Pierson," Spengler corrected. "Lee Pierson. He's still with the bank, and so is Goddard. I was a witness at the trial, Mr. Taylor. I know what is in the records. When the bank closed, the tellers began to count their cash. Pierson and Goddard were finished and out of the bank by three-thirty. Mathias had trouble getting his cash to balance. I went over it with him twice before we caught the error. Sam Kern was in the vault checking the Dyer payroll against the remaining funds. The payroll went out on Friday, and the balancing usually kept us at the bank until four or later."

"But at three-forty," Lowden said, "you received a telephone call from your housekeeper, Mrs. Holmes. Now here's a section of testimony Mathias had brack-eted. Mrs. Holmes was on the stand being examined by the District Attorney. His object was to pinpoint the situation which resulted in Mathias being left alone in the bank.

Q. Mrs. Holmes, will you please tell the court what you did following Mrs. Spengler's heart attack on the date in question?

A. I got the medicine Dr. Clinton had left and gave her a spoonful.

Q. Was Mrs. Spengler subject to such attacks?

A. Yes, sir. Mrs. Spengler had been a semi-invalid for more than twenty years. We knew it was only a matter of time. I gave her the medi-cine and got her into bed, and then I called Dr.

Clinton and told him this one seemed worse than the others. He asked me to call Mr. Spengler right away, and that's what I did.

"Mr. Taylor," Spengler interrupted. "I told you that I'm familiar with the testimony at the trial. What are you trying to prove?"

"I'm not trying to prove anything," Lowden answered quietly. "I'm only trying to discover what Arnold Mathias wanted to prove. A few pages later in the transcript is another bracketed section. It's the testimony of Samuel Kern being questioned by the District Attorney. Kern states that he, Mathias, and yourself were alone in the bank when Mrs. Holmes called. He was in the vault. Hearing the telephone, he stepped outside because he thought it might be his wife calling to remind him of the basketball game.

Q. When you stepped outside, Mr. Kern, did you lock the vault?

A. No, I didn't. I wasn't finished checking the payroll. The call was from Spengler's housekeeper informing him that his wife had just suffered another heart attack. He left for home immediately. That is, he started to leave. He put on his hat and coat and went out to the parking lot at the side of the bank; but he came right back. He couldn't get his car started. I offered to push him, but he said it would be better if Arnold pushed him. I had a new car with an automatic shift. Arnold had an old one with a standard shift. When the pavement is icy, it's hard to get a start from an automatic drive.

Q. And so Mr. Spengler left the second time with Arnold Mathias.

A. No, sir. Not then. Arnold never parked in the lot behind the bank. I think he was sensitive because Mr. Spengler had kidded him about his old car giving the bank a bad name. He always parked on the side street around the corner. While he went to get his car and drive it back, Mr. Spengler came into the vault to help me; but he was too upset. Finally, he asked me to call Dr. Clinton for him. I did, but the doctor had already left for Mrs. Spengler's house. By the time I finished the call, Arnold was back. Before Mr. Spengler went out with him he said to me, 'I know how much it means to you to see your son play his first game tonight, Sam. You clear out and let Arnold lock up.'

Henry Lowden finished reading. When he looked up Spengler was watching him closely. "That section of testimony is not only bracketed," Taylor added, "but a few words of it are underlined. '. . . *Mr. Spengler came back into the vault to help me,*' and again, '. . . *he asked me to call Dr. Clinton for him.*' That makes an interesting coupling, don't you think?"

Spengler simply ignored the question.

"What about your second point, Mr. Taylor? You said that Mathias could have done three things with the money."

Lowden smiled. "A subject does get tedious when it's pursued too hotly, doesn't it? The second thing Mathias could have done was to hide the money, as you suggested. But where? His room was thoroughly searched by the police at the time of his arrest, and his car was all but torn apart. Moreover, although the theft occurred on Friday when Mathias locked the vault, and wasn't discovered until the following Monday, Mathias made no attempt to leave town—as would have been expected of a man with a very warm $200,000 on his hands. He went to a movie Friday night, alone. He caught cold and, according to his landlady's testimony, stayed in his room Saturday and Sunday. On his way to the movie, he had the tank of his car filled at the Center Street station. Less than a gallon of fuel had been consumed when the police examined his car. By their tests, that car made less than fourteen miles to the gallon, which means that Arnold Mathias drove less than fourteen miles after the money was taken from the vault. Where—and when—did he hide it, Mr. Spengler?"

"You're quoting almost verbatim from Ira Casey's summation to the jury," Spengler said sharply. "All you've omitted was the sentimental reference to his tragic childhood."

"Sentimental? Does that denote disapproval?"

"I hired Casey!"

"Unfortunately for Mathias. Casey was your personal friend, with a friend's loyalty and a friend's blindness. William Spengler, respectable citizen, had lost his wife on the day a large piece of the Dyer payroll was stolen. Convention wrapped him in immunity. Another lawyer, to whom William Spengler was just one of three men who had access to the vault, would have pounced on what Mathias discovered after three years in prison. Mrs. Holmes, under oath, testified that she had called Dr. Clinton and then, at his request, called you at the bank. Samuel Kern, under oath, testified that you asked Mathias to start your car in spite of his offer——"

"Because Sam had a car with an automatic drive!"

"Because Mathias had parked his car around the corner, and you knew it! He had to walk—let's say 200 feet, get his car started, drive around the lot and then come back inside the bank for you, Mr. Spengler. It was cold and so, naturally, you waited inside for him. You went to the vault to help Kern; then you asked him to call Dr. Clinton. Didn't Mrs. Holmes tell you that she had called the doctor? It must have been a tremendous oversight if she didn't. But Kern, another sympathetic friend, was willing to do anything to help. He left the vault and made the telephone call. Now here's a map Mathias drew of the bank—exterior and interior. He marked the location of the telephone Kern used, and the location of where his car was parked when he went to get it. With Mathias outside and Kern on the telephone, there must have been a period of several minutes when you were alone in the vault."

William Spengler hadn't touched his brandy. Now he lifted the glass and drank slowly, never taking his eyes from Henry Lowden's face. When he put the glass down, empty, he said,

"And what was your third possibility, Mr. Taylor?"

Lowden placed the sheet of paper back in his suit-case.

"I wasn't certain until I came to Kirkland this afternoon," he said, "but the station master gave me a clue. I understand that the late Senator Dawes had a great many mourners at his funeral."

"Senator Dawes——?"

"And even deeper mourners when it developed that he had left no fortune. But what if one of those would-be beneficiaries had stolen $200,000 and wanted to pass it off as an inheritance? The idea has possibilities, don't you think?"

Tightly, Spengler replied, "If you're thinking of the coincidence of my wife's death at the time of the theft, you can forget it. She left me nothing. Everything, even this house, is in her father's name."

"But he won't live forever, will he? A tight-fisted old tyrant like Wingate must have accumulated quite a fortune."

"That's not true! My father-in-law has been ill for many years, and my wife was an invalid for most of our married life. Illness is expensive even in Kirkland."

"And frustrating," Lowden reflected, "particularly for a man with a taste for fine brandy and French painting."

"The third possibility," Spengler insisted.

"The obvious, Mr. Spengler. The Dyer deposit must have been a temptation from the beginning, knowing that you had a ready-made suspect working in the bank. A record is tough to live down, even a juvenile record. The public is seldom in a forgiving mood when someone has made off with its unearned cash. And then your wife had a heart attack on Friday afternoon. Her timing was perfect."

"My wife was dying——"

"That couldn't have surprised you. She'd been near death for twenty years. But it did give you an excuse to leave the bank early on the same day Sam Kern was eager to get off to a basketball game. All you had to do was get Kern and Mathias out of the way for a few minutes—just long enough to transfer $200,000 from the Dyer account to your own box. The money was never found, Mr. Spengler, because it never left the vault."

Henry Lowden might have been reading from the court records. He finished his quiet accusation and waited. Spengler's response was electric.

"Is that what Arnold Mathias told you when you were cellmates at State Prison, Mr. Henry?"

"You made that mistake once before. The name is Taylor. Henry Taylor."

"There is no Henry Taylor! I suppose you thought it was too late for me to check on that letter of credit this afternoon. It wasn't. I telephoned the Chicago bank while you were waiting in my office. That letter was a fake."

"You were frightened, Mr. Spengler."

"I'm a good businessman!"

"Who keeps a two-day old newspaper in his desk. You didn't hear of Mathias' death on a newscast. You read about it over and over——"

"What are you trying to do, Henry? Sell me those records and that ridiculous map? Do you think I care what a dead convict suspected?"

The man who called himself Henry Taylor didn't lose control.

"We're not discussing what a *dead* convict suspected," he said. "Innocent or guilty, when a man tries to break out of prison he's courting sudden death. But there's something you don't know about Thomas Henry, who did escape. He wasn't serving time for anything as minor as grand theft. He was in for murder. He's got nothing to lose."

"All I have to do is pick up this telephone——"

"Absolutely nothing, Mr. Spengler. And he's rough. He could make the Sphinx talk if the Sphinx could lead him to $200,000. Go ahead and pick up the telephone. The number of the police station is 110. I looked it up in the directory in my hotel room."

William Spengler was reaching toward the telephone. He paused, bewildered, and in the instant of hesitation Henry Lowden's right hand flicked inside his coat pocket and came out grasping the snubnosed .38.

"No—don't," Spengler said weakly.

"Have you ever been worked over by a desperate man, Mr. Spengler? A really desperate man?"

"But I don't have the money here!" Spengler gasped.

"Where is it?"

"At the bank. I can't get it until tomorrow."

"Is it all there?"

"Most of it. Henry, be reasonable. Everyone thinks Mathias took the money, and he's dead. We can make a deal."

"Thank you, Mr. Spengler. We already have."

The man who called himself Henry Taylor shifted the gun to his left hand and took up the telephone with his right. Carefully, he dialed 110. There was time to explain while the operator rang.

"I'm not Thomas Henry, Mr. Spengler; but I knew I could get a confession out of you and clear Mathias if I reached you before Henry. Lucky for you, I succeeded. My name is Lowden. Henry Taylor Lowden. I'm the guard at State Prison who had to shoot Mathias."

On the other end of the wire, a voice was answering. Lowden's mouth set in a grim smile. The case of Arnold Mathias was almost closed.

THE ENORMOUS $10

Jack Ritchie

The state auditor clicked his tongue. "See here, Mr. Webster, we just can't have this."

I experienced some alarm. "Can't have what? Is there a shortage?"

He shook his head. "Not that. But your bank has ten dollars more than it's supposed to have."

I leaned back in my swivel chair. "Well, that's nothing to worry about. As long as we're not short."

He waggled a finger. "You can't dismiss it so lightly, Mr. Webster. You know very well that your books have to balance to the penny. The very last penny."

I smiled ingratiatingly. "Now, Mr. Stuart, after all it's just ten . . ."

He set his lips. "I'll have to make a report to the commission."

I sat up. "But, Mr. Stuart, there'll be an investigation."

"Do you have anything to hide?"

"Of course not," I said stiffly. "My books are in perfect order."

"More than that," he said dryly. "You've got ten dollars too much in your cash reserves." He lit a thin cigar. "You've got to face it, Mr. Webster. Somebody's been putting money into your vault and perhaps——"

"Impossible," I said firmly. "Both Mr. Barger and Mrs. White have been with me for years. I trust them implicitly."

His face remained skeptical. "Are they your only employees?"

I nodded. "We're a small-town bank."

"And they both have access to the vault?"

"Yes," I admitted. "But I just can't conceive that any one of them would do something like that."

"Nevertheless, one of them is guilty."

I thought it over. "Are you absolutely certain you made no mistake?"

His teeth clamped the cigar. "I never make a mistake."

I brooded a few moments more. "Mr. Stuart, you have been auditing my books for ten years. This is the first time you've found anything wrong."

He nodded.

"Well, just for old time's sake, couldn't you go over the books again tomorrow? Merely to be positive before you send in your report?"

He tasted the idea and then spoke grudgingly. "All right. I'll come back tomorrow. Nine o'clock, on the dot."

When he was gone, I walked into the bank proper. It was after hours, but Mr. Barger and Mrs. White were still at the desks behind the walnut railing.

"You know what Mr. Stuart found?" I asked.

They nodded and looked down at their folded hands.

"You realize what this means," I said. "There'll be an investigation. Word will get out that we do sloppy bookkeeping. I wouldn't be surprised if there's a run on the bank."

Their eyes still avoided me.

"I just can't understand it," I said. "Both of you have been with me more than twenty years. I thought that we were more than just employer and employees. I thought we were friends."

Mrs. White swallowed. She had graying hair and she was a grandmother eight times over.

"I don't know which one of you is responsible," I said. "Or what circumstances prompted you to do something like that. However, since it is, after all, only a matter of ten dollars, I think we can easily rectify the matter right now."

Hope came to their faces.

I smiled. "Luckily, I managed to persuade Mr. Stuart to agree to come back tomorrow for a recheck. And now I'll simply step into the vault and remove a ten dollar bill. Thereby our cash reserves will be at their proper level."

The light faded from their eyes.

"It isn't actually stealing," I said quickly. "I'll give the ten to the Red Cross or some other worthy charity."

Barger was a thin stooped man a few years older than Mrs. White. He cleared his throat. "It isn't that, Mr. Webster. But I just closed the vault and set the time clock. It won't open again until nine o'clock tomorrow morning."

I exhaled and closed my eyes.

Mrs. White spoke. "Perhaps we could take out the ten dollars in the morning?"

"No," I said wearily. "Stuart said he'd be here at nine. I've never known him to be late."

In the evening, I was in my apartment over Hanson's drugstore, when my door buzzer sounded.

It was Barger and he removed his hat. "Could I talk to you, Mr. Webster?"

"Of course, Henry. Come in."

We went into the living room and I turned off the television set.

Barger sat down on the edge of a chair and put his hat on his knees. "I've been thinking things over and I wouldn't want you to be thinking that Mrs. White could be responsible for the bank's troubles." He gulped and had difficulty continuing. "Mr. Webster, I'm the one who put the ten dollars in our cash reserves."

I think my eyes widened. "But, Henry, how could you do something like that?"

He looked down at the rug. "I didn't really mean to do it. It was an accident."

His fingers worked at the hat brim and his face was pale.

"Henry," I said soothingly, "would you care for some water?"

He shook his head. "No, thank you. I'll be all right in a minute."

After awhile I said, "How did it happen?"

He took a deep breath. "The races."

I frowned. "The races?"

"Yes. There's what they call a bookie joint over in Clinton. A pretty big place, Mr. Webster. A dozen people or more talking at the telephones all the time. They take bets from all over, like New York and Philadelphia too."

The shock showed in my voice. "You played the horses?"

He hung his head. "There were hospital bills, and I was having trouble meeting the mortgage payments, and I don't really get much of a salary."

"I'm sorry about that, Henry," I said. "But you know that we're a small bank and. . . ."

He held up a hand. "Oh, I'm not complaining, Mr. Webster. I know how it is."

I sighed. "But, Henry, you know you can't beat the horses."

He looked at the floor again. "First it was two dollars, then five, then ten. I had some winners, of course, but I kept getting in deeper and deeper."

I had a growing suspicion. "Where did you get the money?"

He licked his lips. "From the bank, Mr. Webster."

In the silence I could hear the refrigerator in the kitchen click on.

Barger's fingers turned the hat around two or three times. "Well, after I took about two thousand dollars, I realized that I'd never be able to repay the bank unless I made a killing."

"And so you took more money," I said grimly.

He nodded. "I made a two thousand dollar bet."

"And lost that too," I said. "That's the way it always . . ."

He interrupted. "No, Mr. Webster. My horse came in and paid ten to one. I took care of the hospital bills, paid off the mortgage, and replaced the money in the bank." He sighed. "I guess I just put back ten dollars too much."

There was nothing I could think of to say.

Now that Henry had confessed, he seemed almost cheerful. "A week ago I washed the Venetian blinds at my house and all that night I dreamed of nothing but Venetian blinds, Venetian blinds." He smiled. "And you know what, Mr. Webster? The next morning when I looked at the racing form, there it was! Venusian Blonde, a filly in the third at Hialeah."

"That isn't exactly the same as Venetian blind," I said sourly.

"Mr. Webster," Barger said. "When you receive a message from up there, you don't quibble about the spelling."

He watched me rub my eyes. "I suppose you'll fire me?"

"I'd like to," I said gloomily. "But as long as the money's back in the bank . . ."

"And more," Barger said eagerly.

I began pacing the room. "Somehow we've got to get into that vault before Stuart does."

Barger contributed sympathetic and silent aid to my thinking and eventually an idea came to me. "I have it. We've simply got to see to it that Stuart isn't at the bank when the vault opens."

Barger was entirely in agreement. "Yes, Mr. Webster, but how?"

"When Stuart stops in town, he always takes a room at the Ames House. It's seven blocks from there to the bank and I know that he always walks."

Barger blinked happily. "Yes, Mr. Webster?"

"I'll pick him up in my car and somehow on the way to the bank I'll develop motor trouble. I'll see to it that we don't arrive there until after nine."

Barger nodded. "And I'll be there when the vault does open, dash in, and take out ten dollars."

"But remember," I cautioned. "I may be able to give you only five minutes."

Then I frowned at him. "One thing, Henry. You've got to promise me that that's the last time you dip into the bank's money."

He put a hand over his heart. "Believe me, Mr. Webster, I've learned my lesson. It just doesn't pay to play the horses."

In the morning I was just finishing breakfast in Jake & Millie's Restaurant, when Mrs. White appeared in the doorway. She paused hesitantly until she saw me and then came to my table.

She sat down and clutched her purse. "Mr. Webster, I haven't been able to sleep all night. Just from worrying."

"Mrs. White," I said. "I think we can stop worrying about this whole . . ."

"I've simply got to face up to it," she said. "I can't have you even thinking that Mr. Barger might be to blame."

I was about to take a sip of coffee, but the cup stopped halfway to my lips.

She looked at me with earnest blue eyes. "Mr. Webster, I'm the one who put the extra ten dollars in the vault."

I put down the cup.

"You see, Mr. Webster, I have six children, eight darling grandchildren, and I'm related to just about everybody in town."

I stared out of the window and waited.

"And, well, times aren't as good as they could be . . . and everybody needed a little help . . . now and then."

I sighed.

"Their credit ratings weren't really good enough for any one of them to get a legitimate loan from the bank, so . . . here and there . . . I would try to ease the way for them a little."

"How much did you take?"

"They're all really good people, Mr. Webster. God-fearing and deserving, and seeing as how I work in a bank where there's all kinds of money just lying . . ."

"How much?"

She took a firmer grip on the purse. "Two thousand five hundred dollars and ninety-eight cents."

I felt a momentary curiosity about the ninety-eight cents, but dismissed it. "Mrs. White, you've been foolish, foolish."

She agreed contritely. "Twenty dollars here, thirty there. It all added up."

I shook my head. "And naturally not a single one of them ever paid back a cent."

She looked up. "But they did, Mr. Webster. Every one of them. And I thought I had kept track of all the money I took, but when I put it back, somehow an extra ten must have slipped in."

She straightened her shoulders. "I'll take full responsibility for the ten dollars. I've led a full life and have no regrets. I only hope they'll let my grandchildren visit me."

I was recovering slowly. "I don't think it will come to that."

"But you'll fire me, of course. I've broken a sacred trust."

"No," I said moodily. "I've already established a precedent."

"You'd be surprised how much good the money did instead of just mouldering away in that old vault," Mrs. White said. "Emmy was able to get a washer-dryer and she needs one so much with those three young children, and Mary Ann was able to get a dress for the high school prom. Her life would have been utterly ruined if she hadn't been able to raise the forty-five dollars and ninety-eight cents."

I glanced at my watch. "I think we'll be able to straighten everything out."

"Do you really think so, Mr. Webster?" she asked eagerly.

I patted her hand. "Yes. I'm going to pick up Mr. Stuart in my car and on the way to the bank I'm going to develop motor trouble." I winked. "And in the meantime Henry will be at the vault when it opens and he'll see to it that our cash reserves come down to their proper level."

Her eyes sparkled. "What a brilliant idea, Mr. Webster." Then she frowned slightly. "But you'd better hurry if you want to catch Mr. Stuart."

"Plenty of time," I said. "It's only quarter after eight."

She checked her small gold watch and then looked over my shoulder. "I'm afraid your watch is slow, Mr. Webster. According to the wall clock behind you and my watch, it's fourteen to nine."

I verified that and grabbed my hat. "We can still make it! But we've got to hurry."

We rushed out of the restaurant to my car parked at the curb and then we stopped.

It was about thirty seconds before I could talk.

"Mrs. White," I said wearily, "if you'll just take a seat in the car, I'll get at that flat tire."

We arrived at the bank ten minutes after nine.

Barger's face was pale. "Stuart was here when the vault opened. What happened, Mr. Webster?"

"Never mind," I said irritably.

And then we sat down to wait.

The time passed slowly and our eyes followed the second hand of the electric clock go around and around.

At ten-thirty, Stuart stepped out of the vault, and his face was pink with embarrassment. "Just one of those things," he said. "Could have happened to anybody."

I sighed. "What could?"

He waved the pack of ten dollar bills in his hand. "Somehow one of these tens got folded in half and so when I went through the stack yesterday I counted the same bill twice. Both ends, you know." His laugh was almost a giggle. "If I'd leafed through the other end of the stack, it would have looked like you were ten dollars short."

Barger and Mrs. White and I looked at each other and then back to the embarrassed, red-faced Stuart.

"It could happen to anybody," he said again.

I took a breath. "Then our cash reserve . . . ?"

"At the proper level," Stuart said. "To the penny."

At noon I went back to Jake & Millie's for lunch and Mr. Sprague, who used to live in New York, sat down at my table.

He took out a pad and pen. "What's your horse for today?"

"None," I said. "I'm through playing the horses."

His face showed surprise. "Quit now? And just after you made a killing on Venusian Blonde? Ten thousand, wasn't it?"

"Nevertheless I quit," I said firmly and I meant it. Playing the horses can be dangerous.

For awhile there, I thought I was the one who put the extra ten in the vault.

FIRST COME, FIRST SERVED

Rog Phillips

It was only Friday noon, and already George Mobray was irritable, in anticipation of the evening. He glared at the new waitress and she remained blithely unaware of him, waiting on customers he was sure had come in after him. Finally she paused in front of him, her pencil and order pad ready.

"Your order, sir?" she asked in a pleasant, subdued voice.

"Are you sure there's no one else to wait on before me?" George asked. "That couple at the end of the counter that just came in, for example?"

She blinked into his baleful eyes. "Sorry," she said. "First come, first served. Your order, please?"

"Franks and noodles," George said. "And please remember me? I wouldn't like for you to say, a half hour from now, that you forgot me and gave my order to someone else."

Her lips parted in a half-smile. "How could I forget you?" she murmured. "Coffee now?"

"Yes," George growled, and was uncomfortably aware of the waitress' clean curves and serene expression as she brought his coffee and went about her business.

Now, if Madge were *half* that attractive, and . . . George's eyes followed the contours of the waitress speculatively. When he finished his lunch he left her a fifty cent tip as a tribute. Maybe, if Life were different . . . But why hope?

Eight hours later, at home, the memory of the waitress added just a shade to his resentment toward Madge. Madge had been drinking again, since dinnertime. George had sat in the sprawling front room of the house reading the paper, marking time until a quarter to nine when he would leave.

Madge came into the front room, slightly unsteady on her feet. She had done the dishes and drunk gin tonics while doing so. Looking at her, George suddenly *knew* he would kill her tonight.

"I suppose you're going out again tonight," she said.

"And why not?" George said, lowering his newspaper and glaring at his wife.

She was years older than he—how many he couldn't guess. Theirs had been a swift romance and courtship, stemming from a dude ranch vacation in California. Madge had seemed almost a child during that summer. A child with fifty thousand dollars in P.T.&T. stocks, other assorted stocks and bonds, and cash. She had said she was thirty-four. Forty, he had felt almost guilty of robbing the cradle when he married her; but the fifty thousand dollars had enabled George to take advantage of certain business opportunities, and in five years he had built it up to almost a quarter of a million.

During those five years Madge had gradually let down, with less and less frequent trips to the beauty parlor, a gradual abandonment of her kittenish personality, until her true age began to emerge—somewhere in the fifties. Sometimes the gray roots of her deliciously seductive red hair were a quarter of an inch exposed, through lazy delay on beauty appointments. Sometimes she neglected the beauty creams, and the wrinkles of old age were visible around her lips and eyes. Tonight her age was especially apparent.

"Sometimes I think you married me just for my money," she snapped, her eyes shrewish.

"One thing about money," George said, putting the paper aside, "it is ageless. A wrinkled fifty dollar bill is as good as a crisp new one."

He stretched elaborately, and stood up, glancing at his wristwatch meaningfully.

"Besides," he added, "if I married you for your money, haven't I more than quintupled it since we got married? Why, this house alone, with all its antiques and knickknacks, is worth more than the fifty thousand you had when you met me."

"And don't think I don't know it!" Madge shouted. "Try and divorce me! Community property laws will give me my original fifty thousand plus half of what you've made on it. Think of that!" She leered at him drunkenly.

"I've thought of it," George said. "Don't wait up for me. You need your *beauty* sleep, you know."

He closed the door quickly, cutting her shouted reply to a whisper. In the three-car garage he touched the smooth wood of his fifteen thousand dollar cabin cruiser, fondly. Madge had bought it for him the second year of their marriage, making the three thousand dollar down payment. He had made the rest of the payments himself—but the contract had been in Madge's name and if he divorced her she would claim the boat just to spite him.

Well, there wasn't going to be a divorce, with all he had worked so hard to get being sliced up like a pie between Madge, her lawyer, and his own lawyer, leaving him with practically nothing. The answer had come to George six months ago while he was rained in for three days at the lake.

He had been in a rented cabin at Lake O' The Ozarks, a planned week of fishing with Tom Braley, Pete Bushini, Harry Hall, Don Madrick, and Al Montgomery. When it started to rain it really came down.

Dealer's choice poker had helped pass some of the time, but there had been hours when even poker was suspended and there was nothing to do.

In desperation George had started to read the various magazines left in the cabin by former occupants. Suddenly he found the story that gave him the answer to his problem.

Murder with a perfect alibi—once you got around the things the murderer in the story overlooked, that tripped him up. The perfect alibi in the story was a poker game and a tight schedule for the murder so that six or seven men would swear you had never left the table. In the story the murderer had found a back door he could sneak out of, drive to the scene of the crime, commit the murder, and get back into the poker game in a little under ten minutes. Then the murderer had tripped himself up by going through a stop sign on the way back to the poker game, and the traffic citation had been his ticket to the gas chamber.

George had never been particularly interested in gambling, nor had he ever played at any of the local games known to be going on behind locked doors. It was an open secret that one game went on in the back room of the barber shop on Third Street and another in the back room of a place called Swanky Hamburgers, run by a tall skinny fellow named Marvin Swank, who packed a roll of bills that was always fat.

George went to both places and played poker, during the month after the fishing trip, finally settling on Swanky Hamburgers as a base of operations because it was the only place that had a never used back exit beyond the rest room so that he could appear to go to the rest room and sneak out, leaving the back door unlocked while he was gone and locking it again when he came back. The stakes were high. You couldn't hope to last out an average session of poker without at least two thousand in cash on you, but during the five months George had been a regular he had come out over seven thousand dollars ahead of the game.

For the past four months George had played at Swank's every Friday night, and every Friday night he had made a "dry run," as he called it in his mind— sneaking out the back door, driving to his house and back to Swank's place again, learning all the stop signs on several different routes, timing himself, etc., and always prepared to abandon the whole scheme if the slightest possible hitch developed.

No hitch had developed. And *tonight was the night*. Madge, acting true to form, would drink herself to sleep by nine o'clock. With luck the players would be the usual bunch: himself, Marvin Swank, Pete Bushini, Al Montgomery, Gordon Godlove, Niel Sorenson, Paul Korvis, and perhaps a newcomer. A sort of team spirit had grown among the regulars, against newcomers. It was a logical thing. Marvin took a dollar every half hour from each player "for the house." Unless the newcomer lost the regulars were out the cost of the evening's play plus whatever the newcomer won.

Last week the stranger in the game had been an out-of-town salesman, and he had lost fifteen hundred dollars. He probably wouldn't be back!

George smiled at the memory. He had won eight hundred dollars, himself . . .

He parked in the supermarket parking lot well toward the back so that when he came from the alley he could slip into his car without being seen from the street. There were other cars there even though the supermarket closed at seven.

George went to the sidewalk and walked past the lighted windows of the deserted supermarket to the Neon front of Swanky Hamburgers.

The place was busy. George walked between the counter and the booths, past the door labeled *Gals,* and pushed open the door labeled *Office*.

"Hiya, Georgey, my old fishin' buddy," Pete Bushini called out from across the room.

"Hi," George said, and nodded to include the others. The game hadn't started yet. Only Pete and Al and Paul were there, besides Marv.

"We're five-handed now," Marvin Swank said. "We could get started."

The game quickly settled down to grim earnest. George set a pace of bluffing with fifty dollar raises that took the conversation out of the game. He wanted to lose a couple of thousand, but instead he won steadily.

By midnight every one at the table had been to the rest room at least twice, and with great inner satisfaction George knew that no one would be able to recall later who had been absent from the table when, or for how long.

He finished his deal, not playing a hand that would have won. Three Aces. But he wanted to leave the table clean, with nothing to point up the fact that he was gone, like a pile of unstacked poker chips in front of him. He wanted to get away and be back before it was his turn to deal next. Then Al Montgomery, sitting to his right, could swear that George had never missed the deal during the whole evening.

Pushing back his chair he got up and headed toward the short hallway leading to the rest room and the back door. He paused in a well-rehearsed act of putting on gloves. No fingerprints of his had ever been on the back door. He paused briefly at the rest-room door and locked it with a dime store skeleton key so that anyone else who tried the door would think the rest room occupied.

He twisted the lock on the back door and pushed down the pin so it would remain unlocked, and slipped out into the alley. He walked swiftly to his car in the supermarket parking lot. The motor started instantly.

When he drove out of the parking lot the street was completely deserted. No cars, and no pedestrians.

He drove at just under the speed limit of twenty-five miles, getting the gun out of the hidden space between the seat and the backrest and, with one hand, unwrapping the plastic cover that kept it free of dust.

Five blocks north, a stop sign, then four blocks east, and two blocks north again, pulling quietly to the curb a block from his house. George slipped out of the car and hurried up the street. He could see no lights on anywhere in the neighborhood. With the gloves still on he unlocked the front door and slipped into his house.

In the bedroom he made sure the curtains were drawn, then turned on the lights. Madge was sprawled out, dead to the world. With an expression of disgust George shot her through the center of her frilly yellow nightgown, tailored for a younger and more seductive body.

Putting the gun in his pocket, he turned her over and pulled back the covers so that it would appear she had been disturbed and tried to get out of bed. He stripped the diamond rings off her fingers, swiftly emptied her jewel box on the dresser and picked out the few really valuable pieces of jewelry, stuffing them into his pocket with the rings.

He was completely in the shadows as he went from the front door to the car. A light had been turned on in a house or two. Some of the neighbors had evidently been awakened by the sound of the shot. George didn't turn on the car lights until he was two blocks away.

He paused at a corner to shove the gun and jewelry through the grating of a curb drain. The gloves followed. When he got back into the car he sighed with relief. It had been more of a nervous strain than he had anticipated. More of a risk, too. What if some neighbor had been awake without the lights on, heard the shot, and had been waiting on the sidewalk when he came out of the house? Now that the murder was done—and couldn't be undone—a dozen weaknesses appeared in his plan.

When he pulled into his parking place in the supermarket lot he glanced at his watch and saw that he had been gone only six minutes. That was half a minute better than rehearsals, but it seemed impossible.

Hours *must* have passed. So much of life couldn't be compressed into six minutes!

He walked swiftly down the alley to the door he had left unlocked, and inched it open, half-expecting the police—the whole town—to be waiting for him inside. Instead, there was no one.

He unlocked the door to the rest room, went inside and inspected himself in the mirror. He stood there a moment, looking at himself, giving himself common sense and courage. There was nothing to fear but fear itself. Fear could color his judgment with nightmares.

He left the rest room and went out to the poker table. Surprisingly, the game was still going on. No one looked up at him as he sat down. No one asked where he had been. No one studied him suspiciously. He was dealt to automatically.

After ten minutes he felt sure that none of the others would remember that he had left the table. He relaxed inside, and to make up for the good hands of poker he had not played, he played two nonsense hands in a row as though they were pat hands, and won both times because no one called his final bet.

The hours passed slowly. George visualized Madge sprawled in death on the bed, rigor mortis setting in, so that the time of death could be established well within the time that seven men would swear he had never left the card table.

He began to feel a sense of bubbling well-being that he had not felt in years. His consistent winning streak could not be the only reason for it. With a shock, he realized that it came from the realization that Madge was dead.

George felt almost drunk with relief, even though the worst job lay ahead—the "discovering" of the body, the calling of the police, and answering their questions in such a way that they wouldn't suspect him.

He toned down his joy by an effort of will. It was a good thing he was the big winner tonight. The others would have wondered about his being so happy if he were losing.

At four o'clock he looked around the table, and he was the only winner. Even Marvin Swank was out a few hundred bucks, and was chewing on his cigar viciously. Pete Bushini was out over a thousand, and Al Montgomery was out at least five hundred. Neither were "old fishing buddies" anymore.

At four-thirty when George won a six hundred dollar pot with a king full on threes against Al Montgomery's flush Al cashed in.

"I've had it for tonight," he said, sighing wearily.

"Shall we break up?" Marvin asked.

"Why?" George said, suddenly reluctant to face what lay ahead. "The night is young—and look at all the beautiful chips I hold in my arms." He wrapped his arms around his stacks of poker chips and grinned.

"He can't stay lucky forever," Pete Bushini said grimly.

So the game continued after Al left. Five, five-thirty. At a quarter to six Marvin Swank said, "You were wrong, Pete. This is George's night, and we can't stop him. Let's call it quits. Next week he won't be so lucky."

Marvin cashed in the stacks of chips while George had a cup of coffee, reluctant to leave. It was beginning to hit him now. "Discovering" the body, calling the police at six in the morning, answering questions . . .

"Why not come home with me and have a nightcap?" George invited Marvin after the others had gone.

"Not me," Marvin said. "I have to open this place in the morning, remember? I'll take a nap on the cot, then when I get things going I'll go home and sleep all day." He was definitely not in the best of humor.

"Okay," George said, straightening out his winnings into a neat pile of fifty dollar bills and inserting them into his billfold.

Then there was the short walk to the supermarket parking lot, and the short drive home. The dawn light was already more than adequate to see by. As George crept along in his car he had an impulse to keep going, turn his back on the whole thing and start a new life. But it was too late for that. Flight would be evidence of guilt.

He made the turn into his own street and his heart hit his ribs with a hammer blow. A police car was parked at the curb in front of his house. Had Madge's body been found already? Had neighbors called the police after hearing the shot, and the police broken in and found her?

So much the better, he decided. It would save him the nerve-wracking job of "discovering" the body himself and calling the police. He turned into the driveway without looking at the police car, pressed the dashboard button that opened the garage doors, and drove into the garage.

He unlocked the door from the garage to the kitchen, half-expecting to see the house swarming with police. The house was silent, except for the ticking of the grandfather clock and mantel clock. Madge had collected clocks.

Moving swiftly, George started a pot of coffee, plugging it in just as the front door chimes sounded. He went through the huge living room cluttered with restored antique furniture Madge had collected, and opened the door. Both policemen were there.

"Well, good morning!" George said. "Come in. Come on into the kitchen. I have a pot of coffee brewing. My wife isn't awake yet." He smiled and added, "I just got home. An all night card game."

"Yes," one of the officers said. "We know. We've been waiting for you. I guess it wouldn't do any harm for us to have a cup of coffee with you."

They followed George to the kitchen.

The percolator was bubbling now. George took three cups and saucers from a cabinet shelf and put them on the table. He got cream and sugar out, and spoons. Then, as an afterthought, he took some sweet rolls from the breadbox, and went back to the refrigerator again for the butter.

Why didn't the policemen talk? Had Madge's body been taken away already? Had they been left behind to break the news to him gently?

"My lucky night . . . won enough for a down payment on a new mink coat for my wife . . . tempted to wake her up and tell her, but she'd kill me if I woke her up this time of the morning . . ." He winked at the cops and added, "But I may not tell her. Keep it a secret and tell her I just broke even."

The coffeepot stopped snorting. George unplugged it and poured coffee in the three cups.

"Sit down," he said. "What's on your mind? Help yourselves to the sweet rolls."

"Thanks," one of the cops said as both reached for the sweet rolls. "So you were playing poker all night?" He began buttering the sweet roll.

George resisted the impulse to say yes and he could prove it. Instead, he grinned. "So maybe it's against the law," he said. "Everybody does it."

"We aren't concerned about that," the cop said. "What time did the game start? When did it break up?"

"It started about nine last night," George said. "It broke up just a few minutes ago."

"Were you there the entire time?"

"Sure," George said. "Why?" He looked at the two cops with round-eyed innocence, forcing a questioning expression onto his face. He resisted the impulse to add that he could prove it.

"Good," his questioner said. "Who else was playing?"

"Oh, come now!" George said. "It's just a friendly game. We play every Friday night. If you're going to clamp down on us far be it from me to stool on the others!"

"Nothing like that. Besides, we know the names of everyone who played. Why do you think we were waiting for you? Was Mr. Montgomery there when the game started at nine?"

"Why, yes!" George said. "He got there before I did, and I was in on the first hand."

"What time did he leave?"

George frowned. "He did leave early," he said. "He had bad luck. I think it was about four-thirty when he quit. Why?"

"Did he leave any other time?"

"No," George said. "None of us did."

"You'd swear to it in court?"

George hesitated. "Of course," he said. "I was there every minute and none of us left. I'd swear to it. Why?"

"Well, that's all right then," the policeman said, putting the last bite of his sweet roll in his mouth with obvious relief. "If you're that positive the others will be too—so Al Montgomery is telling the truth. We thought he was anyway, but we have to check these things out, you know."

The two policemen gulped the last of their coffee and stood up to leave.

"What things do you have to check out?" George asked.

"His wife was shot between eleven o'clock and midnight," the cop said.

"Oh NO!" George said.

"Apparently she was shot by a burglar," the cop said, "but only her jewelry was missing. Nothing else was touched, and there's no indication of forcible entry. Under the circumstances we had to consider the possibility that he shot her himself. But if he has seven witnesses able to swear that he never left their sight for a minute that rules him out."

George sank weakly into a chair.

"You're taking it pretty hard," the other policeman said. "Good friends of yours?"

Staring into space George nodded. "We went fishing together six months ago, we've been playing poker together every Friday night since then." He thought bitterly, *We have the same reading tastes,* but he didn't say it.

"Sorry," the policeman said. "Don't get up. We can let ourselves out."

George heard the front door close a moment later. He got to his feet and went to make sure the police were gone. Then, in a daze, he went to the back hallway and opened the door to the bedroom.

The light was still on, the curtains drawn shut, and Madge still lay as he had left her—except that now it was obvious even from the doorway that she was dead and the bloodstained sheets were dried.

"Why didn't he kill his wife *last* Friday?" George groaned. He went slowly to the side of the bed, a thousand amateurish plans for getting rid of the body forming in his mind and being abandoned.

He thought of calling the police, of bluffing it out. But the two bullets wouldn't match. They hadn't come from the same gun. And two husbands with the same alibi? On the same night?

"What will I do now?" George whispered, staring at the corpse.

THE EXPLOSIVES EXPERT

John Lutz

Billy Edgemore, the afternoon bartender, stood behind the long bar of the Last Stop Lounge and squinted through the dimness at the sunlight beyond the front window. He was a wiry man, taller than he appeared at first, and he looked like he should be a bartender, with his bald head, cheerfully seamed face and his brilliant red vest that was the bartender's uniform at the Last Stop. Behind him long rows of glistening bottles picked up the light on the mirrored backbar, the glinting clear gins and vodkas, the beautiful amber bourbons and lighter Scotches, the various hues of the assorted wines, brandies and liqueurs. The Last Stop's bar was well stocked.

Beyond the ferns that blocked the view out (and in) the front window, Billy saw a figure cross the small patch of light and turn to enter the stained-glass front door, the first customer he was to serve that day.

It was Sam Daniels. Sam was an employee of the Hulton Plant up the street, as were most of the customers of the Last Stop.

"Afternoon, Sam," Billy said, turning on his professional smile. "Kind of early today, aren't you?"

"Off work," Sam said, mounting a bar stool as if it were a horse. "Beer."

Billy drew a beer and set the wet schooner in front of Sam on the mahogany bar. "Didn't expect a customer for another two hours, when the plant lets out," Billy said.

"Guess not," Sam said, sipping his beer. He was a short man with a swarthy face, a head of curly hair, and a stomach paunch too big for a man in his early thirties—a man who liked his drinking.

"Figured you didn't go to work when I saw you weren't wearing your badge," Billy said. The Hulton Plant manufactured some secret government thing, a component for the hydrogen bomb, and each employee had to wear his small plastic badge with his name, number and photograph on it in order to enter or leave the plant.

"Regular Sherlock," Sam said, and jiggled the beer in his glass.

"You notice lots of things when you're a bartender," Billy said, wiping down the bar with a clean white towel. *You notice things,* Billy repeated to himself, *and you get to know people, and when you get to know them, really get to know them, you've got to dislike them.* "I guess I tended bar in the wrong places."

"What's that?" Sam Daniels asked.

"Just thinking out loud," Billy said, and hung the

towel on its chrome rack. When Billy looked at his past he seemed to be peering down a long tunnel of empty bottles, drunks and hollow laughter; of curt orders, see-through stares and dreary conversations. He'd never liked his job, but it was all he'd known for the past thirty years.

"Wife's supposed to meet me here pretty soon," Sam said. "She's getting off work early." He winked at Billy. "Toothache."

Billy smiled his automatic smile and nodded. He never had liked Sam, who had a tendency to get loud and violent when he got drunk.

Within a few minutes Rita Daniels entered. She was a tall, pretty woman, somewhat younger than her husband. She had a good figure, dark eyes, and expensively bleached blonde hair that looked a bit stringy now from the heat outside.

"Coke and bourbon," she ordered, without looking at Billy. He served her the highball where she sat next to her husband at the bar.

No one spoke for a while as Rita sipped her drink. The faint sound of traffic, muffled through the thick door of the Last Stop, filled the silence. When a muted horn sounded, Rita said, "It's dead in here. Put a quarter in the jukebox."

Sam did as his wife said, and soft jazz immediately displaced the traffic sounds.

"You know I don't like jazz, Sam." Rita downed her drink quicker than she should have, then got down off the stool to go to the powder room.

"Saw Doug Baker last night," Billy said, picking up the empty glass. Doug Baker was a restaurant owner who lived on the other side of town, and it was no secret that he came to the Last Stop only to see Rita Daniels, though Rita was almost always with her husband.

"How 'bout that," Sam said. "Two more of the same."

Rita returned to her stool, and Billy put two highballs before her and her husband.

"I was drinking beer," Sam said in a loud voice.

"So you were," Billy answered, smiling his My Mistake smile. He shrugged and motioned toward the highballs. "On the house. Unless you'd rather have beer."

"No," Sam said, "think nothing of it."

That was how Billy thought Sam would answer. His cheapness was one of the things Billy disliked most about the man. It was one of the things he knew Rita disliked most in Sam Daniels, too.

"How'd it go with the hydrogen bombs today?" Rita asked her husband. "Didn't go in at all, huh?"

Billy could see she was aggravated and was trying to nag him.

"No," Sam said, "and I don't make hydrogen bombs."

"Ha!" Rita laughed. "You oughta think about it. That's about all you can make." She turned away before Sam could answer. "Hey, Billy, you know anything about hydrogen bombs?"

"Naw," Billy said. "Your husband knows more about that than me."

"Yeah," Rita said, "the union rates him an expert. Some expert! Splices a few wires together."

"Five dollars an hour," Sam said, "and double time for overtime."

Rita whirled a braceleted arm above her head. "Wheeee . . ."

Like many married couples, Sam and Rita never failed to bicker when they came into the Last Stop. Billy laughed. "The Friendly Daniels." Sam didn't laugh.

"Don't bug me today," Sam said to Rita. "I'm in a bad mood."

"Cheer up, Sam," Billy said. "It's a sign she loves you, or loves somebody, anyway."

Sam ignored Billy and finished his drink. "Where'd you go last night?" he asked his wife.

"You know I was at my sister's. I even stopped in here for about a half hour on the way. Billy can verify it."

"Right," Billy said

"I thought you said Doug Baker was in here last night," Sam said to him, his eyes narrow.

"He was," Billy said. "He, uh, came in late." He turned to make more drinks, placing the glasses lip to lip and pouring bourbon into each in one deft stream without spilling a drop. He made them a little stronger this time, shooting in the soda expertly, jabbing swizzle sticks between the ice cubes and placing the glasses on the bar.

"You wouldn't be covering up or anything, would you, Billy?" Sam's voice had acquired a mean edge.

"Now *wait a minute!*" Rita said. "If you think I came in here last night to see Doug Baker, you're crazy!"

"Well," Sam stirred his drink viciously and took a sip, "Billy mentioned Baker was in here . . ."

"I said he came in late," Billy said quickly.

"And he acted like he was covering up or something," Sam said, looking accusingly at Billy.

"*Covering up?*" Rita turned to Billy, her penciled eyebrows knitted in a frown. "Have you ever seen me with another man?"

"Naw," Billy said blandly, "of course not. You folks shouldn't fight."

Still indignant, Rita swiveled on her stool to face her husband. "Have I ever been unfaithful?"

"How the hell should I know?"

"Good point," Billy said with a forced laugh.

"It's not funny!" Rita snapped.

"Keep it light, folks," Billy said seriously. "You know we don't like trouble in here."

"Sorry," Rita said, but her voice was hurt. She swiveled back to face the bar and gulped angrily on her drink. Billy could see that the liquor was getting to her, was getting to them both.

There was silence for a while, then Rita said morosely, "I *oughta* go out on you Mr. Five-dollar-hydrogen-bomb-expert! You think I do anyway, and at least Doug Baker's got money."

Sam grabbed her wrist, making the bracelets jingle. She tried to jerk away but he held her arm so tightly that his knuckles were white. "You ever see Baker behind my back and I'll kill you both!" He almost spit the words out.

"Hey, now," Billy said gently, "don't talk like that, folks!" He placed his hand on Sam Daniels' arm and felt the muscles relax as Sam released his wife. She bent over silently on her stool and held the wrist as if it were broken. "Have one on the house," Billy said, taking up their almost empty glasses. "One to make up by."

"Make mine straight," Sam said. He was breathing hard and his face was red.

"Damn you!" Rita moaned. She half fell off the stool and walked quickly but staggeringly to the powder room again.

Billy began to mix the drinks deftly, speedily, as if there were a dozen people at the bar and they all demanded service. In the faint red glow from the beer-ad electric clock he looked like an ancient alchemist before his rows of multicolored bottles. "You shouldn't be so hard on her," he said absently as he mixed. "Can't believe all the rumors you hear about a woman as pretty as Rita, and a harmless kiss in fun never hurt nobody."

"Rumors?" Sam leaned over the bar. "Kiss? What kiss? Did she kiss Baker last night?"

"Take it easy," Billy said. "I told you Baker came in late." The phone rang, as it always did during the fifteen minutes before the Hulton Plant let out, with wives leaving messages and asking for errant husbands. When Billy returned, Rita was back at the bar.

"Let's get out of here," she said. There were tear streaks in her makeup.

"Finish your drinks and go home happy, folks." Billy shot a glance at the door and set the glasses on the bar.

Rita drank hers slowly, but Sam tossed his drink

down and stared straight ahead. Quietly, Billy put another full glass in front of him.

"I hear you *were* in here with Baker last night," Sam said in a low voice. "Somebody even saw you kissing him."

"You're *crazy!*" Rita's thickened voice was outraged.

Billy moved quickly toward them. "I didn't say that."

"I know you were covering up!" Sam glared pure hate at him. "We'll see what Baker says, because I'm going to drive over to his place right now and bash his brains out!"

"But I didn't even see Baker last night!" Rita took a pull on her drink, trying to calm herself. Sam swung sharply around with his forearm, hitting Rita's chin and the highball glass at the same time. There was a clink as the glass hit her teeth and she fell backward off the stool.

Billy reached under the bar and his hand came up with a glinting chrome automatic that seemed to catch every ray of light in the place. It was a gentleman's gun, and standing there in his white shirt and red vest Billy looked like a gentleman holding it.

"Now, don't move, folks." He aimed the gun directly at Sam's stomach. "You know we don't go for that kind of trouble in here." He looked down and saw blood seeping between Rita's fingers as she held her hand over her mouth. Billy wet a clean towel and tossed it to her, and she held it to her face and scooted backward to sit sobbing in the farthest booth.

Billy leaned close to Sam. "Listen," he said, his voice a sincere whisper, "I don't want to bring trouble on Baker, or on you for that matter, so I can't stand by and let you go over there and kill him and throw your own life away. It wasn't him she was in here with. He came in later."

"Wasn't him?" Sam asked in bewildered fury. "Who was it then?"

"I don't know," Billy said, still in a whisper so Rita

couldn't hear. "He had a badge on, so he worked at the plant, but I don't know who he is and that's the truth."

"Oh, no!"

"Take it easy, Sam. She only kissed him in that booth there. And I'm not even sure I saw that. The booth was dark."

Sam tossed down the drink that was on the bar and moaned. He was staring at the automatic and Billy could see he wanted desperately to move.

A warm silence filled the bar, and then the phone rang shrilly, turning the silence to icicles.

"Now take it easy," Billy said, backing slowly down the bar toward where the phone hung on the wall. "A kiss isn't anything." As the phone rang again he could almost see the shrill sound grate through Sam's tense body. Billy placed the automatic on the bar and took the last five steps to the phone. He let it ring once more before answering it.

"Naw," Billy said into the receiver, standing with his back to Sam and Rita, "he's not here." He stood for a long moment instead of hanging up, as if someone were still on the other end of the line.

The shot was a sudden, angry bark.

Billy put the receiver on the hook and turned. Sam was standing slumped with a supporting hand on a bar stool. Rita was crumpled on the floor beneath the table of the booth she'd been sitting in, her eyes open, her blonde hair bright with blood.

His head still bowed, Sam began to shake.

Within minutes the police were there, led by a young plainclothes detective named Parks.

"You say they were arguing and he just up and shot her?" Parks was asking as his men led Sam outside.

"He accused her of running around," Billy said. "They were arguing, he hit her, and I was going to throw them out when the phone rang. I set the gun down for a moment when I went to answer the phone, and he grabbed it and shot."

"Uh-hm," Parks said efficiently, flashing a look to-

ward where Rita's body had lain before they'd photo-
graphed it and taken it away. "Pretty simple, I guess.
Daniels confessed as soon as we got here. In fact, we
couldn't shut him up. Pretty broken."

"Who wouldn't be?" Billy said.

"Save some sympathy for the girl." Parks looked
around. "Seems like a nice place. I don't know why
there's so much trouble in here."

Billy shrugged. "In a dive, a class joint or a place
like this, people are mostly the same."

Parks grinned. "You're probably right," he said,
and started toward the door. Before pushing it open,
he paused and turned. "If you see anything like this
developing again, give us a call, huh?"

"Sure," Billy said, polishing a glass and holding it
up to the fading afternoon light. "You know we don't
like trouble in here."

I HATED THE HIRED MAN

H. A. DeRosso

Pa found him one morning sleeping in the haymow
when he went to milk the cows. It was not the first
time someone had taken shelter in our barn overnight.
This was during the Thirties, the time of the Depression, when many men were on the bum throughout
the land, and now and then one of them would stop
at our farm for a handout or, if it was after dark, go
to sleep in the barn and Pa would find them there in
the morning. He would always send them on to the
house and Iris would fix them a meal and some sand-
wiches to take with them when they left.

And that is how Evans came to us.

I was in the house eating breakfast when he rapped
on the door. Iris opened it and then grew red as she
stood there staring at him and him staring back at her
with a smile on his mouth. He went on staring at Iris
until she stepped back and invited him inside.

He told her his name and she told him hers. I noticed how his eyes followed her as she moved about the kitchen. A couple of times she caught him watching her and she got red all over again and real nervous. This didn't seem to bother Evans at all. The smile grew on his mouth until two long dimples showed in his cheeks.

He asked me who I was, but I wouldn't tell him. So Iris said I was her stepson. Evans kind of nodded as if that meant something to him. He tried to get me to talk, but I didn't like him. I didn't know why. Of all the tramps who had ever stopped at our farm I liked Evans least of all.

I got up to go.

Iris said, "Tommy. You haven't finished breakfast."

"I ain't hungry no more," I said.

"Well, finish your milk at least."

"I'm full."

"You know you should drink more milk. Tommy! Come back here! I'll tell your father."

"Go on and tell him," I sassed back, running out the door.

I heard Evans chuckle and then Iris say something in a mad voice. But I didn't care. I was out of the house by then and that was all that mattered.

It was spring. The snow was all melted except for a few spots in the woods where the sun couldn't get at it. The grass was turning green and the plowed fields were drying out. Pa had said he might start picking rocks and I knew he was going to when I saw the horses in the barn.

I never liked picking rocks, but it had to be done before the fields could be cultivated and seeded. So I was happy because after the rocks had been hauled away, Pa would sometimes let me ride on the drag and the disk with him and teach me how to drive and handle the machines though he said they were still a little too much for an eleven-year-old kid to handle by himself.

I went in the barn to say hello to him. He was busy

milking away, the sound of it a steady swishing in the foaming milk pail, and he showed me that special smile he'd had for me ever since my real Ma—not Iris—had died. He squirted a stream of milk that hit me in the face and he laughed as I hollered in surprise and went running into the horse barn.

I climbed up on the manger and petted King and Queen, our team. They nosed me with their soft muzzles and Queen nipped playfully at my arm. Pa said she was a mean one, but she was like a pet with me.

After I got tired of playing with the horses I went outside. There was a crow on a fencepost and I put a rock in my slingshot and let fly at him. He took off, flapping his big black wings, and I tried another shot. Though I was pretty good with a slingshot, I never was able to get close enough to hit a crow.

Pa called me then. He was done milking and was going to let the cows out. It was my job to chase them to the pasture. When I got back from that he was in the barn, harnessing the team, and he had Evans with him.

"I don't know how good a hand I'll make, Mr. Dietrich," Evans was saying. "I've never worked on a dairy farm before. I picked fruit in California and Oregon last fall. All I want is a place to sleep and three meals a day for awhile."

"I don't know," Pa said, "if I can afford to keep you on after spring planting, Evans. I just can't afford wages."

"No need to pay me. Just three squares a day and a place to bunk."

"Okay," Pa said.

Evans noticed me then. "Hello there," he said to me. "Find your tongue yet?"

I turned and ran from the barn. I heard Pa say something about me being shy and Evans laughed. I went and climbed up on the wagon and sat there, wondering why Pa had to go and hire Evans. Couldn't he have found someone else, anyone else? Just so it wasn't Evans.

Pa led the horses out of the barn and then showed Evans how to team them and hitch them to the stone-boat. They were all set to take off for the fields when Pa noticed me.

"Aren't you coming, Tom?" he called.

I didn't answer.

"Tom." Pa's voice had changed. When he spoke like that he meant what he said. "You come here this minute. Mind me now."

I climbed down real slow from the wagon and walked over and got on the stoneboat. When it started with a jerk, Evans was caught by surprise and went stumbling off. But he just laughed and jumped back on.

"First time I ever rode one of these," he said, and Pa laughed with him and explained how to brace himself when the horses started.

Evans dropped a hand on my shoulder, but I shrugged it off. Pa handed me the lines then and let me drive and though this was what I liked best of all it didn't thrill me this time . . .

That evening, after supper, Pa took me for a walk over the farm. This was the time he liked best, when the air was soft and warm and there was the rich smell of growing grass and stirred up soil.

He put an arm around my shoulders as we walked along. "What's wrong, Tom?"

I didn't answer.

His grip tightened a bit. "How come you acted the way you did today?"

"I don't like Evans," I blurted out.

He chuckled. "Why?"

"I don't know. I just don't like him."

He sighed. "Your Ma told me you sassed her this morning. And in front of Evans."

"She ain't my Ma."

His grip tightened hard for a moment, then eased. "She's my wife, Tom. I know she'll never replace my Laura and I don't expect her to. That's something you've got to accept, too. She's young and not too bright and kind of foolish at times, not the steady woman your Ma was."

"What did you marry her for then?"

He sighed again. "A man somehow has to have a woman with him. His life isn't complete if he hasn't. There's a loneliness, a—when you're older you'll understand." He ruffled my hair. "And you need a woman to look after you."

"I don't," I said fiercely. "Me and you were doing all right after Ma died. Iris didn't have to come."

He laughed a little sadly. "Don't you remember all the pork and beans we ate, the meat I burned? Iris isn't much of a cook, but she's better than I am."

"I never complained about what you fixed to eat."

"I know you didn't, but it wasn't good for you." His hand dropped and squeezed my shoulder. "You've got to learn to like Iris because she's going to be around a long time."

"Well, I'm not going to learn to like Evans."

He laughed.

"Will he be around long, too?" I asked.

"I don't think so. His kind have itchy feet. He'll move on as soon as spring planting's over . . ."

But Evans didn't move on. And no matter how hard I tried I could not make up to Evans. Not that he did anything to me. He tried to get me to play games with him; he made a dandy kite for me, but it was no use. There were too many outsiders around now. First Iris, then Evans. I longed for the old days when there had been just my Pa and my Ma and me.

I heard Pa and Iris talking about Evans once. Pa said Evans was green, that he had a lot to learn about farming, but he was a willing worker. For that reason Pa let him stay on. Evans didn't want any money and haying season was coming on and Pa would need a hired hand worse than ever then.

Iris liked Evans. When they were in the house together and Pa was gone doing something and they thought I wasn't around to hear, they'd talk and whisper and laugh. Iris especially would laugh in a way she never did when talking with Pa. Since Evans had come, she'd taken to wearing nice clothes all the time and to fixing her hair and sometimes to putting on rouge and powder even if she wasn't going in to town.

Pa liked Evans, too, and that always made me mad. I heard Pa say once that Evans was a smart man, that if it wasn't for the Depression Evans would be sitting pretty. Pa began to take Evans fishing with him in the evenings, on the small lake that bordered our south forty. I went along a couple of times, but because Evans was there I didn't enjoy myself though I loved to fish.

I thought that summer would never come. I wanted the grass to grow real fast so it would be ready for mowing and drying and storing in the barn because maybe then, when haying was over, Evans would move on.

It was the middle of June when it happened. The timothy was up to my waist and the clover had the rich, thick smell, but Pa never started to cut hay until the first of July. Spring came late to northern Wisconsin where we lived and so did summer. Though haying was a couple of weeks away Pa started getting the machinery in shape, replacing the nicked and broken knives on the sickle and seeing that the rake and hay loader were in good shape.

I'll never forget that day. It was hot and muggy and the sun seemed to burn wherever it touched your skin and you had to sweat even when you were sitting still. Pa and Evans were repairing the hayrack and I snuck away and went through the pasture and on down to the lake where I stripped off my clothes and went swimming.

The water was nice and warm and it sure was much more comfortable in the lake than sweating in the sun. Thunderclouds began to pile up to the south and I figured by nightfall we would have a storm. Time went by real fast and all at once I heard voices and recognized one of them as Pa's.

I just barely made it out of the water and grabbed my clothes and ducked behind some bushes before Pa and Evans came into sight. I thought that Pa might be looking for me because I had snuck away and so I crouched there naked behind the bushes with my teeth chattering from the sudden change out of the warm water into the cool shade of the bushes. But Pa wasn't looking for me. Him and Evans were going fishing.

They got into the boat and rowed out on the lake. I remembered that my real Ma had never liked the idea of Pa going fishing in a boat because he couldn't swim. I watched them awhile, waiting to dry, and then pulled on my clothes even though I was still damp. I was ready to sneak back to the farm when I heard a cry, faint and frightened, out on the lake.

When I looked, the boat was upside down with Evans hanging on to it. He just seemed to be waiting. There was no sign of my Pa. No sign at all . . .

I ran all the way back and hid up in the haybarn. At times I cried, the tears running hot and stinging down my cheeks. Then all at once I would grow cold and start to shiver and think that now I was all alone. Even my Pa was gone. Only Iris remained—and Evans.

I heard him when he returned from the lake, breathing hard as he passed close to the barn like he'd been running. I crawled down the ladder and snuck around to see what he would tell Iris. I knew he had told her when she screamed.

Evans tried calming her. He raised his voice and shouted at her and then there was a sound like a slap and Iris quit howling. After awhile, she came out the door and started calling me. My legs didn't want to move; I wished I could run but I didn't know where. Evans was standing there, watching me, and I knew if I tried to run, his long legs would catch me sure. So all I could do was go to Iris.

She put her arms around me. "Oh, you poor little lamb," she sobbed. "Oh, Tommy, Tommy, how am I going to tell you? Oh, my little lamb."

I looked up into Evans' eyes and it was like looking into those of the Devil. If he knew I'd seen what had happened out on the lake, if he guessed—I shuddered. Iris held me tighter.

"Do you know? Did you hear when we were talking?"

I nodded.

Evans was watching me real close. "Why doesn't he cry?" he asked Iris. Then to me, "Don't you know your Pa is dead?"

I nodded again.

Iris said, "Hush, now, Lloyd. Don't you see the poor lamb's in shock? He'll cry later on. You better go and report this to the sheriff."

I could hardly wait for the sheriff to get there. He would look after me; he would see that no harm came to me. He would take Evans and lock him up in a deep, dark hole and never let him out. But all the sheriff did was listen to Evans.

Evans told how the boat got upset when Pa stood up to change seats and Evans went flying out into the water and when he came up and looked around he couldn't see Pa anywhere. So he kept diving and swimming around, looking for Pa, but couldn't find him. So he finally gave up and swam to shore and ran to report the accident.

I opened my mouth to say it wasn't so, that Evans hadn't dived or swam or looked for Pa at all, but had hung on to the boat all the while. But the sheriff was nodding like he had believed Evans and then I caught Evans watching me with that hard, cruel look I'd seen in his eyes earlier. So I shut my mouth, but the sheriff had seen I'd wanted to talk.

"Yes, son?" he asked in a soft, gentle voice so much like Pa's I could have cried. "Did you want to say something?"

I looked at Evans. He was watching me, but he was smiling now though not with his eyes. "Go ahead, Tommy. If you want to ask the sheriff something go right ahead. He won't bite you." Then, chuckling, to the sheriff, "He's very shy. You can't get a word out of him when there's strangers around."

I'd never seen a sheriff before. I thought he'd be a big man, even bigger than Evans, but this sheriff was small and old with a little round belly and he didn't even have a gun. Evans could squash him with one blow of his big fists.

"Go on, Tommy," Evans said, smiling, but watching me with those Devil's eyes, "speak up. You were going to say something, weren't you?"

I knew the sheriff wouldn't believe me. Iris wouldn't either. She believed only what Evans told her. Evans never took his eyes off me. I knew I had to say something to keep him from guessing that I had seen what had happened out on the lake.

"Is—is my Pa really dead?"

The sheriff looked at Evans and at Iris and then cleared his throat. "I'm afraid so, son." Then to Iris, "Are you caring for the lad?"

"I should say so. After all, Sam Dietrich was my husband. I've always been like another mother to you, haven't I, Tommy?"

She put her arms around me and started to cry again. The sheriff cleared his throat once more and looked uncomfortable.

Evans said, "He'll be in good hands, sheriff. I've never seen a finer foster-mother than Mrs. Dietrich. Now, don't you think we'd better go see about the dragging operations?"

The days turned lost and empty for me after they recovered the body of my father. There was no place for me to go because I had no kin. I had to stay on the farm where everything I saw, everywhere I went reminded me of Pa. A few people came to say they were sorry. The men patted me on the head or shook my hand and told me I was a little man. The women sighed and twittered over me while their eyes turned wet.

Iris was nicer to me than she'd ever been and I began to think that maybe she had loved Pa after all. But then I'd hear her whispering and laughing with Evans and a couple of times I saw how he touched her and I knew even then, as young as I was, that she hadn't cared too much for Pa who had been quite a bit older than her.

I begun to catch Evans watching me. No matter where I went, what I did, I'd look up or around and find him there, looking at me with a strange, measuring light in his eyes. He would smile and say something nice and kind, but I knew his words were empty. I knew he was the Devil himself and nothing he could say or do would ever fool me.

I could hardly wait for haying to begin, because of what I was going to do to Evans. That was all I lived for, the day that the bloom came out on the timothy and it was time to oil the mowing machine and hitch the horses to it and then go around the fields, dropping the tall grass in long, fragrant swaths.

I was happy when Iris said to me, "Tomorrow Lloyd is going to start cutting hay and you've got to show him how to operate the mowing machine. You used to follow your Pa around all the time so you should know how it runs. You've got to start cooperating and helping around here, young man. Lloyd needs you and we need him. I don't know what I'd do if Lloyd wasn't around."

That morning I had to help him harness the horses. Queen was real mean and laid her ears back every time Evans came closer to her. He was afraid she'd bite him, so I had to slip the bit in her mouth and the bridle over her head. Then we led the horses outside and hitched them to the mowing machine.

I showed Evans how to drop the sickle and use the foot lever to raise it when he came to a rock and how to put the machine in gear. He gave me a big grin.

"You're real helpful this morning, Tom," he said. "I like that. I've got a hunch we're going to get along real good from now on. How about it?"

"Sure," I said. "We're going to get along fine."

He asked me where to start and I told him the section by the spring. The land was low and wet and Pa had always had trouble with the mower there. The grass was thick and tough and always choked the sickle and Pa had to back up the mower and raise the sickle halfway while I cleared it. I was hoping the sickle would get clogged up today.

Evans dropped the sickle and kicked the mower in gear and started off. I followed in the lane made by the sickle as it dropped the tall, scented timothy. I had always liked this walking behind the mower, listening to the chatter of the Pittman shaft as it drove the sickle, hearing the snorting and coughing of the horses as some of the bloom on the timothy got in their nostrils. But today there was no pleasure in me, only sadness, because it wasn't Pa up there riding the mower.

Sure enough, when he got to the low spot by the spring, where the reedy swamp grass mingled with the timothy, the sickle choked. Evans backed up the team and then, with racing heart, I walked around in front of the sickle and pulled out the grass where it was clogged between the knives and the guards. I told Evans that was how it was done.

I followed him around the field a couple of times and each time the mower clogged up at the spring and I walked around in front of the sickle to clean it. The third round I said I was tired and would rest until he came around again. Evans just shrugged that off and clucked the horse into motion.

I waited hidden in the brush around the spring with my slingshot in my hands and a pocket full of rocks. When Evans had completed another round, the mower choked again. He started to call me, but I stayed hidden, hoping he wouldn't come looking for me. I heard him mutter something as if he was sore at me, and then he got off the mower and stood in front of the sickle like I'd stood and started to clean it.

I had a sharp rock in my slingshot. I took careful aim at Queen's rump and let her have the rock as hard as I could. Then, quickly, I let King have one on the rump, too, and the team burst into a run.

Evans let out one startled yell, then began to scream as the sickle hooked him in the middle and doubled him and carried him along with the horses' stampeding rush. He screamed quite a long time and that was the sweetest sound I've ever heard.

When the sheriff came to look into the accident and asked me questions, I pretended to be scared and shocked. All I ever said was, "The horses ran away. They just ran away . . ."

A SINGULAR QUARRY

Ed Lacy

After a timid knock, the woman half-opened my office door and asked, "Mr. William Ash, the private detective?"

About forty, she was tall and on the slim side, with brownish hair cropped in an old-fashioned bob to frame a plain but interesting face, minus makeup. Her modest short dress and fancy sandals, all a golden tan, were hard to judge as to their cost, but the wedding ring, a jade ring and pin could all have been trading stamp stuff. No money here, I decided with resignation.

I stood up. "That's my name. Come in." Up close, the hazel eyes were nervous, with tense lines around the thin, red mouth. Maybe she was fifty. I pegged it for a husband-shadowing job.

She sat on the one chair alongside my desk, crossing very nice legs. She could be thirty-five. "I'm Mrs. Daisy Davis." Opening her clutch bag, she dropped a $1000 bill on my battered desk.

"Mrs. Davis, you have an enchanting way of opening a conversation," I said, staring at the big bill, "but you seem to have misread my door. It reads *private investigator,* not *thug.* I don't go in for strong-arm stuff, even for a grand."-

"I want a detective, not a goon," she said calmly. "When I tell people about it, they react as if I belong in a ha-ha institution. So whenever you think I'm talking wildly, Mr. Ash, look at the money. It will bring you back to reality."

"Okay, I can hardly take my greedy eyes off it. What people have you been talking to, Mrs. Davis? Talking about what?"

"I've been talking to the police, but when they started staring at me with that she's-a-nut look, I couldn't tell them about it. Mr. Ash, I'm hardly a crime buff, but I've traveled over three hundred miles to see you because I remembered reading about a case you worked on several years ago, where a gambler was arrested for murder and even after he was convicted, even though you were off salary, you kept working on the case and found the real killer. I like that sort of work attitude."

I shrugged, keeping an eye on the grand green sight. "Once you get started, you want to see the finish. What's your trouble, Mrs. Davis?"

"Nick, my husband, was killed a month ago. He died a horrible death; he was tortured. I want you to find the killer or killers. My husband was murdered either by a man named Carlos, who represents a South African diamond syndicate, or by somebody—keep your eyes on the money—from outer space."

I tried not to blink. The last thing she looked like was a loon. "Outer space? Don't tell me flying saucers are involved?"

"They definitely are," she said.

I managed to take my eyes from the money to stare at her. She stared back, soft eyes very steady. I said, "Take it from the top, Mrs. Davis."

"Nick and I had been married for twenty years, but never had children. I worked as a telephone operator, while Nick was a morgue keeper at a U.S. airbase. I think we were a very average couple. Our joint income was about $9,000. We had a comfortable little house, an old car, and about a thousand dollars in the bank. Today I have a Caddy and over $46,000 in cash. All this happened over the last four months. In short, Nick came into a bundle."

My palms were sweating slightly; I rubbed them on my pants. "Why does a stateside airbase need a morgue keeper?"

"If a pilot is killed in a crash, the body is kept in the morgue pending an investigation. Actually, it was a minor civil service job; Nick was a sort of glorified porter. Now, Mr. Ash, I've never seen a UFO, but in our area several sightings have been reported in the last year. People claim they have seen lights—flying saucers—hovering over the power lines. Whether it's true or merely their imagination, I frankly don't know. I do know the airbase sends out fighter planes trying to find these saucers after each sighting.

"Well, about seven months ago Nick came home quite excited one night, told me it was top secret and all that, but four small bodies, about the size of boys, had been brought to the morgue, each sewed up in a canvas bag. Nick told me rumors had it that the bodies were humanoids, a form of human life, from a saucer. Nick never opened the canvas bags, of course, but merely kept them in the refrigerated vaults.

"About a month later a UFO was reported over an abandoned quarry one night and again the following night. On both nights Nick was out of the house, and he was fired the day after the second UFO sighting. He never told me why. The official reason was 'inefficiency'. Nick was only six years away from his pension but he didn't seem upset at losing his job. He showed me a heavy hunk of what looked like cloudy glass, which must have weighed ten pounds. He warned me not to talk about it, said it was a huge, rough diamond. I never saw the stone again, and Nick flatly refused to tell me what had happened at the airbase. My theory, and it's only a *theory,* is that Nick was given the diamond by somebody from a UFO in return for smuggling out one or all of the bodies in the morgue. The Air Force won't discuss the case."

"Hold it. This ten-pound stone, was it really a diamond?"

"I assume so. Nick was very mysterious about it, claimed I would be safer not knowing too much. All I know is that Nick went to see a jeweler in Springfield, which is the nearest city to Eastville where we live. The jeweler, a Mr. Frank Simpson, has now vanished, but prior to his disappearance he told me Nick had brought him several rough diamonds to sell, weighing a total of 109 carats. A week later Nick suddenly had thousands of dollars, told me to quit my job. A week or so after that, Nick had more money, and bought the Caddy. Now, this is only my *theory,* but Nick would go out to the quarry and then ride to Springfield the next day. Later, he would go to Springfield again and return with thousands of dollars. I'm sure he was cutting up the big diamond and selling bits of it to Mr. Simpson, who cut and polished them and, in turn, sold them to diamond merchants in New York."

"Did Nick know anything about diamonds?"

"No."

"Cutting a diamond calls for great skill."

She nodded. "I think Nick was merely chipping off bits of the stone somehow, and taking the chips to Mr. Simpson. Nick was very happy, told me he would soon be a millionaire and then we'd take a trip around the world. Mr. Simpson told me——"

"When did he tell you all this?"

"The day after Nick's body was found. I went to see Simpson and he was packing, ready to take off, badly frightened. He told me the diamonds were flawless, the finest stones he'd ever seen, and that a Mr. Carlos of a large South African diamond syndicate had questioned him as to where the diamonds had been found. He wanted Simpson to agree to sell only to the syndicate. I know that on the day before—before Nick was found murdered, he received two phone calls from this Mr. Carlos, I overheard Nick shouting that he wasn't interested in any deal, and flatly refused to say where the rough gems came from. I don't know what was said on the phone, but Nick was very angry and the second time, before he hung up, he said, 'You can't threaten me!' When I asked, Nick told me not to worry. He went to the quarry that night and never returned. The next morning they found Nick's corpse. He had been burned across various parts of his body, died from shock and a heart attack."

Keeping my eyes glued on the thousand buck bill and my sanity, I asked, "What did the police do about all this?"

"Nothing. They claim Nick was killed by a person or persons unknown. You see, the second I started telling them about the flying saucer, well, they reacted like I was crazy. When I mentioned the diamond syndicate, they were sure I'd flipped; diamonds have never been found around this part of the country. I assume that when the police checked with the airbase they ran into 'No comment.' I want Nick's killer or killers found, if possible."

My eyes traced the 1000 on each corner of the bill as I asked, "Mrs. Davis, where were you on the night Nick was killed?"

Her gasp made me look at her. Face flushed, she asked, "Are you hinting I had——"

"All I'm trying to do is get a few facts. You said Nick didn't return all that night. Weren't you worried?"

"I was playing whist at a neighbor's. The police checked on that. I came home at about eleven P.M. and went to sleep. I'm a sound sleeper; it was only in the morning I realized Nick hadn't come home. If I had killed my husband, would I hire you to find the killers?"

"Could be you're hiring me to find the rest of that big diamond?"

Daisy shook her head. "I don't care about that unlucky stone! Of course if you should find it, all right, but I told you I have enough money, plus there's about $15,000 due on Nick's insurance and pension fund money. I want my husband's killers found. Frankly, there is one other reason: I'm frightened. I have this feeling of being watched all the time."

"This Carlos character been calling you since Nick died?"

"No. I never see anybody, but I feel I'm being followed, watched."

"Have you been out to the quarry since? What's out there?"

"The only time I was there was when the police sent for me to identify Nick's b-body. It's a big rocky hole, full of water. I think, at one time, they used to get slate, or something, from the quarry. It hasn't been used for, oh, over twenty years. There's an abandoned shack and parts of rusty machinery around. Kids used to swim there, but there was a drowning a few years back and nobody goes to the quarry now. Mr. Ash, will you take the case?"

As it happened, the only thing I was working on was locating witnesses to a car accident and that had reached the waiting stage, for answers to some letters I'd mailed the day before. "Sure, I'll take the case. I charge a hundred a day plus expenses, and I don't guarantee results. That understood, Mrs. Davis?"

She didn't flinch at the fee, merely said, "All I ask is that you do your best."

I took out a pad and wrote down the exact dates of the UFO sightings, when Nick was bounced, Simpson's address, some data on herself and Nick, which wasn't much as they were both orphans. About Carlos, I asked, "Do you know his full name? The diamond syndicate he worked for?"

"All I know is his name was Carlos. Whether that's

his first or last name, I can't say, nor did Nick ever mention the name of the syndicate he worked for."

"How do you know it's a South African one?"

"Mr. Simpson didn't mention the name, but he did say it was South African."

I typed up a statement, which she signed, stating Mrs. Davis was retaining me. When she said, "Keep the $1000 as a retainer," I told her to put it back in her bag. Then I walked her to my bank, where I had her change it: you have to sign a form when changing a $1000 bill. Daisy Davis really impressed me; while in the bank she also cashed a $500 bill. She was returning to Eastville, but I suggested she stay in the city for a few days as a safety measure. She registered at a good hotel. Leo Klein, the house dick, had once been my patrol car partner, and I told him to keep an eye on her.

Back in my office, I sat at my desk, carefully counting and recounting the twenty $50 bills, sort of mentally pinching myself. In twenty years as a city cop and dick and eight years as a private badge, I thought I'd worked on every kind of a case, but this was my first flying saucer caper.

In investigative work there are things you can do without leaving your desk. I checked Mrs. Daisy Davis with a guy working for a credit bureau who gave me off-the-cuff info in return for a few bottles around Christmas. Then I phoned a reporter whom I had supported for a number of years when he was my son-in-law, and we are still friendly. I asked him to see if the papers had anything on the UFO sightings in Eastville on the dates Daisy had given me. My ex-son-in-law said, "Flying saucers? Bill, have you flipped?"

"I'm not sure myself. But let me know what you find, Sonny."

Then I called a guy I knew on the force who is now a captain and part of our local police brass. After the usual where-have-you-been small talk, he gave me the name of a sergeant on the Eastville police force (10 men, all told) but when I asked who he knew on the New York City force, or if he was friendly with anybody on the New York Jewelers Association security force, he said that would take a little thinking, he'd call me back.

When I long-distanced Eastville, a sergeant said, "So she's hiring private tin? Well, there isn't much I can tell you about the Nick Davis killing. He had no police record, didn't run around, and Mrs. Davis' alibi checked out; she was playing cards that night. So, no motive for the killing. We figure it was the work of a nut. There were lines burnt into his soles and legs, like a tic-tac-toe design. Nick Davis had $167 in his wallet; it wasn't touched. The work of a nut, for sure."

"This tic-tac-toe design, could it mean anything, do you think?"

"Sure, it means a nut with some kind of small branding iron came upon Nick, that's all. Of course, the case is in our open files, but we haven't any working leads."

I tried not to laugh. The case was in their "open" files—I'd give odds this was the only murder case Eastville had in the last fifty years. "Didn't Mrs. Davis have some leads?"

"Look, I've known Daisy Davis for a lot of years, mister, and generally she's a levelheaded woman. But the grief, the shock of losing Nick, sent Daisy out of her mind. Really off. She talked about men from some other planet, South African gunmen, diamonds. Daisy was in a bad way."

"Tell me, have there been any UFO sightings around Eastville?"

"Man, don't you start *that*. We get calls almost every month, some folks so positive they seen one, they're ready to fight if you don't believe them. Ask me, all crackpot stuff. We refer such calls to the airbase, where they forget them. A person sees a star twinkle, or a plane light, and right away they're shouting they seen a UFO."

I thanked him and after I hung up, my bottle pal

in the credit outfit called to tell me Mrs. Daisy Davis had a solid rating. He ended with, "Bill, if she's your client, you've really hooked a live one."

My police captain called to give me the name of the head of security for the Manhattan Jewelers Association, and added, "Bill, I only met this guy once. He used to be an FBI man. If you want info from him, you'd best go see him in New York. Phoning him will only be a waste of money. What are you working on, Bill? We haven't had any stolen jewelry case here in months."

"This is an out-of-town thing. Thanks for the dope. I'll drop in and see how much beer you can drink one of these days."

Minutes later my ex-son-in-law phoned. "Adjust your space helmet, Pops. There were alleged UFO sightings on the dates you mentioned. Several people claim to have seen them, sober folks, too. The fact is, unidentified flying objects have been seen fairly often around Eastville, but the airbase there keeps hush-hush on the whole deal, okay?"

"Thanks."

"What do you hear from Ruthie, Bill?"

"She and her husband are making out fine in Los Angeles. They have a baby girl."

"Good. Ruthie always wanted kids. Bill, how about you and Alice coming over some night, meet my new wife?"

"Sure. We'll make a date, one of these days."

I long-distanced the U.S. airbase at Eastville and finally got the information officer on the other end of the wire. When I asked, "Is it true you have, or had, bodies taken from a UFO in your morgue?" I could hear him suck in his breath, then sputter, "Who the hell are you?"

"Merely a curious taxpayer. Is it true?"

"No comment."

"Why? Why should it be hush-hush? Or are we at war with Mars?"

"It is an Air Force policy that all UFO information must come from Washington."

"Then I take it you have, or had, the bodies at the Eastville Air Base?"

"I never confirmed that, or denied it. Perhaps you didn't hear me. I said I have no comment."

"Oh, I heard you. In fact, this is all on tape," I said to make him nervous. As I hung up I felt a little better; if Daisy was a nut, she wasn't alone in this.

I phoned Mrs. Davis at her hotel and was told she was out. I left a message that I'd call her late tomorrow, then got Leo on the phone.

He said, "How would I know where she went? Maybe shopping, to a movie. Bill, she didn't check out of the hotel, I'm positive."

"Keep an eye on Mrs. Davis. I'll take care of you."

"I bet. Listen, the doc took me off booze and cigarettes."

"Great, Leo, I'll send you a fat box of candy."

At 3:30 P.M. I quit being a telephone jockey with a call to my wife. "Alice, I have to go to New York tonight on a case. How about coming along?"

"Tonight? For how long, Bill?"

"We should be back tomorrow night."

"Too much traveling and packing for so short a time," Alice said, as I knew she would, but she liked to be asked. "Want me to meet you at the airport with a light bag?"

"A great idea, honey. Just a shirt, tie and toilet articles."

Locking the office, I crossed the street to make a reservation on a 10:20 P.M. jet. The wife and I had a good supper at the airport and by midnight I was pounding my ear in a Manhattan hotel.

The Manhattan Jewelers Association's security force had a swank suite of offices and at 11 A.M. I was talking to the head security officer, also on the swank side, a well set-up guy looking like the movie version of an executive, with brushed gray hair, good clothes, even a manicure.

He was good, too. I merely told him I was on a murder case which might be connected with diamonds and he let it go at that. When I asked if his association knew of a Frank Simpson of Springfield, he called the name into the intercom on his desk and a few minutes later a pretty secretary brought in a file.

He said, "Mr. Ash, it's odd you should mention Mr. Simpson. There's much interest in him in the market lately. Mr. Simpson started out in the Diamond Exchange as a cutter and polisher, then became a dealer. When his wife died eight years ago, he gave up the hustle here and opened a general jewelry shop in Springfield."

"Why the special interest in Simpson now? And what did you mean by hustle? Was he legit?"

"Oh yes, he was legit. You see, Mr. Ash, in the diamond trade a fellow can have two feet of window space and part of a counter, yet he can be doing a yearly gross business in the hundreds of thousands, carry a half-million dollar stock, often on him. I used the word 'hustle' because diamonds are one of the most competitive businesses you'll find and a successful dealer really has to go out and hustle. As for the sudden interest in Simpson, he has sold a number of stones recently, which he cut and polished himself, all absolutely flawless, the finest diamonds ever seen. Mr. Simpson refused to reveal the source of the rough stones, but these gems brought top price because of their remarkable purity—no flaws or foreign matter. They are very rare, and have a faint black tinge."

"Could they be manmade gems? I think I once read that diamonds can be made in a lab."

He smiled. "Indeed they can, Mr. Ash. But to make a, say, three-carat diamond would cost three times what a natural gem would sell for. Mr. Simpson has been rather mysterious as to his source and there are rumors that he's in contact with a new mine."

"Have diamonds been found in the States?"

"Oh, yes. Single, alluvial diamonds have been found, of poor quality, and there was a mine in Murfreesboro, Arkansas."

"Is a diamond mine a big affair, like a coal mine? Could it be a one or two man operation, for example?"

He shook his carefully brushed gray head. "Diamonds can be found on the surface, even in river beds, as gold nuggets are sometimes found. But the great diamond mines are as deep and large as any coal mine. A true diamond mine would hardly be a one man operation."

"About South Africa—Suppose Simpson had somehow found a diamond mine here in the States, would the diamond syndicate contact him?"

"Certainly, if he began selling gems in any quantity. The price of diamonds is kept high by carefully limiting the supply."

I asked, "If Simpson refused to sell to them, would they resort to strong-arm stuff?"

He shook his handsome head again. "Mr. Ash, the diamond syndicates are big business, with millions in reserve. If they felt it necessary to get control of a new mine, they would make so large an offer no man in his right mind would refuse. Naturally, there can be other reasons for not selling. The Russians are mining diamonds and there's a possibility they may someday flood the market, a political move to deal an economic kayo to the Union of South Africa. But as for a single mine owner, the syndicate could top any offer the mine owner made. It's strictly business, not a muscle deal, at least here in the States. Certainly the history of diamonds is one of violence. If a native African should stumble upon a mine and refuse to deal with the syndicate, violence might be used. But, as I said, not here in the States, if that is what you're driving at."

"Okay. Now, do these syndicates have some representatives here?"

"Yes. There are three major syndicates but on a price and supply level, they operate as a single organization in the States."

"Do they have a representative here called Carlos? I don't know if that's his first or last name."

"I never heard the name and I personally know all their agents. Mr. Ash, let me paint a clear picture for you. If Mr. Simpson really had found a mine with these superior diamonds, what would he gain by not working with the syndicate? If he flooded the market, the price of the gems would drop. Operating a mine calls for a large overhead. It would be much easier for him to accept an offer of, say, two or three million for his mine, skip the headaches."

He had Simpson's picture in his file, a fat-faced guy, middle-aged. Handsome had a copy of the snap made for me and by two A.M. I was flying home, smugly pleased at the way the case was breaking.

After phoning Alice from the airport, I went directly to Daisy Davis' hotel. Leo met me in the lobby. "Bill, I've been calling you. Your bird checked out an hour ago."

"Damn."

"No way I could stop her. But our switchboard operator says Mrs. Davis phoned the bus terminal a half hour before she checked out."

I took a cab to the terminal, was told the only bus to Springfield, which was the closest stop to Eastville, had pulled out before Daisy left, so she'd had to drive. I got my car from the garage, stopped at the office to pick up my gun, phoned Alice, then started for Eastville, clocking ninety once I hit the throughway.

Eastville has a two-block-long main drag, a supermarket the largest store. The Davis house was a modest deal which had recently been reshingled, new storm windows added. When Daisy opened the door I asked, "Why didn't you stay at the hotel?"

"I didn't have a change of clothing and I thought it silly to buy some when I could come here, pack a bag, and return to the hotel by evening."

"You might have ended up as the best-dressed woman in the cemetery. If you were returning, why did you check out of the hotel?"

"Force of habit, saving a day's room rent. Did you learn anything, Mr. Ash?"

If she had returned to the hotel by night she wouldn't have saved a penny. I said, "We're dealing with a killer, possibly a nut, so . . ."

"A spaceman?"

"Come on, forget that flying saucer stuff, our killer is an Earth man. I'm spending the night here."

"Oh. Really, what will the neighbors think?"

"Daisy, what will the neighbors think if you're found murdered? Skip the gossip, say I'm your older brother, or some such nonsense. I'm hungry and have some questions to ask. Let's go out for supper."

"That would really start gossip. We can eat here."

Daisy wasn't a bad cook, and as we ate I asked, "How long has it been since Simpson closed his store and took off?"

"The day after Nick was killed, about a month ago."

"Did you tell the police about Simpson?"

"No. Soon as I mentioned diamonds, they reacted as if I were crazy. What has Mr. Simpson to do with this?"

"I'll tell you tomorrow. Have you heard from Simpson since then?"

"No."

"Have you any idea where he is?"

"None."

"Did this Carlos guy ever call you?"

"I never spoke to him."

"This morgue job Nick had, did he work alone?"

"Yes. As I explained, it was part of his porter work at the airbase."

"Except for yourself and Simpson, did Nick ever tell anybody else about the diamond?"

"I'm sure he didn't. Can't you tell me what you've found out, Bill?"

"In the morning we'll drive into Springfield. I've a few things to check out, then I'll tell you who the killer is. Let me help you with the dishes."

We sat around and watched TV over a few beers, like an old married couple, but unlike an old couple I slept on the living-room couch. We went to sleep at ten-thirty and at eleven the phone rang. I answered it on the first ring since the phone was on a table next to the couch. I said, "Hello?" and didn't get any answer, although I could hear somebody breathing at the other end of the wire. When I hung up I turned to see Daisy standing in the doorway of the bedroom, the light behind her silhouetting her good figure.

"Who was that, Bill?"

"I don't know. Were you expecting a call? I mean, if a man answers . . ."

She shook her head.

"Ever get any calls before, where nobody answered?"

She shook her head again, said, "Good night, Bill," and shut her door, turning off the light. I moved the chair with my clothes and shoulder holster nearer the couch and stretched out again, thinking hard about Daisy. I was thinking she'd told me she was such a heavy sleeper that she hadn't been aware, until morning, that her husband hadn't returned, the night he was killed. Now, one phone ring had got her up. The case had seemed so simple—but if Daisy was in this with Simpson, why had she hired me?

I fell off into an uneasy sleep and in the morning, after a decent breakfast, we drove to Springfield, which was only twenty miles away. This is a fairly large city with a big shopping complex and several streets of shops. The Simpson jewelry store was a small affair, with a locked steel gate across the one window and the entrance. I noticed a trade magazine and a single letter inside the gate. I waited for the mailman and when he tossed two more letters through the gate, I asked, "Have you any idea when Mr. Simpson will be back? He was repairing my watch."

"There was a sign pasted on the window, saying he was ill, but would reopen shortly. Wind and rain took the sign off last week."

"Did he leave any forwarding address?"

"Nope. Why do you ask?"

"He's been gone a month and there isn't much mail piled up inside the gate."

The mailman stared at the few pieces of mail. "Say, that's a fact. There was a whole pile of mail there the other day. Guess he must have come by and picked it up."

"You know his home address?"

"Sure, here. He lives over the store."

Returning to the car, I glanced at the apartment above the shop, the two windows shut, shades pulled down. I drove around the block. The rear windows sported an air conditioner. By going through an alley and over a fence, I could get to Simpson's apartment, but it wasn't worth the risk. Instead, I stopped at a stationery store, bought paper and an envelope. I wrote:

> *Simpson: I've found the mine. Important I see you at once, re: polishing and cutting some stones.*
>
> *Carlos*

I put this in the envelope and tossed it inside the store gate. Then we drove to the Davis house, by way of the quarry, which was a desolate looking spot even in the sunshine. Over lunch Daisy asked, "Obviously you suspect Frank Simpson. What about Carlos?"

"Carlos doesn't exist, like the flying saucers. I don't know where Nick got the diamond, but I think Simpson was sure your husband had stumbled upon a diamond mine and tortured him in an effort to get the location of the mine. I expect to have a showdown with Simpson tonight."

"You know where he is, then?"

"No, but he'll find me."

I sat by the picture window, watching the street. The phone call came at the end of the afternoon. When Daisy said, "Mr. Simpson, where—" I grabbed the phone from her hand, said, "Simpson, this is Carlos. Be at your store in the morning. I'll have some rough stones ready for cutting. My syndicate has worked out a deal with Mrs. Davis." I hung up quickly and returned to the window.

Daisy asked, "What was that about?"

"You ever go bluefishing?"

She shook her head.

"A blue is a vicious and greedy fish. So you toss out a lot of bait, including one with a hook in it, and hope the blue will be so busy eating he'll take the hook. That's called chumming."

"I still don't understand, Bill."

I smiled at her. "Why should I tell you the secrets of the private-eye racket? You're too pretty to be a good investigator."

"All right, I'll shut up, and you stop putting me on," Daisy said, so pleased that she blushed. I turned to stare at the street again, waiting to see if Simpson would try watching the house. All I saw were neighbors returning from work. I really hoped Simpson showed tonight; it would be a problem spending another night in the Davis house—on the couch. That kind of problem I had avoided, until now.

We had a light snack for supper and at seven P.M. I went to the bathroom, checked my gun, then told Daisy to visit her next-door neighbors, to stay there until I returned, and I turned on the house lights. She gave me a key and I got in my car, drove around the block, returned to watch Daisy go to the next house. When I was convinced she was staying there, I drove to the quarry. The moon was out and the place was spooky as hell. A rough hill of stone rose about a hundred jagged feet above a dark pond some thirty feet across. There was a shack ready to fall apart, the remains of some kind of winch, rusted and busted, a

few trees and large boulders. That was it. I cased the
shack thoroughly, studied the trees and rocks, then
sat in front of the shack until ten P.M. listening to the
intense silence, watching the stars, the trees. Even
though I was sitting in a shadow, I felt exposed. I
went down to the edge of the pond and sat behind a
large boulder, worrying a little about snakes. My back
was to the pond as I watched the shack. It seemed a
secure stakeout. Maybe it was a half hour later when
I heard a faint ripple of water behind me. Before I
could spin around, my head went into orbit.

I came to on the broken floor inside the shack, my
head soaring. When my eyes started working I didn't
have to wonder what I'd been slugged with. Simpson
was standing in front of me, a jagged, dirty rock in
his left hand. It was so heavy he finally put it down
at his weird feet, put it down gently; but the .45 in a
plastic bag, which his right hand held, wasn't heavy:
he kept it pointed at me. Something was tickling my
neck. Keeping an eye on the .45, I slowly raised a
hand to the back of my neck and felt blood.

For a moment I wondered if I were still out, maybe dreaming, for Simpson looked really out of this
world in a black rubber scuba suit, fins, air tanks on
his back, face mask raised onto his dark hair. His pot-
belly in that suit looked comical, if I were in a laughing mood. He said, "Well now, Mr. Ash, you're a
dumb private eye, sitting with your back to the water
and to me. As you see, I found the diamond."

Either his voice was shrill or something was wrong
with my hearing. I was having trouble keeping my
throbbing head on my thick neck, getting the dim
scene in focus. My wallet and gun were lying on the
other end of the busted floor, so Simpson knew all
about me.

"Daisy hired you, of course, but why?"

"To find Nick's killer—you," I said, but not a sound
came out.

Simpson waved the .45. "Perhaps a crack across your stupid head will loosen your big tongue!" he shrilled.

"To find Nick's killer—you!" Now the words came bursting out of my mouth. "Talk about dummies I knew it had to be you from the go. Inventing Carlos was childish." Glancing at the .45, I wondered why I was talking so big.

The jeweler shrugged. "I didn't expect the loon to die. He brought me the finest diamonds I've ever seen, with a cock and bull story about a flying saucer. But I'll find his mine yet. He had this great stone hidden under the pond water, and someplace in this quarry I'll find his mine. It'll be the greatest strike in diamond history. I'll have plenty of time to hunt for it, after I take care of you."

"Knock me off and you're bagged. I left a report with my secretary about looking for you, so don't . . ."

"Don't hand me that garbage, Ash, I'm not buying it. I'll merely tie rocks around your big feet and toss you in. The pond is fifty feet deep and there are fish in there, so you'll be a skelton—should you ever come to the surface. And I have an alibi worked out for tonight, which hardly concerns you. Things are working for me. I'll——"

"You're running in bad luck, Simpson. They haven't abolished the death penalty in this state yet!"

"Enough of this chatter, Ash. I'm going to tie your feet now. I assume you know about a .45; at this range you'll be in shreds. I don't care if I toss you in the pond in one piece or a hundred. If you want to die the hard way, try something, make me shoot you."

He stepped forward, walking awkwardly with the fins on his feet, and pulled a length of heavy rope from around his waist with his left hand. Kneeling in front of my feet, he pointed the gun down my thighs as he said, "Raise your feet, detective, slowly and gently."

In the dim light the .45 seemed bigger than a battleship gun as I stared into the barrel, certain I could see the grooves. I raised my feet a few inches, head fighting to leave my neck with the motion. Simpson got his rope around my ankles, tied them tightly in a clumsy knot with his left hand. Then he stood up, the heavy rubber suit making his face shine with sweat. Staring down at me, he said, "I wonder if you know anything about the mine, Ash? From the secretive way Nick acted, I'm certain Daisy doesn't know its location. Still, you are a detective and no telling what you may have stumbled upon in your snooping. A few jabs in your more tender spots will make you downright loud-mouthed."

"Listen, Simpson, we can work out a deal. Forget Daisy. You and I . . ." I began talking wildly, sitting up for punching room. My head seemed to be working again. There was a long chance I might clip him if he somehow missed me with the gun, the first shot. I might make it if I could pull myself together, get my reflexes going.

Simpson giggled, a high, insane sound. With his fat face framed by the dark rubber headpiece, the face glass on his forehead reflecting the faint light, plus that crazy laugh, Simpson actually looked like some sort of devil in person. When the giggle died he shrilled, "I do believe you are about to try something, detective. Strangely enough, I've always considered myself a meek man, yet when I was trying to make Nick talk, via a small soldering iron in my cellar, I found I enjoy torturing. Fantastic, but there it is. So don't try to con me, detective. There's only one possible deal; if you know the location of the mine, tell me, while you can still talk."

"Stop it, Simpson. Once I tell you, I'm dead." I fell back again. I'd have a better chance kicking him with my tied feet as he came in. "Let's both talk sense. Untie me and I'll take you to the diamond mine."

"Where is it, on the moon?" he cut in sarcastically. "Nick with his flying saucer garbage, and you with this——"

"Untie me and I'll show you the mine, for a forty percent cut, Simpson. Without me, you'll never find it."

"Garbage, detective, pure, low-grade slop!" he shrilled. "If you knew where the mine was, you wouldn't have tried to lure me out here with that stupid letter!"

"Simpson, how else could I have arranged to see you? I keep telling you, Daisy is out. I know where the mine is and you know how to cut the stones, where to sell 'em. Forty percent for me and you take sixty. Just untie me and——"

"No! I've wasted too much time with you, detective. Now, I'm going——"

Suddenly, we both became aware of a faint humming sound, like the noise of a giant generator. The interior of the shack turned a blinding red and there was the smell of burning oxygen, a blanket of heat. Through the one broken window I saw that the entire outside was a flashing red. Simpson spun around and headed for the door. He shifted the .45 to his right hand, picked up the diamond with his left as he stepped through the doorway, out of my sight.

The red turned even brighter, and I had to close my eyes. Then I heard this short but piercing scream, the light dimmed, and it was night again. Bending forward, I untied my ankles, stumbled toward the doorway, picking up my wallet and gun on the way.

Speeding up toward the stars was a large, spinning, red ball, rings of blue blinking on and off underneath it. It was going at such incredible speed that within a few seconds it looked like a red star. Then it vanished.

I shut my eyes for a second, opening them slowly to accustom myself to the pale moonlight. I looked around quickly for Simpson—but he had vanished! Simpson had simply vanished! Without knowing why, I knelt and touched the dirt. It burned my fingertips. With a muffled scream of panic, I raced for my car. For a second the battery seemed dead. Then the lights came on, the starter turned over. I kept the gas pedal on the floor all the way to Daisy's house.

Once inside I ran to her liquor cabinet, took a big swig of the first bottle I touched. It didn't do a damn thing for me. My nerves, my whole being, were drum tight.

Daisy came in, and gasped, "Bill, what's wrong? You're so pale, so terribly white."

"Listen, listen," I heard a strange voice mumble, then I got myself under control, told her what had happened. I finished with, "Whether you believe it or not, it's the truth! Simpson killed your husband, and the—the spaceship took him away!"

"I believe it," Daisy whispered, staring into my eyes.

"You really do? I'm not positive I believe it, but it's over. You're safe, Daisy. I'm driving back now. Wheeling a car relaxes me, and I'll explode if I don't do something. Tomorrow, or soon as I pull myself together, I'll return the balance of your $1000. I put in three days, plus traveling to New York and——"

"No," she whispered, touching my face gently with a finger. "You're trembling, Bill."

"I'll calm down soon, I hope."

"Keep the money, Bill. You did your job, risked your life. What about the police? Are you going to tell them what happened?"

Shaking my head, I squeezed her hand as I pulled it from my face. "I should report it, but they'd never believe me. If I tried telling them, they'd fit me for a straitjacket."

"Of course. I understand. Neither of us will ever say a word about tonight. We can't."

"Right. Except for that letter I signed Carlos, there's no possible connection between us and Simpson. And the letter doesn't mean a damn thing. Simpson's clothes must be someplace around the quarry, but that's no link to us. Daisy, should you ever be questioned, you hired me to look into Nick's death, I found nothing, gave it up. That's it."

She nodded. There was an awkward moment as we walked toward the door. We shook hands. Then Daisy suddenly kissed me, hard, on the mouth, and whispered, "That's something else we'll never talk about again. Goodbye, Bill."

Once in my car, I started for home, driving fast. My nerves were still taut and I was so wide awake I doubted if I'd ever be able to sleep again. There was always the possibility of a humming, bright red nightmare awaiting me.

SLEEP IS FOR THE INNOCENT

Henry Slesar

Cavender made another contribution to the butt pile in the cloverleaf ashtray, and under his hand the mountain of crushed cigarettes wriggled like white worms. He drew away in disgust and pushed his bare feet into the slippers by the bed. On the nighttable, the luminous hands of the alarm clock had moved mercilessly to four o'clock, and he knew that he hadn't beaten the problem by medication. If anything, the depressing effect of the Nembutal had made his insomnia worse; he felt leaden and even feverish, all the pulses in his body united in one continuous throb, his ears ringing, his eyes dry and gritty. He told himself that he wouldn't report for work the next day, and that started a chain of thoughts about the office. At four-fifteen, he gave up the effort completely and tried to read. The words crashed into each other in a jumble of ink. At five, he dozed off and awoke ten minutes later. At six, he decided to take the advice of Dr. Steers and see a head-shrinker; the decision alone was enough to give him some peace; he slept the short hour before the alarm clock jangled.

The name on the door was Tedaldi.

"Did you have an appointment?" the girl at the desk said. She was appraising him, and Cavender didn't like it. He felt ashamed, embarrassed, as if she could read his problem by looking at his face. "No," he muttered. "I was told to come here by Dr. Steers."

"I see. Would you like to make an appointment?"

"I'd like to see Dr. Tedaldi now. I took off from my job to see him."

She looked doubtful, but picked up the pad and pencil from her desk and bore them like shield-and-mace into the private office behind her. A moment later, she emerged and seemed pleased with herself.

"All right. Dr. Tedaldi will see you."

"Damn nice of him," Cavender said.

"Dr. Steers and I went to school together." Tedaldi was a round, jovial man with a face that looked like a collection of perishable vegetables. Cavender didn't like him, and regretted coming. "What seems to be your trouble, Mr. Cavender?"

"Insomnia."

"How's that?"

"Insomnia. I can't sleep. I haven't slept for months."

Tedaldi rubbed his carroty nose. "Lots of people say that. Claim they never sleep." He chuckled. "Not really true, of course, it only *seems* that way."

"I sleep sometimes. Maybe an hour, two hours. But it's not enough."

"No, I guess it isn't. And since you came to see me, I gather that Dr. Steers doesn't believe your trouble is organic." He pulled a pad towards him. "Let's get the details out of the way, shall we? Then we'll talk."

He gave him details. Name: Charles Cavender. Age: 36. Occupation: Steamship line executive. Marital status . . .

"Single. No, widowed."

Tedaldi shot an eyebrow upwards. "Your wife died young?"

"In an accident," he growled.

"What sort of accident?"

"Does it matter?"

"It might."

Cavender sighed.

"A fire," he said, and leaned back in the plush chair with a sense of release, the desire for sleep almost overcoming him, the gentle voice of the round man behind the desk receding into the distance, becoming nothing more than the faint sound of an overheard conversation that had nothing to do with him . . .

Then he was talking. He talked for the duration of twelve cigarettes, pausing only to take long drags, telling Tedaldi what he wanted to hear, about Linda, about the fire, about the dream.

"My dream's back like it was a year ago," he said. "We're in the old house on Grassy Heights; I can see every stick of furniture in the living room, the shiny cherry red breakfront and that fuzzy rug that always messed up my trouser cuffs . . . I'm sitting down, not reading or anything, just sitting there. Linda's upstairs. I go to call her, from the foot of the stairs, and she comes out in that gypsy skirt of hers, smiling, her hand on the bannister, and then, behind her, I see the flames . . ." He rubbed his eyes. "She doesn't seem to be aware of them. They come licking out of our bedroom towards her; she keeps on smiling. I yell at her, scream, until my throat dries up and I can't yell anymore. Then the flames grab her and pull her backwards; I can hear them roaring, crackling . . ."

Tedaldi was patient. He was a good listener. He waited until Cavender was composed again.

"That's the way the dream goes," he said finally. "But it isn't the way it happened, not for real."

"How did it happen?"

"It was the middle of the night. We were asleep. It was early winter, and something had gone wrong with the furnace; I had a portable heater I kept for emergencies, and we had it set up in the bedroom. Somehow, the draperies caught fire; that's what the experts said later." No point in mentioning that his smoking in bed might have caused it. "Neither of us woke up until the whole room was blazing. It seemed like everything was on fire, everything . . . the room was full of smoke, I could barely see. I called Linda's name, but she didn't answer. I stumbled to the door, but I couldn't get it open. The doorknob was white-hot. Then I found the bathroom door; it was halfway open; I went inside; I don't know why myself. I was hysterical, that's the only word for it. I slammed the door shut and began to work on the window. It opened, and I jumped out. It wasn't much of a drop, and there were bushes to break my fall. I wasn't even bruised. When I hit the ground, I started running, like a crazy man. I was almost to the road when I looked back and saw the house, the whole thing covered in flames, swallowed up. It was an old house, wood-framed, a tinder box . . ."

He had said enough. He closed his mouth, and wouldn't even answer Tedaldi's next question.

"Your wife was killed?"

Cavender lit another cigarette.

"Do you think you could have saved her?" Tedaldi asked. "Has it troubled you that you didn't try?"

He took a long puff, and looked at the books on the shelves of the doctor's office.

"Do you feel guilty, Mr. Cavender? Is that your problem?"

"No!"

"It wouldn't be unnatural. Even if you had done the only sensible thing, even if there was no chance of saving your wife, it's inevitable that you would feel *some* guilt. After all, *you're* alive."

"That's not it," Cavender said quietly. "I know it wasn't my fault. I don't blame myself."

"Perhaps not consciously."

"Consciously or unconsciously. It wasn't my fault, doctor. No matter *what* he says."

Tedaldi blinked.

"No matter what *who* says?"

"Jack Fletcher. Her brother."

"Your wife's brother?"

"Yes." He stomped out his cigarette and lit another. "There's the man who ought to see you, doc."

He laughed coldly. "He's the guy who needs the head-shrinker, more than I do."

"Why do you say that?"

"Because he's crazy, that's why. Because he's got this nutty idea in his head and he can't get it out."

"What idea is that? Does he hold you responsible for his sister's death?"

"Yes."

"Do you know why?"

Cavender shrugged. "How should I know? I never met the guy; I don't even know what he looks like. He was a million miles away when the fire happened, but the way he talks you'd think he was right next door."

"Where was he?"

"In Denver. At a veteran's hospital. He's been there eight, nine years, since Korea. He was informed of Linda's death, naturally, and he got hold of newspaper clippings about the fire. I guess that's how he got the idea about me. Some of those articles, they were pretty unfair——"

"What idea is that, Mr. Cavender?"

"That I saved my own skin. And let Linda burn."

"Is that what he thinks?"

"That's what he thinks. That's what he wrote me, while he was still in the hospital. A real psychotic letter, doc, you'd be interested in it. Only I threw it away."

"And where is this man now?"

Cavender stabbed out his cigarette.

"He's back in the city. He got back last month."

"Has he contacted you since then?"

"Once. By telephone."

"What did he say?"

"Just what you'd expect. He said a lot of nasty things, doc. He even threatened me."

"Threatened you? With violence?"

Cavender didn't answer.

"Did you tell the police about it?"

"No."

"Why not?"

"I don't know!" He stood up, and began pacing the floor. "Look, the guy's half out of his head. He was close to his sister, both of them grew up without parents, you know what I mean? I don't blame him for being upset about it. Only he's wrong, you know, absolutely wrong. I couldn't have saved her, not in a million years. He wasn't in that room, doc, he didn't know what it was like! It was hell, absolute *hell*. For all I know, Linda was already dead when I woke up. There wasn't a chance in the world, not a chance!" He was sweating.

"You don't have to explain yourself to me," Tedaldi said soothingly.

"Sure, I know it's all connected up, my insomnia and everything. But I slept okay after the fire, doc, that's the thing that bothers me. I slept okay after the fire."

"Then when did your insomnia begin? When Jack Fletcher returned from the hospital?"

Cavender paused, and shut his eyes.

"Yes," he said. "Come to think of it, yes."

At three A.M., he crushed the empty pack of cigarettes and went rooting about his bureau drawer for a fresh replacement. The drawer was empty, and he cursed his forgetfulness. He examined the butts in the cloverleaf tray by his bed, and found none over an inch in length. Sleeplessness was bad enough; smokelessness made the situation intolerable. He dressed quickly, and went out of the hotel room to the night elevator. It was automatic, and brought him silently to the ground floor. The lobby was deserted, a pale yellow light shining on the desk. He walked out into the cold west side street and looked up and down, shivering inside his topcoat, trying to remember where he had seen an all-night drugstore.

He found one after six blocks of walking. The sleepy-eyed old man behind the counter sold him four packs and then asked if there were anything else. He almost asked him for an insomnia cure, and then decided against it. If Steers didn't know how to make him sleep, how could an aging pharmacist do better?

On the slow walk back to the hotel, he thought about his visit to Tedaldi, and knew that it had been fruitless. Confession may be good for the soul, but it hadn't done his body any good. Tedaldi had wanted him to return on a regular basis; he said he would think about it. Well, he had thought about it; the answer was no.

Back in his room, he lay sleeplessly on his bed until the alarm clock rang. Then he dressed and went to the office.

Jameson wanted to see him.

"Now, look, fella." Uneasy smile on his boss's face. "Better get hold of yourself. One mistake, two mistakes, that's understandable. But when you louse up a whole schedule, that makes the whole office look bad. Know what would have happened if I hadn't caught the error? We'd have ships going out without passengers."

"Sorry," Cavender mumbled. "Haven't been well lately."

"You *look* bad," Jameson frowned. "You've been looking bad for weeks. Sure there's nothing wrong with you, Charlie?"

"I've been to a doctor. Nothing wrong. Just insomnia." He smiled feebly. "Maybe I need an ocean voyage."

Jameson laughed heartily. "Better take care of yourself, Charlie. We can't afford to lose you, not during the season." Then, without laughing. "But watch what you're doing, fella, huh?"

That night, he thought about the office, during his sleepless hours. By morning, he knew that the office wasn't at the root of his problem. The root was Jack Fletcher.

He called him the next day.

"Jack? It's Charlie, Charlie Cavender."

A grim pause. He had never known that silence

could convey hatred, but he knew it now.

"Listen, Jack, I don't like the way things are between us. What do you say we get together and talk about it? Once and for all."

"I've got nothing to say to you, Cavender."

"Look it's no use acting like a couple of kids. Best thing for us to do is lay our cards on the table. That's the only grownup thing to do."

"Flake off," Jack Fletcher growled. "I haven't forgotten you, buddy. Don't worry about that."

"Now what kind of talk——"

"Flake off," Linda's brother said. "I'm thinking about you all the time. All the time, Charlie."

He hung up.

That night, the cloverleaf ashtray clattered to the floor, no longer able to sustain the weight of the cigarettes, and broke in four pieces. Cavender kicked at it angrily, and found himself sobbing in the process.

"Let me sleep," he whimpered. "Oh, God, can't you let me sleep?"

He was talking to Fletcher. He knew that it was Fletcher who had murdered his sleep. Fletcher had conceived this torture for him, out of his hatred and malice. Fletcher. Fletcher.

"Damn you!" Cavender shouted.

The next morning, Sills, the hotel manager, an oily man with fluttering hands, stopped him at the elevator in the lobby. Cavender only half-listened to what he was saying, but he knew it was a complaint about his nighttime behavior, about the noises in his room. Sills was apologetic, but he had his duty. Cavender muttered at him, and walked away. Complain to Fletcher, he thought. Fletcher's the one responsible.

The thought clung to him all day. *Fletcher's the one responsible* . . .

When closing time came, he decided to pay Linda's brother a visit.

Fletcher was living in a rooming house on the Lower East Side. Brownstone was a misnomer; the facade was black with a century of untouched dirt. It gave the house a gloomy, threatening look. Cavender was actually afraid when he punched the door buzzer over the grimy nameplate. Yes, he was afraid of Fletcher, he admitted the fact to himself; but the time had come to face that fear.

The door buzzed back at him, and he walked into the dingy hallway. Fletcher's apartment was on the ground floor; he hesitated a moment before knocking, but he didn't have to announce himself. The door opened, and he saw Linda's brother for the first time. He was a thin young man with fiery red hair and a narrow pinched face. He was in a wheelchair, and there was a blanket in his lap. He was a cripple, a paraplegic; Linda had never told him that. Cavender looked down at him and almost laughed in relief. No sympathy, just relief. He had feared a cripple. He had lain awake, staring into the darkness, because of half a man. Cavender smiled.

"Jack Fletcher?" he said. "I'm Charlie Cavender."

"I know you," the young man said hoarsely. "What do you want here?"

"To see you. Like I said on the phone."

"Flake off, mister." His hand went to the door and started to push it shut. Cavender put his toe in the way.

"Don't act like that. It's about time we got to-gether——"

"I don't want to see you."

"Five minutes. Just give me five minutes."

Fletcher scowled, and pushed back his chair. It wasn't a cheerful welcome, but it would do. Cavender came into the room.

"I'm sorry," he said. "Linda never told me what was wrong with you."

"Don't be sorry for me, buster. Be sorry for yourself."

"It must have been rough. I was in the air corps myself, during World War Two . . ."

"Bully for you. Any decorations for bravery?" He sneered at him.

"I wish you wouldn't talk like that. I know the way those newspaper stories made it sound, only it wasn't like that at all. You never gave me a chance to tell you my side——"

"Flake off," Fletcher said wearily. "Go away, will ya?"

"Not until you understand."

Fletcher gripped the wheels of his chair and spun them ferociously, thundering across the thin carpeting of his room to the corner, braking to a sharp halt on the other side. "Get out of here," he said raspingly. "Get out before I do what I wanted to do. When I first heard——"

"You wanted to kill me, didn't you?"

"Yes! I wanted to kill you, you dirty coward! I wanted to see you squirm——"

Cavender snorted. "How?" he said.

"You think I need legs? You think I needed legs to get you, you crud?"

Cavender couldn't stop himself. He laughed aloud.

Fletcher was opening the single drawer of a writing table. He was making a lot of noise in the process, but it didn't bother his visitor. Even when he wheeled around and flashed the automatic, Cavender didn't flinch.

"This don't need legs," Fletcher whispered. "This has its own legs, mister. Now you know how."

"That's stupid," Cavender said contemptuously. "Just plain dumb." All fear had left him. He walked toward the boy. "Put it away, Jack. Let's be sensible."

"I can still do it, Cavender. I can still pull the trigger——"

"Put it away." Cavender reached out his hand, proving his own courage to both of them. "Put that damned thing away, Jack."

"I'll kill you!"

Cavender caught Fletcher's wrist and held it firmly; there was more strength in the thin arm than he suspected, but he knew he was stronger. The chair wheels began to slide around during their exertions;

Fletcher threw back his other arm to balance himself. Cavender twisted, and the gun's mouth pointed towards the younger man's head. Fletcher's eyes moved wildly; Fletcher tried to take his finger from the trigger. It was then that Cavender realized that all the fear had been transformed to his tormentor, and the feeling was one of power and satisfaction. Fletcher said something, his last words, and Cavender squeezed until the gun fired. A terrible, bloody thing happened to the young face, and Cavender released his hold.

He stood back, watching the body droop in the chair, the right arm dangling over the side and dropping the automatic to the carpet.

Fletcher was dead, but Cavender wasn't sorry. It was Fletcher's own hand that had held the weapon, squeezed the trigger; if he hadn't brought the gun into play, it would never have happened.

Cavender listened; there was no reaction to the booming sound of the gun.

He gave a minute's thought to his predicament. Should he wait it out, and claim self-defense? Or should he leave now, and let the story speak for itself; the miserable war cripple, the souvenir automatic, the last, hopeless gesture of a defeated man . . .

He waited a moment longer. When nothing happened, he went to the door.

He spent the evening in the balcony of a neighborhood movie; even before the feature's end, he felt a delicious drowsiness. He got up, and went back to the hotel. At ten o'clock, he called room service for a sandwich and a bottle of beer. He ate greedily, then lit a cigarette and stretched out on the bed with his clothes on.

He knew it was going to happen. He could feel it happening. It was like a caressing hand. It was like the gentle touch of a summer breeze. His eyes grew heavy. He smiled. He was still smiling when sleep came, only minutes later.

Sills, the manager of the hotel in which Cavender lived, fluttered his hands and pleaded with the inspector.

"Please. The report . . ."

"I wouldn't worry about it, Mr. Sills, if it's the insurance that's on your mind. The fire wasn't your responsibility; you were in good standing."

Mr. Sills sighed with relief.

"No, it wasn't your fault," the inspector said grimly. "Seems like people never get any sense. You warn 'em a million times not to smoke in bed, but what good does it do?" He turned to watch the stretcher bearers move off with their blackened burden, and shook his head pityingly. "Must have been a real heavy sleeper, that one."

SORRY, RIGHT NUMBER

Charles Einstein

Considering that they'd never met them, the Sloanes knew a great deal about the Martinsons. It was inevitable that they should, because for the past twelve years they had shared the same party-line telephone in a rural area where the houses were spread out and people could pick their friends, even if not the cousers of their telephones.

Though neither Mr. nor Mrs. Sloane ever purposely listened in when the Martinsons' phone was in use, there had been by now literally hundreds of times when, picking up the phone, they had heard one or the other of the Martinsons talking. Occasionally, when Mrs. Martinson talked for an hour or more during the course of a single call, Mrs. Sloane might pick up her receiver four or five times in a weary effort to put through a brief call of her own. "Will you *please* stop listening to my conversations?" Mrs. Martinson would snap. You could usually hear the sound of the other party's phone being picked up when you were talking—unless the other party was very quiet about it.

And, in truth, the Sloanes got to be quiet about it, over the years. It was habit by now; you did not want to pick up the phone, for no matter how legitimate a purpose, for no matter how brief a period of time, and have that shrewish Mrs. Martinson chew you out. So the Sloanes picked up their telephone softly. And, over the years, got to know the Martinsons—and to dislike them very much. Mrs. Martinson was a battle-ax of the old school, and Mr. Martinson was gruff, unpleasant and uncouth. To the Sloanes, it seemed the best thing that could be said about the Martinsons was that they were well matched.

But finally, late one Saturday afternoon, it suddenly appeared that not even this was true. For Ed Sloane, picking up the phone to make a call—picking it up softly, out of inevitable habit—heard the unmistakable voice of Mr. Martinson saying: "So my wife dies. It's not the end of the world. She's outside now. We can talk."

"I just wanted you to know," a woman's voice said, "what a serious thing you're doing."

Ed Sloane's eyes widened.

"It's going to be in her food. She'll never suspect."

"Poison is poison," the woman's voice said.

"Only when somebody guesses. And nobody's going to guess, are they?"

"No," the woman said. "It's still murder, though. We shouldn't be talking——"

"By tomorrow morning," Mr. Martinson said, "it'll be death due to natural causes." He laughed. "Nothing more. Nothing less."

Frozen-fingered and silent, Ed Sloane hung up the phone. He went into the kitchen where Betty was and poured himself a stiff drink.

"What's the matter with you?" she asked.

He told her.

"My God," she said. "What are we going to do?"

"I don't know," Sloane said. "He's going to do it at supper. There isn't much time."

"You've got to call the police," she said.

"I suppose so."

"What do you mean, you *suppose* so? Maybe I think Mrs. Martinson would be better off dead, too—but that's not for us to decide."

"I know. But suppose that conversation wasn't—Well, I mean, if we get the police out there, what will happen? Martinson will deny the whole thing; we can't prove it . . . unless they actually find the poison, and I don't know how likely that would be. They'd say we'd been listening in on their phone calls for years and causing trouble and this and that—and you and I'll be in a real jam."

Mrs. Sloane shook her head. "I don't care. You can't just sit there."

"I'll call the police," Sloane said dimly, and strode to the telephone.

What he heard when he picked it up—lifting the receiver violently this time, without thought to being quiet about it—was Mrs. Martinson's voice. Obviously, she had come into the house from outside, and was now jabbering away on the phone.

". . . and, wait just a minute, Dorothy," she was saying, "there's somebody—on—our—line. Will you *please* hang up this telephone?"

Sloane cleared his voice. "Mrs. Martinson," he said. "This is Mr. Sloane. I'm afraid this is something of an emergency."

"Oh?" Mrs. Martinson was querulous. "So that's it now. A new one. Would you mind very much, so long as you're listening to my private conversations which are, by the way, protected by the Fourth Amendment to the Constitution of the United States, telling me the nature of your so-called emergency?"

"Look," Sloane said to her, "somebody's going to be murdered."

"Oh," Mrs. Martinson said, her voice in mimicry.

"Somebody's going to be murdered. Who?"

"You."

"What?" Mrs. Martinson said. "Well, I— Did you hear that, Dorothy?"

"I think he's drunk, whoever it is," the voice named Dorothy said. "But, honey, if he says it's an emergency, don't you have to give up the phone? Couldn't he make trouble for you?"

"It is just as illegal," Mrs. Martinson said triumphantly, "to pretend that an emergency exists, as a means of getting the other party to relinquish the telephone. What have you got to say to that, Mr. Snoop?"

Sloane said, "Mrs. Martinson, listen, you——"

"Get off my line!" she shrieked. "Get off!"

Slowly, Sloane hung up the phone. His wife came out of the kitchen and said, "Well?"

"It's out of our hands now," he said. "I did what I—" A look came into his eye. "How long have we been on the party line with them?"

"Twelve years," Betty said.

"Twelve years is a long time," Sloane said. "Is supper ready?"

FREE ADVICE, INC.

Michael Brett

Charlton McArdie took his first step toward becoming a millionaire as the result of a woman who dialed a wrong telephone number.

The way it happened, Charlton and myself, I'm James Hamilton, were trying to muster strength to leave the office and go home—not that we'd done anything to make us tired, but you can get tired doing nothing. We were the eastern sales representatives for Cool-Cool, a new Midwestern air-conditioning firm, and it was the coldest, dampest summer in twenty years. Most of the few shoppers purchased name brands. Those who had bought Cool-Cool called back to complain about breakdowns, excessive noise, over-heating, short-circuiting and exploding sets. A fan blowing across a chunk of ice would have been more efficient than a Cool-Cool air-conditioner.

Charlton and I had already decided to sever connections with the firm when our contracts terminated at the end of the month. However, since we were on straight salary we came to the office every day and put in our time.

Frankly, the prospect of being without a job worried me more than it did Charlton. I've got a wife and a small house. Charlton, on the other hand, is single and lives in a fleabag hotel over on Forty-third Street. He keeps talking about how he's going to get a duplex apartment and a fancy girl friend someday.

Charlton does a lot of daydreaming.

He also spends his time doing newspaper crossword puzzles and commenting disparagingly on the columnists who give advice to the lovelorn, on health, on finance, on not getting old—on just about everything.

His attacks were usually preceded by an explosive horse-laugh which shattered the silence in the office. Then he'd say, "Now look at this. You'd never believe that people can be so naive. Here's a college girl, writes to this Miss Common Sense. She's a college girl who believes in free love. Sex is an important part of marriage and she wants to be the perfect wife when the time comes. So Miss Common Sense tells her, 'Insofar as sex is concerned, practice does not necessarily make perfect.' That's just common sense. Now she didn't need Miss Common Sense to tell her that. Isn't that so?"

So I said, "Sure."

"And take this one here, for instance," said Charlton. "Here's a gal who writes that her husband is overweight and how can she make him lose weight. So Miss Common Sense gives her a diet to follow and tells her to broil his food instead of frying it. Then she says, 'Send for my booklet, How To Keep Hubby From Becoming Tubby.'

"Here's another one. Somebody writes in and wants to know if it's all right to neck. So Miss Common Sense says, 'I will be glad to help you with your problem. Send fifty cents in coin and a self-addressed envelope for my booklet, How to Cool It.' Did you ever hear anything as silly as all this business about people writing in and asking for advice?"

He walked over to the window.

"Now look down there. There's thousands of people and the one thing you can be sure of, each and every one of them needs advice. Don't you think so, Hamilton?"

I was a little tired of the way he kept attacking the newspaper columnists, so I said, "You're probably right, Charlton. Why don't you go into the advice business? With your attitude, you'd probably make a fortune."

"You're telling me," said Charlton, and he gave out a loud guffaw.

Of course I had no idea that he was going to take me seriously when the telephone rang just then, or I might not have said it.

Charlton got it and said, "Hello." Then he listened for a minute and said, "One moment, Mrs. Abernathy." He covered the mouthpiece and said, "You know what? This is a wrong number. I'm talking to some dame who thinks she's talking to her psychiatrist, a guy named Doctor Kazoola." He winked. "You told me to go into the advice business. Okay, I'm going to give her some." He uncovered the mouthpiece.

"Mrs. Abernathy, now what can we do for you, dear?" He listened, nodding sympathetically and repeating bits of what she was saying so I could follow the conversation. "I see, the pills haven't worked. You still haven't been able to sleep . . . Well, that's bad . . . Ummm . . . Your life is confused . . . I do understand . . . I want you to remember one thing. There is absolutely everything in life but a clear answer . . . Yes, of course I sympathize with you over your husband's peculiar behavior, but many men think they're Hollywood idols. People are people, Mrs. Abernathy. When it comes to people there aren't any cut and dried answers . . . I agree, the situation with your husband is deplorable."

I laughed and said, "Cut it out, Charlton."

He ignored me and went on. "What I want you to do, Mrs. Abernathy, is place yourself completely in my hands. You may not approve or agree with what I'm about to say, but that's beside the point. Remember, it's for your good, no matter how unorthodox it may sound to you. Actually, what it is is a famous Far East method which is based upon the theory of taking strength from within. A form of mysticism. To make it work, you have to accept the treatment without question. Through it you'll be able to gain insight into your own character. The first act of insight is to completely throw away all of the accepted methods of psychiatric treatment. Now, Mrs. Abernathy, when I say go, I want you to take the telephone receiver and move it in a circle around your head, all the while chanting, *ah-zo, ah-zo.*" He coughed. "I know it must sound ridiculous, but please believe me, it has a definite function. Now *go!*"

Then he covered the mouthpiece again, looked at me and said, "Hamilton, she's doing it. She's waving the telephone around in the air."

I said, "What's with you, Charlton? You nuts, or something?"

"Not me. She's the one, waving that telephone around and chanting. All I'm doing is proving something. You told me to give advice, right?"

"Charlton, you're crazy. I was kidding."

"You think *I'm* crazy? *She's* waving a telephone."

"She's crazy too."

He glanced at his watch. "The way I figure it, in about three minutes her arm is going to get tired and then I'm going to give her another routine. The point I'm trying to make is that people will listen and believe almost anything as long as they think the advice they're getting is from a competent source."

He moved his hand off the mouthpiece and spoke to Mrs. Abernathy again. "All right, Mrs. Abernathy, you can stop the ah-zo. Now what I want you to do is walk around the block in sneakers." He paused, listening. "Yes, house slippers will do. When you've done that, I want you to take a hot bath, then I want you to drink eight ounces of Scotch and go right to bed. I guarantee that you'll sleep." A pause. "All right, since you don't drink, you can make it four ounces. You'll sleep wonderfully . . . Yes, tomorrow I want you to call me. Thank you very much, Mrs. Abernathy."

He hung up and looked at me thoughtfully.

"Do you know the last thing she said? She said, 'Thank you, Doctor. I'll send you a check.' How do you like that?"

I had to laugh. "Wonderful. She's going to send this Doctor Kazoola, whoever he is, a check for nothing, and tonight the poor woman is going to run around the block and fall into bed potted. You ought to be ashamed of yourself, Charlton."

"Ashamed nothing." He crossed the room mumbling to himself and came back again. "Mrs. Abernathy gave me an idea. How to get *rich*. We can both get rich. Think of what happened. I gave a woman advice over the telephone and she's going to send her doctor a check. Now what does this mean? Do you have any ideas?"

"It means she's paying for services rendered. So what?"

"That's true, but what's important is that she's sending him a check for advice."

"Listen, Charlton, I'm beginning to get a headache. What are you driving at?"

"I'm going into the business of giving advice. I've given it lots of thought and the potential is great."

"That's good. In what field do you intend to specialize, law, medicine, finance? What?"

He sat down behind his desk and closed his eyes. With his eyes closed he said, "Medicine and law are out. The Bar Association and the Medical Association would crack down on me. Finance would be okay, though. I'll be a *stock market analyst.*"

I thought he was losing his mind. "Charlton, we've been here for too long, business has been bad for too long."

He opened his eyes. "That's right. Time for a change. I'm tired of not doing business, of being in hock, of worrying where next month's rent is coming from, of not being able to buy a new car. I'm going to give people advice and they're going to pay me for it."

"Yeah, I'd like to see it. Tell me something, what qualifies you as a stock analyst?"

"Your trouble is that you're negative. I'm a financial expert because I say I am. I've been reading about some guy, the leading exponent of transcendental meditation. It's a theory which says that people can do anything if they really think about it and tell themselves they can. It's like self-hypnosis. Okay, I tell myself that I'm a stock expert and I am. It's as simple as that."

"That's fine. Why don't you announce that you're a brain surgeon—are you something merely because you say you are? Be sensible."

"I didn't say anything about being a brain surgeon, did I? All I want to do is give people financial advice. Think of the possibilities. Do you know anyone who doesn't need advice on one matter or another? Everybody wants advice. There are people who don't make a move without consulting their horoscopes, and if the signs aren't favorable they won't get out of bed, much less leave their homes. What does it mean? They're following advice. And what about the millions of dollars spent with public relations firms, promotional attorneys, financial advisors, crystal ball gazers, mediums, psychics, goonies and loonies? Name it and you've got it—there's somebody to give advice."

I could see that I wasn't getting anywhere. "Granted, but why should people come to you? Who knows you? What makes you qualified?"

"Nothing. I have no qualifications, but the one thing I can do is give advice, and the way I'm going to advertise it we'll make a million dollars. The advice I give will be free."

I thought he was demented. "Free advice, you'll go broke."

"Wrong. We'll clean up. They'll just think the advice is free. Let me explain my plan. Let's assume a man buys a certain stock. Okay, then what happens?"

"It goes up or it goes down. He makes or he loses money."

"Very good. You're getting the idea. There are two things that can happen, and right off the bat as far as you're concerned, the odds you're working with are fifty-fifty. Now suppose you predict a winner. The guy who's got it is going to send you a small donation for putting him onto a good thing. Or suppose you tell a stockholder to sell off or to purchase additional stock. Without knowing anything about the stock, you're bound to come up with the right advice merely through the laws of chance and probability."

"That's all fine and good. Now what about the guy who follows your advice and comes up a loser?"

"You can't worry about him. There's a hundred guys selling books on how to beat the market. More guys go broke following the tips in those books than you can count. Let's face it. If the guys who were writing those books really had a surefire way of predicting the market, they wouldn't be writing books in the first place. They'd be wheeler-dealer speculators."

"What about collections? What makes you think that a guy, even if he makes money on your advice, is going to send you money?"

"The honor system," he said.

"That isn't business."

"Exactly. But if I were going to follow the rules of business, this gimmick wouldn't work." He looked at me. "Hamilton, all it costs us is the price of an advertisement and we're in business. What do you say?"

I doubted that anything would come of it, but I

said yes anyway. We went to work on the ad immediately. He took it to a newspaper and I went home. I didn't say anything to my wife about it.

We'd taken a good-sized ad, a square, heavily outlined. FREE ADVICE, INCORPORATED. STOCK ANALYSTS; a phone number and address. I kept thinking that I'd simply thrown away my share of the advertisement's cost. I also thought about the idea catching on. The prospect was bewildering. I couldn't sleep.

After breakfast, I rushed off to the office. Charlton was already there. "Any calls?" I said.

He whooped with laughter. "It's eight o'clock. Give people time to read it."

At nine the phone rang. It was a man threatening to sue unless we took back a Cool-Cool air-conditioner he had purchased a month ago.

At eleven, when I was beginning to think that the advertisement was a washout, the phone rang. It was the first reply to our ad. Charlton took it and said, "Free Advice, Incorporated. Yes, ma'am, there's no charge for this. This is a public service function. We need your name and phone number for our files. We'll give you a reference number. We are not responsible for any information that we dispense. This is a nonprofit organization. However, if you feel that our advice has benefited you in any way, your donation allowing us to continue will be appreciated."

He wrote down the information and then said, "All right, ma'am, what can we do for you?" He listened, interrupting from time to time. I could follow the drift of the conversation. "All right you've got a thousand shares of Santa Maria Railroad stock. It's gone up five points during the past month and you want to know whether to sell. My advice to you is, sell and take your profits . . . No ma'am, it's against our policy to reveal the information we use. However, I will say this, Santa Maria is negotiating two hundred million dollars in new loans from banks and insurance companies to refinance millions of dollars in outstanding debts. My advice is to sell. Your number, incidentally, is B 28." He hung up.

I was stunned. "Is that true about Santa Maria Railroad?"

"How do I know?" he said. "It could be. Railroads are always negotiating loans. It really doesn't matter. The main thing is that I've told her something." He wrote B 28 next to her name and the advice he had given her.

I took the next call. It was from a man named Summerfield. After I'd taken down the necessary information and had assigned him a number and had gone through the policy spiel, he told me that he had five hundred shares of Northern Tractor, which he planned to sell, and then he was going to invest the money in a Florida land development company.

"What's the name of the company, Mr. Summerfield?" I asked.

"Flamingo Land Development Company."

"Flamingo Land Development Company?" I shouted. "Forget it. Stay away from Flamingo Land Development Company."

"What is it?" he asked excitedly. "Do you know something?"

"Sell off the Northern Tractor, deposit the money in a bank and then call me at the end of the month. Ask for Mr. Hamilton," I said, and ended our conversation.

Charlton looked at me incredulously. "What do you know about the Flamingo Land Development Company?"

"About as much as you know about Santa Maria Railroad," I said. "That isn't important, though. What counts is that Mr. Summerfield thinks I know something about it. That land could be under water."

"It certainly could," said Charlton. "It probably is."

There were fifty-four calls the first day. The second day brought an even heavier response to the ad. We became more scientific. In giving advice on a specific stock, we advised fifty percent of those who called to sell and the other half to buy additional stock. We kept records. We watched the progress of our stock tips for a month. In that period the last number we assigned was B 5028. We had advised five thousand people. Charlton was right. Money began to roll in from the winners who were eagerly seeking new ways to make additional monies. We had a good thing going. Those who had followed our advice and made big money were generous in their donations. To them we were heroes. We forgot completely about the others who had followed our advice and lost. To them we were bums.

Some good had come from our advice. We had advised prospective purchasers of an oil company stock to buy as much as they could. Drilling for oil, the company had inadvertently hit a vast underground source of natural gas and the stock had skyrocketed. The stockholders had become wealthy.

The woman Charlton had advised to sell off her Santa Maria stock called, angrily. The stock had gone up ten points.

"Don't worry about it," Charlton told her. "I have inside information that the bottom is going to fall out."

The man I'd warned about Flamingo Land Development Company called. I'd saved his life's savings. It was an out and out land swindle. "I'm sending you a hundred dollars, so you can continue with your good work," he said.

At the end of two months we were making big money. Charlton moved out of his room into a six-room duplex, got a fancy girl friend and bought her minks and diamonds. And all around us people were becoming wealthy. We began to study the market and the more we studied it the less we knew.

Charlton kept going through the records, talking to himself. Look at this B 336. Here's a guy I made into a millionaire. He didn't know what to do and I was the guy who tipped him off. It's absurd, Hamilton. We're making people into millionaires and not doing it for ourselves. I knew this stock was going to rise. The trouble with us is that we're not smart enough to follow our own advice."

"What about people who listened to us and lost their shirts?"

"What about them?" Charlton shouted. "You're being negative again. Try to look at the good we've done for the rest."

I could already see what he had in mind.

At the end of the week he told me that he knew of a stock selling at four and a half dollars that was going to go to fifty.

"How do you know?" I said.

"How do I know? I know, that's all."

I really believed he did, but I didn't want any part of it anyway. "What do we need it for, Charlton?" I said. "We're doing all right, the way things are going."

"I'm going into it with every cent I have," Charlton said. "It's going to hit and it's going to make me a millionaire."

"I'll sit back and watch," I said.

"Suit yourself, but I want to tell you something. This is something that happens once in a lifetime." He laughed. "The difference between us, Hamilton, is that a guy like you doesn't really have imagination. Two years from now you'll be back selling air-conditioners."

I went home and thought about it. I didn't sleep all night. Six months ago I had nothing, and today I had fifty thousand dollars in the bank. One thing was sure, no matter how scatterbrained his schemes had sounded I hadn't lost anything by listening to him.

In the morning I withdrew my money from the bank without telling my wife, and Charlton and I bought fifty thousand dollars worth of the new issue apiece.

That was on Monday. By Friday my investment was worth ten thousand and by the following Monday the stock had gone off the board. It had all been a swindle.

Charlton was going to ask his girl friend to return the mink coat and some of the diamonds he'd bought her, but she'd heard about what had happened and had gone somewhere.

My wife left me.

Charlton went slightly mad. He came in on Wednesday and pointed a gun at me and said it was all my fault. If I hadn't invested with him he never would have gone in all by himself. "Look what you made me do," he said. "I'm going to kill you."

"Let's talk it over," I said. "Now put the gun down. Look, let's not lose our heads. We still have a good thing going for us. We made money. We can do it again."

"I don't know how," Charlton said doubtfully.

"Think positive, Charlton. We can do it."

He burst into unexpected laughter and put the gun down. "I must be losing my mind. What was I thinking of? Sure we can do it again."

We were both laughing so hard by then that we didn't see the little man who stepped into the office.

"Are you Free Advice, Incorporated?" he asked.

"That's us," said Charlton exuberantly.

"You told me to sell off my oil shares. I had three thousand shares at a dollar. Do you know what the price is now? Ninety-four dollars. You ruined me."

When he drew a gun and started firing, I took cover behind a desk. I could hear Charlton fall, and the gunman running away.

I got up, walked over to where Charlton lay dead, and unthinkingly picked up the gun that his murderer had used.

When people came running, that was the way they found me, with the gun in my hand.

Explaining it to the police was very difficult. They didn't believe there was a little man with a gun. They found Charlton's gun on the desk and they came up with the theory that Charlton and I had an argument and that I'd killed him.

When I asked permission to check through my

records—we were up to B 7800—on the chance that I might learn the identity of the man we'd misadvised, they sent me to a police psychiatrist, who had an overbearing manner until I described the scheme Charlton and I had used to found Free Advice, Inc. He thought I was crazy.

I believe he would have committed me to a mental institution if Charlton's killer hadn't come forward then and surrendered to the police.

I was released. As I was leaving the psychiatrist's office, he said, "I'm lucky. If I had known about Free Advice, Incorporated, I might have been tempted to call you. I own three hundred shares of something called Western Pump. What do you know about Western Pump?"

I'd never heard of Western Pump, but, I thought, why should I tell him that? "Buy as much as you can get," I said. "That one is going to go to the moon. It has great potential."

He leaned forward eagerly. "Do you really think so?"

I nodded and went out, wisely.

A SWEET YOUNG THING

Mary Linn Roby

The trouble with you," Mildred Cross said, her face scarlet with rage, "is that you're absolutely convinced that girl is a sweet young thing."

"But she is," Ken retorted. "I can't understand your attitude, Mildred. I thought it was the understanding that when she came here we were to be like a mother and father to her, but that hasn't been the way it's worked out. She might just as well be a servant."

Mildred laughed, scornfully. She was a tall, well-built woman with hair that had been bleached to a silvery white. Everything about her was immaculate, from the highly polished leather of her Italian sandals to the crisp white silk of her blouse.

"She wasn't a responsibility that I wanted to take on," she said sharply. "How do you think I felt when she just turned up here? I hadn't even seen her mother for fifteen years, not since June was a baby. We never were close, Frances and I. Not like real sisters."

"June is still your niece," Ken protested.

"What you mean is, she's my responsibility," Mildred snapped.

They were standing beside the oval swimming pool. The mid-afternoon sun was hot. Ken pulled his sweater over his head and sat down on one of the deck chairs.

"I'm thirsty," Mildred said, reaching for the bell on the table. Ken caught her hand.

"Don't ring for that poor kid," he said. "She's at your beck and call all day. If you want a maid, Mildred, why don't you hire someone? There's nothing to stop you."

She looked at him, her green eyes narrowed.

"It's not a question of money, is it, darling?" she said with acid sweetness. "My money. It will buy anything as far as you're concerned, won't it?"

Ken looked away. Why did she always have to bring her money into the discussion? After all, he had a good business and didn't ask her for anything. If she wanted to spend some of her small fortune on extras for the house, it was no concern of his. She had a maid before June came, but he noticed that it had not taken her more than a week to fire the girl. Then, gradually, June had taken over all the duties except those of the cook, and Mildred kept talking about what a good thing it was for young people to earn their way.

"She wants to go back to college in the fall," Ken said now. "What are you going to do about that?"

"She doesn't have a bean," Mildred reminded him, "and colleges cost money."

"You've got plenty of that."

Ken got out of the deck chair and stared down at her.

"Don't talk to me that way," Mildred flared. "THAT girl comes along with no more claim on me than the fact that she's my niece and just—just settles in. Now, don't interrupt me, Ken. I know that I told her mother that I'd be the girl's godmother, but I hadn't planned on anything like this. How did I know she was going to be an orphan? All right, so she's here. I don't want her, but she's here. I ask her to help around the house, and she does. At least, I guess you'd call it help. She's a bit slovenly, in case you hadn't noticed, but she rearranges the dust."

Lighting a cigarette with quick, sharp movements, she continued, "And what's she getting in return? All this, that's all."

Mildred turned and pointed up at the house. It was set on a slight rise beyond the pool, with terraced lawns between. It was a showplace, and Ken hated it. He had paid for it himself, because Mildred had insisted this was where she wanted to live, but he knew that everyone in town imagined it must have been bought with her money.

"And now," Mildred said scornfully, "she wants to go back to college. Well, things aren't the same as they were when her parents were alive, and she'd better get that through her head pronto."

She went walking off across the lawn, a slim figure, beautiful—from a distance. In a few minutes Ken heard the car start and knew that, as always when she was angry, she was going to drive along the highway too fast, risking her life and that of everyone else. He closed his eyes and lay back, feeling the sun beating against him. Gradually, through the drowsiness which was engulfing him, he became aware that someone was standing nearby. He opened his eyes and saw June.

She was wearing a red bathing suit, too brief, but what all the young girls wore now. Where Mildred was angular, June was gently rounded. Her skin was tanned to the color of bronze. Her long black hair hung straight about her shoulders. She had a bathing cap in her hand.

"I hope," she said slowly, "that you and Aunt Mildred haven't been fighting over me."

Her voice was sweet, low, gentle, as unlike Mildred's as a voice could be. Sweet, that was the word that always came to his mind. She was very, very sweet.

"I know Aunt Mildred doesn't want me here," she was saying now. Her voice broke just a bit, and she turned to stare out over the pool.

"Don't be absurd," Ken told her. "We want you very much."

He was going to say something about the daughter they had never had, but suddenly the girl was in his arms, sobbing. He touched the soft black hair, gingerly at first, and then contentedly, as though she were a child—and that was what she was, a child. He held her tighter.

That was the beginning. His motives were flawless. He wanted to make the girl feel at home, make her feel that they loved her. Of course it was perfectly clear that Mildred didn't love her, and that left only him; and June was so sweet, so affectionate.

After that day by the swimming pool, Ken never touched June—not for weeks—but he planned little expeditions now and then, in the afternoons, places to go that he thought would amuse her.

Of course, he always asked Mildred to go along, too, and she just as consistently laughed at him. He knew it seemed silly, the places they went; the zoo, for one. He hadn't been there since he was twelve, and he had been afraid after they had started out that it would be dull. Instead, they spent four hours wandering from cage to cage, laughing uproariously at the monkeys, eating cotton candy. It was as though, suddenly, he was a boy again.

That was the way June treated him, sometimes; and sometimes he was the older man of whom she asked advice. Sometimes he was a father, and she would playfully run her long fingers through his hair.

She liked to touch him. When they walked, she wanted him to hold her hand. She was so very innocent; so very sweet.

Ken didn't know when it was, actually, that they abandoned places like the zoo, and began to go out evenings instead. June told him that she was nineteen and had never been inside a nightclub. She sounded so wistful, so he had taken her. He felt this sort of outing would be a little more difficult to explain to Mildred, so he made excuses; not lies. June pretended she had a boyfriend whom she met down in the village. Mildred was glad to have her out of the way and didn't ask awkward questions, and it was easy for Ken to get out.

June met him at the corner of the road, and got into the car, laughing, her hair glistening in the moonlight. There was nothing wrong in what they were doing. It was so much fun to show her the nightlife of the city, so exciting to hear her low laughter, intriguing to hear her giggle when she was allowed to have a glass of champagne.

It was strange that all of this was not enough for Ken. He was restless. He wanted June to have more. That was why he took the pin.

It was Mildred's, technically. Actually it was his. He had bought it for Mildred ten years before but she had thrown it into her jewelry box and never worn it. It was not her sort of thing, she had said casually; but it was just right for June, a tiny blue diamond in the center of a rose fashioned out of gold.

June was delighted with the pin, and kissed him gravely on the cheek. It was odd how her attitude toward him had changed. She was not often the little girl any longer. Instead, there were flashes of the mature, understanding woman she could be. More and more often Ken found himself telling her about Mildred, how unhappy she made him, and June was a wonderful listener, sitting close beside him in the car on some deserted road. Sometimes it was very difficult to remember that she was a child.

Then the whole thing came to an end. Mildred appeared in his office one day, carrying a manila envelope. She told his secretary that she didn't want to be disturbed. *She* didn't want to be disturbed. It was humiliating, coming into his office, taking over.

"I don't know what's the matter with you," Ken told her, hanging onto the end of the desk to keep himself from grabbing her by the throat. "If this sort of thing ever happens again, I'll leave you. I swear it."

"You'll leave me on top of the biggest scandal this town has ever had," she said, thin-lipped.

She tore open the manila envelope and reports tumbled all over his desk, reports from a detective agency. Obviously Mildred had been having him and June followed right from the beginning, right from the zoo to the afternoon movies to the clubs to the deserted roads.

"And now she has the nerve to flaunt herself in front of me," Mildred shrilled, "wearing that pin; that diamond pin you gave me."

"What are you going to do?" Ken asked her, his face white.

"Divorce you," Mildred said through her teeth. "With lots of publicity. You're going to lose me and the money as well. And she'll lose, too. She was my heir, I suppose, after you. I don't have any other relatives. She might have had everything I have one day. But not now! And, furthermore, the little witch is going to know about it tonight!"

She was screaming now. Ken took her by the shoulders and shook her until she stopped. As she went running through the outer office, he watched the clerks turn and stare after her. She had promised to make a scandal. As far as he was concerned, it was already made.

Ken stayed in the office until everyone had left. He stayed until well into the evening. There was a bottle of Scotch in his desk drawer, and he drank it and smoked one cigarette after another. Finally he decided he would go to Mildred, plead with her. It was bad enough for her to destroy his business, ruin his life, but she could not be allowed to spoil everything for June.

So he went home. It was nine o'clock when he opened the door. The clock in the hall was just striking the hour. There was a light in the library and Ken went there, forcing himself, one foot in front of the other, like a dazed man.

He found Mildred there—dead—on the floor. Her white-blonde hair was spread out around her head almost as though it had been arranged. When he raised her head, he saw that the back of it had been beaten into a bloody pulp. The poker with which it had been done was on the floor beside her.

He called the police. Matt Haskell, in charge of homicide, came. Ken had known him ever since they were boys together, and he saw the odd look in Matt's eyes when he introduced him to June.

She had been in bed, and Ken had gotten her up only when Matt insisted. He had broken it to her gently, and she was crying quietly now, a childlike figure in a long white robe, her black hair streaming around her shoulders, her feet bare. Ken noticed the way Matt patted her arm and made her sit down in a corner, well away from the body.

It was easy to get the story out of her, what story there was. Matt sat opposite her in a chair, leaning forward, speaking gently as a father would to his daughter. She told him how she had heard Mildred come in and go into the library, obviously upset. She had knocked once to see if she could help, but Mildred had told her to go away. Later she had gone back to see if Mildred wanted anything to eat, and her aunt had said no.

"Are you sure it was your aunt's voice you heard, June?" Matt said.

"Oh, yes." June's eyes were round, like blue spangles. "In fact she told me to come in. She was sitting right here. She . . ." The girl went white and put her hand to her head.

"That's all right, dear," Ken said. "Take your time."

"She'd been crying," June told him. "Her makeup was all smeared. She said she didn't want to be bothered for the rest of the evening, so I ate something, watched television for awhile, and then I went to bed."

"Are you certain that she didn't say anything else?" Matt probed gently.

June's eyes widened. "Of course, I'm sure," she told him. "What else should she have said?"

Ken thought it strange that Mildred had not told June that she was disinheriting her as she had threatened to do that afternoon in his office. Mildred usually did exactly what she said she would do. He supposed he should be grateful that this once she had not. Now June need never know about the hatred her aunt had felt for her.

"Do you know what your aunt might have been unhappy about?" Matt asked.

June stared at him and shook her head back. "Not that unhappy."

"Had you ever seen her cry before?"

"Oh, yes. When she and Uncle Kenneth—well, when they argued."

Ken stared at the girl incredulously. Uncle Kenneth! She had never called him that before. It had been Ken between them, right from the beginning.

"I think you ought to put off answering any more questions until tomorrow, June," he said. "You're obviously very upset."

Matt stared at him, his eyes cold. "You don't mind talking, do you, June?" he said.

"No. Not if I can be of help."

Matt smiled. "That's a good girl. You say that your aunt and uncle quarreled?"

"Yes."

She looked at Kenneth uncertainly, as though he should tell her what to do. He shook his head at her, but Matt saw him.

"I'd prefer it if you'd go out into the hall until I finish questioning Miss Gray," Matt said. "If you'll just go along with that officer."

"She should be informed of her rights!" Ken protested. "She has a right to get a lawyer."

"*She* doesn't need a lawyer," Matt said slowly.

Only later, when Ken was standing in the hall with a policeman on either side of him, did he realize exactly what Matt had said. He couldn't mean that! He couldn't suspect him of murdering Mildred. He had been at the office. Someone must have seen him. Someone . . .

Ken was told to go back into the library. June was sobbing, and Matt was running his fingers across her hair. Ken knew how that felt. He remembered all too well how that felt.

Matt straightened when he saw Ken. "I'm sorry," he said, "but you're going to have to come down to headquarters with me."

"What's she been telling you?" Ken demanded. "I'm not responsible for this. I was at the office until a few minutes ago. June was the one who was alone here with Mildred. She——"

"Don't try to involve this child," Matt said between his teeth. He was obviously an outraged man. "One thing before we go. Do you recognize this?"

He pulled something out of his pocket. It was the diamond pin.

"We found this in your wife's hand," Matt said to Ken. "The pin was open, as though she had just pulled it off. Was it hers?"

"Oh, yes!" June exclaimed before Ken could say a word. "It was one of Aunt Mildred's favorite pieces. She wore it all the time."

Over Matt's head, Ken's eyes met the girl's. An aching coldness settled in his stomach. He could see Mildred telling her that she would lose any chance of inheriting that money as soon as she could get the will changed; and he could see June picking up the poker and bringing it down on Mildred's head again and again, while Mildred, clutching out in panic, pulled the pin from the girl's dress.

"Now, my dear," Matt was saying, "you'd better get some rest. I don't think you should stay here alone, though. Why don't you come home with me? You'll like Alice. She's my wife."

He smiled down at the girl in a fatherly way, as she moved across the room toward him, avoiding the place where Mildred's body lay.

"Alice will be happy to have you," Ken heard Matt say as he and the girl went through the door into the corridor. "You know, it's a darned shame that anything like this had to happen to a sweet young thing like you."

THE PRICE OF FAME

Richard Deming

Harry Cannon always cased his jobs carefully. For ten days he had studied the layout of Gilbert's Liquor Store. He knew what time the place opened in the morning and when it closed at night. He knew the busiest hours of the day, and that the period just before the nine P.M. closing was the deadest. He knew what hours the two clerks worked and that the second-trick clerk left at eight P.M., leaving proprietor Arthur Gilbert alone for the last hour. One night he had even followed Arthur home to Long Island, so that he knew where the man lived.

But best of all he knew that Arthur Gilbert went to the bank only on Friday morning. Which meant that Thursday night, somewhere in the place, an entire week's receipts were hidden.

Cannon pulled up in front of the liquor store at exactly 8:55 P.M. Through the glass front window he could see the plump, balding proprietor checking out the cash register. There were no customers in the place.

From the seat alongside of him Cannon lifted a false rubber nose attached to some black frames without lenses. When he fitted the frames over his ears, his appearance totally changed. His thin face seemed broader, and the contraption gave him a bulbous-nosed, owlish look in place of his usual pinched, scowling expression. It also added ten years to his bare twenty-eight.

It was both an effective disguise and a safer one than a mask, for from a distance it didn't look like a disguise. There was always the danger of a mask being spotted from some nearby window or passing car. As he was, casual passersby, unless they got too close, would merely take him for a rather ugly man.

Slipping from the righthand door of the car, Cannon shot a quick glance in both directions, straightened his lanky form and strode briskly into the liquor store. The plump proprietor glanced up from his register with a customer-welcoming smile which disappeared the moment it began to form. His expression turned wary and he slowly raised his hands to shoulder height even before Cannon drew the thirty-eight automatic from his pocket. The instant reaction made Cannon feel a bleak sort of pride in his growing reputation.

"I guess you know who I am," he said between his teeth, stepping behind the counter and aiming the gun at the proprietor's belt buckle.

"Yes," the plump man said without fright, but still wearing a wary expression. "I won't give you any trouble. The money's right there in the drawer."

Contemptuously Cannon motioned him through a door immediately behind the counter, followed as the man backed into the storeroom, his hands still at shoulder height. After a quick glance around the room to make sure no one else was there, Cannon pushed the door partially shut to block the view from the street but still allow him a view of the main part of the store.

"Turn around," he ordered.

The man presented his back. "You won't have to shoot me," he said quietly. "I'm not going to try anything."

"You think I shoot people for nothing?" Cannon inquired sourly.

When there was no reply, Cannon said in a sharp voice, "Well, do you?"

"I know you have shot people," the plump man said carefully. There was no fear in his voice, but it was extremely cautious. "I was merely pointing out that you have no cause to shoot me. I intend to cooperate fully."

"Well, now. Then you can start by putting your hands down."

Slowly, carefully, the man lowered his hands to his sides.

"Get on your stomach," Cannon directed.

Without haste, but without delay either, the man dropped to hands and knees, then stretched full-length on the floor.

"Stay there until I tell you different," Cannon directed.

Glancing through the partially open door of the storeroom, he saw that no one was passing on the street. Opening the door wide, he thrust the gun into his belt and stepped out to the cash register. The counter blocked the view of the prone man by anyone who might pass the front window, or even come into the store, but Cannon could still see him from the register. He kept flicking glances that way as he scooped bills from the open drawer and stuffed them into his suit-coat pockets. He ignored the change.

When the register was empty of bills, Cannon stepped back into the storeroom and partially closed the door again.

In a cold voice he said, "I guess you've read about me in the papers, haven't you, mister?"

"Yes," the man admitted.

"Tell me what you've read."

After a momentary hesitation, the man said, "They call you the Nose Bandit."

"I mean everything you've read."

"Well, you've held up a lot of places. I believe you've killed three people."

"You'd better believe it. What else?"

"The police advise not to resist you in any way."

"That's right. Why?"

The prone man said quietly, "I have no desire to make you angry."

"The only way you'll make me angry is not to do exactly as I say. Why do the cops advise people not to resist?"

With a sort of resigned caution, the man on the floor said, "They say you're a psychopathic killer. That you'll kill on the slightest provocation."

"Now you're coming along," Cannon said with approval. "Do you believe that?"

"I only know what I've read. If you want me to believe it, I will. If you don't, I won't."

"I want you to believe it," Cannon said coldly. "That psycho stuff is window dressing because the fuzz is too dumb to catch me, but you'd better believe I'll kill you if you give me any lip. You know why we're having this little conversation?"

"I have no idea."

"Because I figure it will save me a lot of time in the long run. You wouldn't refuse to tell me anything I wanted to know, would you, Mr. Gilbert?"

"I doubt that it would be safe," the proprietor said quietly.

"You *are* Arthur Gilbert, aren't you?"

"Yes."

"I cased this job real thoroughly, Arthur. You keep a money box with the real cash in it. That chickenfeed in the register was just today's receipts. You bank once a week, on Friday, and this is Thursday night, so that money box ought to be real full. I figure

I'll get to it faster if you tell me where it is than if I have to hunt for it while you lie here dead on the floor. But it's up to you. I'm going to ask you once. If I don't get a fast answer, I'm going to blow your brains out. Understand?"

"Perfectly. It's behind the cognac on the bottom shelf over there in the corner."

"Point," Cannon instructed.

Raising one hand from the floor, Gilbert pointed.

Cannon had to remove two rows of cognac bottles before he found the square metal box behind them. It wasn't locked, so he was spared the irritation of having to make Arthur Gilbert produce the key. There was nearly five hundred dollars in bills in it, plus a stack of checks. He pocketed the bills only.

Walking over to the storeroom door, he glanced out, then drew back again when he saw a young couple slowly walking past the plate-glass front window. He waited a few moments, looked again and saw that the street in front was now clear of pedestrians. Pulling the door wide open, he momentarily turned back to the man on the floor.

"You stay in that position for five minutes, Arthur," he instructed. "If I see your head above the counter, I'll blow it off. Understand?"

"I understand," Gilbert said.

Without hurry Cannon walked from the store, climbed into the car in front of the store and drove away. A quarter block away he removed the fake glasses and false nose, folded them and put them into his inside breast pocket. Six blocks farther he abandoned the car in an alley across the street from a subway entrance, first carefully wiping the steering wheel and shift lever with a handkerchief. Ten minutes later he was on a subway to Brooklyn.

Within a half hour of the time he had left the liquor store, Cannon was ascending to the street from the Fulton Street station. He found his car parked where he had left it, a dozen yards from the subway entrance. He parked in front of his rooming house exactly at ten P.M. Tiptoeing past his landlady's room, he went up the stairs without her hearing him. He always left for a job surreptitiously and returned as quietly. You never knew when a landlady's testimony that you had been in your room all evening might come in handy.

In his room he counted the take. It came to five hundred and sixty-two dollars. It wasn't exactly in a class with the Brinks robbery, he thought, but with his simple needs it would carry him for weeks.

Part of the enjoyment Harry Cannon derived from his chosen profession was the newspaper writeups he got. There was a scrapbook in a suitcase at the back of his closet containing news clippings of every job he had pulled. There were twenty-two news accounts in all, the coverage on each progressively more detailed. The first, dated a little more than two years earlier, was a back-page, one-paragraph item describing a Bronx drugstore stickup by a man wearing a dime-store false nose and lensless frames. The latest was a full-column front-page spread headlined: NOSE BANDIT STRIKES AGAIN.

Cannon spent many quiet evenings in his room reading over his scrapbook. He particularly enjoyed comparing the sensational treatment his more recent exploits received with the routine coverage of his early jobs. Three kills had made him about the hottest news copy in town.

On Friday morning he was up early to buy all the New York papers. Back in his room again, he went through them one by one with growing puzzlement.

There wasn't a single mention of last night's robbery.

After some thought, it occurred to him that it was possible Arthur Gilbert had died of a heart attack after he had left the store, his body had been found and no one knew there had been a robbery. The man hadn't appeared particularly frightened, but that may have been mere surface control. Beneath it, he may have been scared to death. Then too, he had read that fat people were more subject to heart attacks than others.

He searched all the papers again, this time for obituaries. There was no mention of Arthur Gilbert.

At noon he went out to buy the noon editions, again for the late afternoon editions, and later for the evening papers. There was still no mention of the robbery and no obituary item on Arthur Gilbert.

By then he was so puzzled, he would have been tempted to drive over to Manhattan and drive past the liquor store to see if Gilbert was still in evidence, except for one thing; he couldn't have gotten there before nine-thirty P.M., and he knew the store would be closed. It would have to wait until tomorrow.

Saturday morning he bought all the papers again. When there was still no report of the robbery, he searched through each paper item by item to see if there was mention of Arthur Gilbert's death, for he could conceive of no other reason that it hadn't been reported. He didn't find an obituary on the liquor store proprietor, but he did find something of interest in the personal column.

The item read: "If N.B., who visited my liquor store at closing time Thursday night will phone Circle 1-62006, he will learn something of great financial advantage."

"N.B." could stand for nose bandit, Cannon reflected. "A.G." could be Arthur Gilbert. Checking the other papers, he found the same ad running in all of them.

In the hallway outside his room there was a pay telephone, and on a small table next to it was a stack of telephone directories. He checked the Manhattan liquor store, and there it was: Circle 1-62006. He returned to his room to think the matter over.

It was evening before he came to the decision to phone the number. By then his curiosity was so aroused that he couldn't resist. But, in the event that it was some kind of police trap, he took the subway to Grand Central Station and phoned from one of the booths there. He made the call at 8:45 P.M.

When a pleasant voice said, "Gilbert's Liquor Store," Cannon said tersely, "I saw your ad."

There was a swift indrawing of breath, then Arthur Gilbert said with a peculiar mixture of relief and eagerness, "There's no one else here, so we can talk."

"Then start talking."

Gilbert said, "You noticed there was nothing in the papers about our—ah—meeting, I suppose."

"Uh-huh."

"I didn't report it. As a demonstration of good faith in case you saw the ad, I have a business proposition for you."

"Yeah? What kind?"

"A job for you. No risk, and the take is twenty thousand. We split fifty-fifty. Interested?"

Cannon was silent for a moment. Then he said, "This is a new one. A victim wanting to go partners with the guy who knocked him over."

In a reasonable tone the liquor dealer said, "You're the only person in your—ah—profession I've ever had contact with. If I had known how to contact someone with your talents, I would have done it long ago, because this plum has been waiting to be plucked for some time. I risked forgetting the amount you took the other night in the hope that I could get in contact with you. It was a real risk too, because it's going to take some fancy bookkeeping to cover the shortage."

There was another silence on Cannon's part. Then he said, "Why didn't you mention this job the other night?"

Gilbert said dryly, "You have a reputation for being rather trigger quick. I thought of it, but I'm a cautious man. I thought it probable that if I tried to shift the subject of conversation, you'd put a bullet in my back before you understood what I was getting at."

"I might have," Cannon admitted. "I like people to listen and not interrupt when I've got a gun on them."

"I was still thinking of it five minutes after you left,

and regretting that there was no way to get in touch with you. Then, just as I was reaching for the phone to call the police, I thought of placing a personal ad."

Cannon said abruptly, "We've talked enough for now, in case you've got cops tracing this call. I'll phone you Monday."

He hung up.

Back in his room Cannon considered the conversation from all angles. If the police were using Arthur Gilbert to set a trap, it seemed a rather far-out scheme. Cannon had never heard of a case where a victim was employed in an attempt to gain the confidence of a stick-up artist.

The more he thought about it, the more he was inclined to believe that Arthur Gilbert actually was prepared to finger some job. Trying to put himself in the liquor dealer's place, he was unable to find any illogic in the man's actions. Convinced that all men were as basically dishonest as himself, it didn't seem in the least odd to Cannon that a seemingly law-abiding merchant would make himself accessory to armed robbery providing he had to take no personal risk. Cannon sincerely believed that fear of consequences was the only thing which prevented many ostensibly honest men from employing his own method of making a living.

Perhaps Arthur Gilbert had often daydreamed of how easy it would be to knock over the twenty grand he was now prepared to finger. He wouldn't have the guts to do it himself, of course, or, as he had pointed out over the phone, the underworld contacts to pass on his information to anyone who could use it. The thought of all that easy money would merely lie in the back of his mind, awaiting an accidental encounter with a real pro to give it concrete substance.

It was worth checking out in any event, Cannon decided. Providing he could make contact with Arthur Cannon without risk.

Turning his thoughts to this problem, it didn't take him long to work out a plan for making safe contact.

If it *was* a police trap, by now Gilbert would have reported to the police that the Nose Bandit had promised to phone again Monday. The fuzz would expect no further attempt at contact before then, and they certainly wouldn't expect it in any way other than a phone call at the store.

The only defect he could see in his plan to make contact was that it involved letting Arthur Gilbert see his face without disguise, something no other victim had ever done. But there was a solution to that. Once their business was finished, he could make another call at the liquor store some night and dispose of Gilbert.

He tabled the matter until Monday morning.

Though Cannon knew what commuter train Arthur Gilbert took home in the evening, because he had once followed him home and had sat two seats behind him on the train, he didn't know which train he took in the morning. It couldn't be a very early one, though, as the man didn't arrive at the liquor store until noon.

To be on the safe side, Cannon was parked at the station on Long Island at nine-thirty A.M.

When Cannon had followed the liquor dealer home, Gilbert had climbed into a parked station wagon when he got off the train. Lacking a car to follow him the rest of the way, Cannon had to content himself with checking the phone book. As only one Arthur Gilbert was listed on Long Island, he knew the man's address, but on the chance that Gilbert's home was under police surveillance, he thought it safer to wait at the train station rather than attempting to trail him clear from his home.

It seemed that Gilbert caught the ten A.M. train, for it was nearly a half hour before Cannon spotted his station wagon pulling into the parking area. The man was alone, and, since no other car followed him into the area, he didn't seem to be under surveillance.

Cannon reached the gate a step behind the liquor dealer. He was on his heels as the plump man entered a car. When Gilbert took a rear seat next to the window, Cannon sat next to him. The liquor store proprietor gave him a casual glance, then opened a morning paper.

As the train started to move, Cannon studied the other nearby passengers. At this time of day there were as many women as men, most of them having the appearance of housewives off on shopping trips. The men all appeared to be businessmen, and none so much as glanced at Gilbert. By the time the conductor had come by to collect Cannon's fare and punch Gilbert's commuter ticket, Cannon was satisfied that no police officer had the liquor dealer under observation.

In a quiet voice Cannon said, "Let's resume our conversation."

Gilbert gave him a startled look. Carefully he folded his newspaper and laid it on his lap. He studied his seat-mate with fascinated eyes.

"Don't look a hole in me," Cannon said.

The liquor dealer emitted held breath. "You gave me a jolt, Mr.—ah—I don't suppose you want to mention your name. It's going to take me a moment to get used to you. I'm not a very courageous man, and frankly you scare me silly."

"You didn't act very scared the other night," Cannon said suspiciously. "And you don't look scared now. In fact, you look pleased."

"Oh, I am," Gilbert assured him. "But nevertheless you make me uneasy. I just conceal my emotions rather well."

This seemed logical to Cannon. Since he had begun to gain news headlines, most of his victims trembled with terror the moment he appeared. Gilbert's calmness had bothered him a little, and he was glad to know it was all front. He liked to be feared.

He asked, "What is this job?"

"Robbing my home."

Cannon stared at him. "Come again?"

"First I had better explain my circumstances," Gilbert said. "My wife has all the money in our family."

"Yeah?"

The liquor dealer gave his head a wry nod. "When you marry for money, Mr.—I keep forgetting you have no name—you earn every cent of it. That little liquor store I run was financed by my wife, a sort of a bone she tossed me to give me something to do. Once a month her brother comes down to audit the books. If there's a nickel short, she knows it. That's what I meant when I told you I was taking a real risk in covering a shortage of over five hundred dollars. The total receipts are turned over to Emily and I get doled out an allowance. The house is in her name, the boat, the station wagon and the other car. Everything."

Cannon frowned. "How come you put up with that? No guts?"

Gilbert flushed slightly. "It isn't quite as bad as I make it seem. I have the use of everything she owns. Plus membership in an exclusive country club. Plus charge accounts in a dozen stores, so I can buy all the clothes I want. But cash I don't have. You'll never find me with more than fifty dollars in my wallet. Just once I'd like some real money of my own to spend without supervision. I'd like to spread my wings a bit before I'm too old to enjoy spending."

Cannon said without cynicism, "You've got some doll lined up, huh?"

Gilbert smiled a trifle sheepishly. "I'd rather not discuss my precise need for money. At any rate, my wife keeps a substantial sum in the house at all times, seldom less than twenty thousand dollars. It's in a wall safe in her bedroom."

"I'm no safecracker," Cannon said dubiously.

"You don't have to be. I'll give you the combination."

Cannon's eyes narrowed. "If you know the combination, why don't you lift it yourself?"

"Because she'd know I took it. No one but the two of us know it. She'd throw me out of the house."

"With twenty grand, you could afford to be kicked out."

Gilbert smiled bitterly. "You don't know my wife. She would have me prosecuted and thrown in jail. And even if I got away with it, it wouldn't be worth it. I'm her sole heir and she's worth three-quarters of a million dollars. She's also not well. I prefer to stay in her good graces."

Cannon nodded. "Okay. What's the setup?"

"My wife is a semi-invalid and spends most of her time in her room. She had a slight stroke a couple of years ago and is paralyzed from the waist down. She has a practical nurse to take care of her when I'm not there, but Miss Prentice goes home as soon as I get in from work. Late at night the two of us are usually alone in the house. We seldom have a guest."

"I see. You want me to walk in some night and stick you up?"

"Not when I'm there," Gilbert said dryly. "It's going to be a little more complicated than a simple stick-up. We'll set a specific time and I'll arrange to be over next door at her brother's. She doesn't object to my leaving her alone for short periods, as long as she knows where I am. She has a bedside phone, so she can always reach me, you see."

Cannon gave him a bleak grin. "All right. Set a time."

Gilbert pursed his lips. "How about tonight? I get home about eleven P.M. and the practical nurse leaves as soon as I get there. Don—that's Emily's brother—never goes to bed until the late show is over, so there will be nothing odd about my dropping in on him at midnight. I do it often. Emily watches it too, as a matter of fact. You'll probably find her in her wheelchair in front of the portable in her room when you walk in. I'll leave by the side door. If you take a station by the garage, you'll see me leave and can use the same door to enter the house. I'll leave it off the latch."

"How do I get to her room?"

"The side door is on the east side of the house. Walk straight ahead down a hall to the stairs. At the top of the stairs turn right. Emily's bedroom is the second door on the right and the safe is behind the picture on the north wall. A word of caution, though. Don't let her hear you until the instant you open her door. That shouldn't be difficult, because there is wall-to-wall carpeting throughout the house. But walk softly anyway. She keeps a gun in her bedside stand, and I don't want any shooting. In spite of her strictness about money, I'm really rather fond of the old girl. I want your promise that you won't harm her."

Cannon said, "I never harm anybody who behaves."

When Gilbert looked a little dubious, Cannon said, "If you're thinking about those three, I had reasons. That smart punk in the filling station tried to jump me. The woman in that drugstore started to scream her head off. And the old man in the delicatessen wouldn't tell me where he kept his cash box. I don't use my gun unless it's necessary."

Cannon's reasons for killing didn't seem to reassure Gilbert much. He continued to look dubious. He said, "Well, it can't possibly be necessary in this case. She can't jump you because she can't move from her chair without assistance. And she can't scream because she speaks only in a bare whisper. Her stroke partially paralyzed her vocal chords. I want your assurance that you won't harm her or the whole deal is off."

"I told you I don't gun people for nothing," Cannon said irritably. "That psycho killer stuff is just to make news. What's the safe combination?"

Gilbert gave his head a slow shake. "You don't get that until the last minute. You might get the idea to walk in before I got home and clean the safe without cutting me in. I wouldn't want you to try it with Miss Prentice there. *She* might try jumping you or screaming. And I don't want anyone killed. You meet me when I walk out the side door and I'll give you the combination."

Cannon shrugged.

"Now you can't simply walk to the safe and open it," Gilbert said. "Emily would wonder how you knew the combination. You'll have to fake being a professional safecracker. Put your ear to the safe as you turn the knob and so on. Will you do that?"

"I'll put on an act," Cannon agreed.

"You won't have to worry about Emily giving an alarm even after you leave," Gilbert said. "If you cut the phone cord in her room, she'll be quite helpless. Her's is the only extension on the second floor, and she can't get downstairs in her wheelchair. She can't even scream. She'll simply have to wait until I return. I'll stay over at Don's until one A.M. in order to give you plenty of time for a getaway. All you have to do is lift the ten thousand dollars from the safe and walk out."

"Ten thousand?" Cannon said with a frown. "I thought it was twenty grand."

Gilbert smiled slightly. "You'll have to forgive me for my lack of trust, but how do I know you'd arrange to get my split to me? I haven't the slightest idea who you are or how to get in contact with you. I'll remove my half before you arrive. Emily always wheels her chair to the stairhead with Miss Prentice when she leaves, so I'll have an easy opportunity."

Cannon's last lingering doubts about the liquor dealer's good faith evaporated. Though his manner hadn't indicated any distrust of the arrangements, ever since the conversation started Cannon had been searching for some hint that the whole thing might be an elaborate police trap. The realization that Gilbert didn't trust him any more than he trusted the liquor dealer settled his suspicions once and for all.

There was one factor Gilbert apparently hadn't considered though, Cannon thought with a grim inner smile. What was to prevent him from cold-cocking the liquor dealer as he came from the side door, relieving him of his ten thousand, then going inside for the rest?

A moment later he was startled to learn that Gilbert *had* considered this factor. The plump man said casually, "Incidentally, in case you have thoughts of getting the entire twenty thousand, the excuse I plan to use for going over to Don's house is to show him my new shotgun. It's a double-barrelled ten-gauge. I'll have it in my hands when I walk out of the house. Loaded. As I mentioned before, I'm not a very courageous man, but I really wouldn't have much fear of going up against a pistol with a shotgun. It would be a pretty one-sided duel."

In spite of himself Cannon began to feel grudging respect for the careful planning Arthur Gilbert had done.

After a moment Gilbert added, "On the other hand, you don't have to fear my double-crossing you by blasting with the shotgun when I walk out. The only way I can stay clear of suspicion is for you to rob the safe and get away clean."

Cannon nodded. "I guess we understand each other. We'll pull it off tonight."

It would have been pointless for Cannon to ride the train all the way back to Long Island to pick up his car, drive it back to Brooklyn, then have to drive to Long Island again that night. He simply left the car there all day and caught the evening train which left an hour before the one Arthur Gilbert took. This gave him an hour to case the layout before Gilbert arrived home.

The home was a broad, two-story brick building set well back from the street with a good fifty feet of lawn between it and the houses on either side. Driving past it slowly, Cannon noted only two rooms were lit. One, on the lower floor, was probably the front room. The other was a front corner room upstairs. He guessed this to be Emily Gilbert's room.

Though he had abandoned all suspicion of a police trap, he searched the shadows beneath trees as he passed anyway. There was no sign of a stakeout. A several-years-old car was parked in front of the house, but he saw it was empty as he passed. He assumed it probably belonged to the practical nurse.

Cannon circled the block, parked a half block away

and cut through several back yards to reach the double garage behind Gilbert's home. The garage doors were open and he could see a large sedan parked in the stall which wasn't vacant.

There was a half moon, but a huge elm near the garage cast the east side of the building in deep shadow. Cannon leaned against the side of the garage and waited. From this point he had a perfect view of the side door fifty feet away.

A few minutes before eleven headlights swung into the driveway. Cannon faded behind the garage until the station wagon drove into it, then moved back to his former position.

A car door slammed and footsteps sounded on the concrete floor. Then Arthur Gilbert's plump form rounded the corner and the man peered toward him in the darkness.

"That you?" Gilbert inquired cautiously.

Cannon said, "Uh-huh."

The liquor dealer made a relieved noise. "All set?"

"Uh-huh," Cannon repeated.

"Just wait here until I come out," Gilbert instructed. "I'll come to you. I'll try to make it by eleven-thirty."

"Okay," Cannon said laconically.

Turning, the plump man walked away and entered the house by the side door. Cannon leaned his back against the garage and waited.

Harry Cannon was a patient man, which was one of the reasons he was so successful in his field. He was capable of standing for hours without boredom, studying the comings and goings of customers, when casing a potential job. The wait the next half hour didn't bother him in the least. He didn't even feel the need of a cigarette.

A few minutes after Gilbert went indoors, a woman in white uniform came from the side door and walked down the driveway to the street. A moment later he heard the car parked in front drive away.

It was just eleven-thirty when the side door opened

again. The plump figure of Arthur Gilbert appeared and moonlight glinted from the twin barrels of the shotgun under his arm. Cannon straightened as the man approached. When Gilbert got within a few feet of him, the barrels raised to center on Cannon's stomach.

"What's that for?" Cannon asked, his eyes narrowing.

"Just precaution," Gilbert said quietly. "I'm going to give you the combination now, and I'll feel safer having you covered once you have that. I plan to keep the ten thousand I have in my pocket."

"You think of all the angles, don't you?" Cannon said coldly. "What's the correct combination?"

"R-3, L-27, R-4, L-2. Better repeat it to yourself a few times."

Cannon soundlessly began moving his lips. After a time he said aloud, "R-3, L-27, R-4, L-2." He gave Gilbert a questioning look.

"You have it," Gilbert said with approval. "Emily is in her chair watching television. Do you have your disguise?"

Reaching into his inside breast pocket, Cannon drew out the false nose and fitted it into place. The shotgun continued to bear on him.

With a frown Cannon said, "Well, get started next door."

The liquor dealer's teeth showed in the darkness. "I don't think I want to turn my back on you, friend. I'll go next door after you're inside."

"You're a trusting soul," Cannon growled.

He circled the man and the shotgun moved with him. He was conscious of it still aimed at his back when he reached the side door. Trying the door, he found it unlocked, pushed it open, then glanced back toward the garage. Gilbert stepped from shadow into moonlight, the shotgun now aimed downward. Lifting one hand in a salute, the man moved off across the lawn toward the house next door.

Cannon entered the house and quietly shut the door behind him.

There was only a dim light on in the hall, which bisected the house from one side to the other. At its far end he could see the stairs. His feet moved soundlessly on the thick carpeting as he went the length of the hall and climbed the stairs to the upper floor. There was a night light on in the upper hall too. Without sound he moved to the second door on the right and placed his ear against it. Inside he could hear a television set going.

Drawing his gun, he flicked off the safety, placed his hand on the knob, turned it and slammed the door wide open.

Directly facing him was a middle-aged, gray-haired woman seated in a wheelchair. She wore a robe over a nightgown and her eyes were burning with rage. Her lips were moving soundlessly in what seemed to be mute curses. Both hands rested on the arms of the chair and the right one held a revolver, its butt firmly set against the wood of the chair arm. The muzzle pointed straight at the doorway.

Cannon reacted faster than he had ever reacted in his life. His finger was squeezing the trigger before the knob of the door crashed back against the wall.

The bullet caught the woman squarely in the heart. Her mouth popped open and her right arm jolted from the chair to hang downward, still gripping the gun. She made a gurgling noise in her throat and her head slowly slumped to her chest.

With one stride Cannon was across the room and had jerked her head up by the hair. One look was enough. She had died instantly.

Flicking on his safety, he shoved the gun into his belt and moved to the picture on the north wall. Jerking it from its hook, he flung it aside. Behind it, just as Gilbert had said, was a small wall safe.

Mouthing the numbers aloud, he rapidly spun the dial. Within a matter of seconds the safe was

His eyes lighted with satisfaction at the thick stack of currency inside. He didn't bother to count it, ramming it into various pockets as rapidly as he could. It took both coat pockets and both side pockets of his trousers to hold it all.

Within a minute and a half of the time he had entered the room, he strode out again and ran toward the stairs.

He came to an abrupt halt as he rounded the corner and reached the top of the stairs. On the landing below him stood Arthur Gilbert with the shotgun aimed upward. He was smiling quite calmly.

Cannon's last thought was the indignant realization that Arthur Gilbert had lied to him. The liquor dealer had said he wasn't a courageous man. In that final moment Cannon could tell by the expression on his face that he was as cold-blooded and emotionless as Cannon himself, no doubt about it.

He made a frantic grab for his belt, got the gun halfway out just as both barrels of the shotgun blasted. He felt a searing flash of pain which seemed to encompass his whole body, then he felt nothing.

Stepping over the dead man, Arthur Gilbert moved to the open door of his wife's bedroom. Viewing the scene inside with satisfaction, he leaned his shotgun outside the door and went inside.

He had some difficulty prying her stiff fingers away from the gun, nearly as much as he had had earlier when he forced them around it. When it was free, he dropped the gun into the drawer of the bedside stand and closed the drawer.

Then he left the room and went downstairs.

The side door burst open just as he reached the bottom of the stairs. A tall, lean man of about fifty stepped in, came to an abrupt halt and stared at Gilbert. Moving toward him like a sleepwalker, Gilbert allowed his face to assume an expression of dazed

"For God's sake, what was all the shooting?" the lean man inquired.

Gilbert said dully, "The Nose Bandit, Don. Miss Prentice must have left the door unlatched when she left. I was in the basement cleaning my new shotgun when I heard the shot. I loaded it and rushed upstairs just in time to meet him coming down. He's dead. I let him have both barrels."

"What about Emily?" his brother-in-law asked.

"That was the first shot," Gilbert said, his face squeezing into an expression of grief. "Her bedroom safe is wide open and she's dead. He killed her."

"Oh, no!" the lean man said in a horrified voice. "Poor Emily!"

If you enjoy the macabre,
the unexpected ...
here are gems of death
and horror from the
world's most unfettered
imaginations.

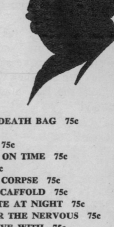

ALFRED HITCHCOCK
presents:

ALFRED HITCHCOCK'S DEATH BAG 75c
COFFIN CORNER 75c
GAMES KILLERS PLAY 75c
GET ME TO THE WAKE ON TIME 75c
HANGMAN'S DOZEN 60c
HAPPINESS IS A WARM CORPSE 75c
A HARD DAY AT THE SCAFFOLD 75c
MORE STORIES FOR LATE AT NIGHT 75c
MORE STORIES NOT FOR THE NERVOUS 75c
MURDERS I FELL IN LOVE WITH 75c
MURDERS ON THE HALF SKULL 75c
NOOSE REPORT 75c
SCREAM ALONG WITH ME 75c
SKULL SESSION 75c
STORIES NOT FOR THE NERVOUS 75c
TWELVE STORIES FOR LATE AT NIGHT 75c
SLAY RIDE 75c

DELL BOOKS